Smoky Mountain Baby
Foggy Mountain Intrigue
Book Two

Ashley A Quinn

TCA Publishing LLC

Smoky Mountain Baby
Copyright © 2020 by Ashley A Quinn
This book is a work of fiction. The names, characters, events, and places are either products of the author's imagination or have been used fictitiously, and are not to be construed as real. Any resemblance to persons, living or dead, actual events, locales, or organizations is entirely coincidental.

No parts of this book may be copied, reproduced, and/or distributed in any way without express written consent from the author.

ISBN: 979-8-9853441-8-9
Library of Congress Control Number: 2022916339

Prologue

Sound reverberated all around Tristan Mabley like an echo in a long tunnel. A steady thwump-thwump vibrated through his chest, a strange accompaniment to the pain that had him in a vice grip. Pressure in his neck and shoulder pushed against the pain to the point it was almost a pain in and of itself. He tried to blink, but could only make his eyelids flutter. What was happening? Why couldn't he wake up?

Gathering every ounce of will he could muster, he forced his eyes open. The face of an angel stared down at him. Warm, cinnamon brown eyes looked back at him from a beautiful heart-shaped face. Long blonde hair scraped back into a ponytail hung over her shoulder. He tried to lift a hand to touch the silky strands, but a pain like he had never known screamed through his shoulder and neck. Bile rose in his throat, and he swallowed hard several times, trying desperately not to throw up.

The angel touched his face softly, her warm fingers sending ripples of sensation through his skin.

"Try not to move, detective. I finally got the bleeding to stop, and I don't want it to start again."

Bleeding? What the hell was she talking about?

Memories niggled the back of his mind, but he was too tired and in too much pain to focus enough to pull them forward.

"You just rest. We'll be at the hospital soon."

Hospital? Why were they going to the hospital?

Must have something to do with the pain he felt. He still couldn't muster up the energy to figure it out, though.

Deciding to take her advice, Tristan let the darkness crowding his mind take over, and he sank into oblivion.

One

"Why the hell are you hiding out in a corner?"

Tristan looked over to see his new brother-in-law, Ben Davidson, approaching, two glasses of champagne in his hands. He reached Tristan's side and held out one of the flutes.

"Thanks." Tristan accepted the glass and took a sip. The cool bite of the tangy liquid was refreshing. "And, I'm not hiding."

Ben just arched an eyebrow.

"All right. Maybe I am. A little. But that woman—Jamie—won't leave me alone. I had to use the 'I need to use the restroom' card to get away. And then she tried to follow me. Said she'd wait in the hall." Tristan shook his head, still in disbelief. He glanced behind Ben, looking for the telltale red hair of the woman who had been following him around for most of the evening. "Why the hell did you invite her?"

"I didn't. She's your sister's friend from college."

"Gemma needs less crazy friends," he mumbled, taking another sip of his champagne.

"You know, if you'd brought a date, you wouldn't have this problem."

Tristan shrugged. "Bringing a date to my sister's wedding seemed like kind of a big deal. There isn't anyone in my life who warrants being my companion to an event like that."

"Not even her?" Ben pointed at the tiny blonde woman talking to Tristan's mother. Her long hair, hanging loose, fell in a shiny curtain down her back. The lavender lace dress she wore highlighted every curve she possessed, of which she had plenty. The woman was a blonde bombshell wrapped in a teeny tiny package.

His jaw worked while his emotions warred with each other as he watched her interact with his mom. "No." His feelings for Laurel Hunt—the paramedic who saved his life half a year ago—were complicated.

Ben tilted his head, looking at him questioningly. "Why not?"

Tristan just pursed his lips and refused to answer. He didn't have an answer. At least not one he wanted to admit—to Ben or to himself.

"You know," Ben started, swirling the champagne in his glass. "Someone once told me not to run from a good thing." He drained his glass. "It was good advice. I'm going to go find my wife. You should go dance."

With a brilliant smile, Ben walked off, leaving Tristan to contemplate what he said. Leave it to Ben to throw his words back at him.

Inhaling deeply, he stared out at the room from his secluded spot, free to observe in the shadows. The party was in full swing. People were talking and laughing and dancing. Everyone was having a great time. As they should. It was a wedding, after all, and his sister's happiness permeated the entire room. From the brilliant violet orchids to the gauzy fabric and fairy lights draped from the rafters of the converted barn, Gemma's vibrant personality was everywhere.

He seemed to be the only one not enjoying all this reception had to offer.

The truth was, he was feeling a bit melancholic. He never thought he would see Gemma married before him. He was six years older than she was, and he didn't even have a prospect for a wife.

Unconsciously, his eyes sought out the blonde bombshell still talking with his mom. Maybe Ben was right to throw his own words back at him. Maybe he was letting something good slip through his fingers. But he didn't know what to say to her or how to approach her. Heaven knows he had tried. He'd asked her to dinner after he was released from the hospital as thanks for saving him, but she shot him down, then proceeded to avoid him at every turn. Every time he saw her in the field on a call, she barely looked at him. She wasn't rude, but she didn't go out of her way to be friendly, either.

It was exasperating. He didn't know why he couldn't get her out of his mind when she obviously never spared him a second thought. Even when he slept, images of her warm, cinnamon-colored eyes invaded his dreams.

He wanted to get to know her better, but he didn't know how without making her uncomfortable. He'd never had so much trouble with a woman before—either getting a date or getting her out of his mind. She had him firmly between a rock and a hard place, and he had no idea how to get out of it.

Slamming back the remaining champagne in his glass, he decided he was being ridiculous by continuing to hide in the shadows. Stepping out from behind the floral spray that kept him concealed, Laurel's laughter immediately drew his attention like a beacon in the night. The tinkling sound was like fairy music.

He meandered past the bar and handed his empty glass to

the bartender. Laurel laughed again, sending his pulse skittering.

This was absurd.

Spinning around, he made a beeline for the two women. A dance wasn't a date. And this was a party. She wouldn't turn him down for a dance at a party.

At least he hoped she wouldn't.

He just knew he would kick himself later if he didn't ask.

As he walked up, both women erupted into giggles. They sounded like schoolgirls.

"Hi, Mom." He bestowed a smile on the older woman before his eyes dropped to the diminutive woman in front of him. She really was very, very small. The top of her head barely cleared his chest. He felt like he could pick her up and lift her like a dumbbell with just one hand. "Laurel. It's nice you could come. You seem to be enjoying yourself."

He watched, completely mystified, as her entire demeanor changed. Where she had been relaxed and open, laughing with his mom, now that he was standing there, she'd grown stiff and wary. The pretty smile that had graced her face was missing as well, along with the sparkle in her warm brown eyes.

"Hello, detective. Yes, I'm having a nice time, thank you."

Tristan frowned. "You're at my sister's wedding. I think you can call me Tristan."

She rolled her lips inward nervously, but nodded.

Eyeing her speculatively, he held out a hand. "Dance with me?"

If he hadn't been watching her so closely, he likely would have missed the miniscule widening of her eyes and the accompanying flash of apprehension. It was there and gone so fast he could almost believe it was a coincidence. Almost. Her abrupt attitude shift told him otherwise, though.

"Oh, I don't really dance. Your mother, though, would make a nice partner." She pointed to his mom, Caroline.

Caroline waved her off. "You go, dear. I'm going to go get off my feet for a bit. These shoes—while gorgeous—aren't the most comfortable things." She gestured to the silver heels on her feet. "I never understood how women could wear these things all day, every day."

Tristan arched an eyebrow at Laurel. "She shot me down. What do you say?" He held his hand out again.

He watched her wage a war with herself as she stared at his hand. Her eyes held both a desire to dance as well as a healthy dose of fear.

Vowing to get to the bottom of that last emotion, he breathed a mental sigh of relief when her desire to dance with him finally won out and she took his hand.

The band had just switched to a slow song as he led her onto the dance floor. Wrapping an arm around her waist, he pulled her close. She held herself stiffly in his arms, touching him only where she had to.

"Relax," he whispered in her ear. "I won't bite unless you want me to," he said, a hint of a teasing smile in his voice.

Laurel stiffened at his words until she resembled a board before she forced herself to unwind a little. She was being ridiculous. Tristan Mabley was not a threat. He was a cop, for heaven's sake. And a nice man. Not all men were scumbags.

She closed her eyes and inhaled a deep breath through her nose.

Bad idea.

The scent of Tristan's cologne flooded her senses. He smelled so *good*. She stared at the knot of his tie, trying to ignore the flare of heat his nearness induced.

Gemma did a good job picking out clothes for the wedding party. Laurel fought a grimace at the absent thought as she stared hard at the wide male chest in front of her and the purple and gray tie he wore. The wedding and reception were both understated and elegant.

Unable to help herself, her eyes wandered over his broad shoulders and up the column of his strong neck, pausing on the long, jagged scar on the left side. It was a stark reminder he nearly died in her care several months ago. "Your scar looks good." Instantly, her face flushed bright red. What an idiotic thing to say.

He pulled back enough to look down at her. "Thanks."

She glanced up at him and got caught in his brilliant blue gaze. Quickly, she looked away, now even more flustered.

"Laurel."

God, she loved the way he said her name. It just rolled off his tongue like music. Her gaze darted upward again, skittering away as she saw he was still looking down at her.

"Hey, is there a reason you seem to be afraid of me? Did I do something in the helicopter? If I did, I'm sorry. I remember very little from that day after the actual shooting."

Startled, she looked up at him, her timidity forgotten. "No, you didn't do anything. You were only semi-conscious and then only for a few brief moments." She could still remember how the blood had poured out of the hole in his neck when she took off the t-shirt bandage Ben strapped on him to stem the bleeding. It had immediately flowed over his shoulder to pool on the leather seat. She'd thought she was going to lose him. If it wasn't for the QuikClot dressings that had become a standard part of her kit, and her ability to tie a really tight bandage, she would have.

"Then why are you acting like I'm about to attack you at any second?"

She shifted uncomfortably. That was a topic she didn't really discuss. With anyone.

Instead of giving him a truthful answer, she just shrugged and skirted the truth. "I'm just shy." That wasn't a lie. She was shy. But that wasn't the only reason he made her nervous.

He stared down at her until she felt like a bug under a microscope. She had a feeling he could tell there was more to the story.

To his credit, though, he didn't push. Just tightened his arms around her and kept dancing.

Laurel felt herself relaxing for real as they danced. His scent, the warmth of his body, and the rhythm of the music all combined to help her forget she didn't like being around men, especially big men.

When the song ended, Laurel was shocked to realize she wanted to keep dancing. As Tristan tried to step back, she tightened her grip on him. Nervously, she looked up into his sapphire eyes. "I'd like to keep dancing. That is, if you want to?"

His smile was soft and charming. "I'd like that too."

Smiling shyly, she settled back into his arms. This time, she laid her head on his chest and closed her eyes, soaking in the feeling of being held tenderly by a handsome man. She'd never had this before and was going to enjoy it while it lasted.

Through several more slow songs, they danced, unhurriedly moving around the dance floor, lost in their own little world. When the music finally switched to something more upbeat, Laurel felt the loss of his arms acutely.

He seemed reluctant to have her leave his side too. Twining their fingers, he tugged her off the floor. "Come on. I'll buy you a drink."

Heart thudding, she followed him to the bar, where she ordered a glass of white wine. Anything stronger and he would have to peel her off the floor. She was not a drinker. He ordered a scotch, neat, then led her to a table on the outskirts of the room.

She perched on the edge of the seat and took a sip of her wine. The cool, crisp liquid helped wet her parched throat and give her an ounce of courage, something which had waned now that they were no longer dancing.

"So how is work going? Did you have any problems with flashbacks when you returned to the field?" She had read studies on the instance of PTSD among police officers returning to work after a shooting. The numbers were staggering. Almost half had symptoms three months after an incident, while ten percent still had severe reactions. Five percent still had severe reactions after a year. Laurel fervently hoped that Tristan fell into the category of those who had fully recovered.

He swirled the amber liquid in his glass. "The first time I had to draw my gun was hard, but otherwise, it hasn't been too bad. A few sleepless nights."

"Nightmares?" She knew all about those.

He nodded. "Yeah. But I haven't had one in a few weeks, so here's hoping they're finally gone." He lifted his glass in a salute before taking a sip.

Laurel took another sip of her wine, looking away awkwardly. God, she hated being shy. She never knew what to say or how to carry a conversation. This was the reason she hid out in her little house and avoided people. She hadn't been able to say no to Gemma, though, when the woman personally invited her to the wedding. Laurel had a feeling not many people could say no to Gemma. Including the man in front of her. She was extremely persuasive. And tenacious.

"So, Laurel, tell me a bit about yourself. I know you work for Northridge Fire Rescue and that you know how to apply a hell of a tourniquet on an awkward wound, but not much else. Are you from Northridge?"

"No. I'm actually from West Virginia. I moved down here about nine years ago."

"What brought you down here?"

He didn't know it, but that was a loaded question. One she didn't want to get into too deeply. "Family stuff. I needed to get away. I saw an ad for a paramedic's course at a technical school in Asheville, so I applied and got accepted. I worked as a housekeeper at a hotel until I finished school and got hired on in Northridge."

He gave her that look again that said he knew there was more to the story. Trying to appear as nonchalant as possible, she willed him not to pry.

"Do you have a big family?"

"Three older brothers and one younger."

"That must have been tough, being the only girl."

Oh, if he only knew. "It had its moments, yes."

Again, that look. She needed to work on her poker face.

"There you are!"

Startled, Laurel looked over as a woman with flaming red hair approached their table, her eyes fixed on Tristan. She heard him groan softly under his breath.

"Jamie. Hi."

"I've been looking all over for you." She took his hand and tried to tug him from his seat. "Come on. I want to dance."

Tristan didn't budge. The woman frowned down at him. Laurel just sat and stared, unsure as to what exactly was going on.

"Jamie, this is Laurel Hunt. Laurel, this is Jamie Sutercliffe. She's a friend of Gemma's from college."

Laurel smiled and waved. "Hi."

Jamie didn't return her smile. She frowned at her instead, seeming to have just noticed her, before turning back to Tristan. "I thought you didn't have a date. Gemma said you came by yourself."

"I came late," Laurel heard herself reply. "I had to work." *What the hell was she doing?* She hoped Tristan didn't mind that she was pretending to be his girlfriend. Considering the look of distress on his face when the woman approached, she didn't think he would.

If possible, Jamie's frown intensified. "She said you were single."

"She's been a little preoccupied with the wedding. Laurel and I have been seeing each other for a few months now. I'm sorry if you had the wrong impression."

"Me too." Disappointment colored her voice. "I guess I'll see you around."

He nodded and Jamie walked off much more slowly than she had arrived.

"Thank you," Tristan said as soon as Jamie was out of ear shot. "She's been following me around all evening."

Laurel smiled, feeling strangely delighted that he would rather be seen with her than the red-haired dynamo who just walked away. "You're welcome."

He finished his drink and stood, holding out his hand. "How about we get some air?"

Laurel tipped up her glass, draining it, and took his hand. "Air sounds good." Maybe it would help her deal with her sudden attraction to this man.

He led her across the room to a set of double doors that led to a deck that ran the length of the barn. The whole structure had been built into a hill, so the deck they stepped out onto was twenty feet off the ground and overlooked a large pond.

Laurel's breath caught at the beautiful scenery. It had snowed a couple of days ago, so the landscape was completely white, and it gleamed in the light from the full moon overhead. Fairy lights wrapped the trees on the path to the pond, ending in a large gazebo at the water's edge. It was like a postcard come to life.

"Wow," she breathed. "This is beautiful."

"Yes, it is."

She looked up at him and found him looking at her, not the view. Blushing, she looked back out over the grounds. The wind kicked up, sending a swirl of snow around them. Even with the heaters on the deck going full-blast, Laurel felt the chill and shivered. She'd left her wrap inside.

Tristan noticed and shrugged out of his suit coat. "Here. I didn't think about the cold when I suggested we come out here." He draped the heavy fabric over her shoulders. The jacket engulfed her in warmth and the scent of his cologne. His hands lingered on her shoulders. Laurel could feel the firm, comforting weight of them through his coat.

Tipping her head, she looked back at him. "Thanks," she said softly.

"You're welcome," he murmured.

Caught in his azure gaze, Laurel slowly turned until she faced him. His hands slid down her arms as she turned, coming to rest on her waist. She laid one palm against his chest, feeling the contours of muscle beneath his dress shirt.

He stared down at her, his eyes turning to midnight pools in the moonlight.

"Laurel." He cupped the side of her face in one large hand, a questioning look in his eyes.

Understanding what he was asking, she nodded. She was tired of being scared. She wanted to feel something other than fear. Her reaction to Tristan when they danced promised that a kiss would lay waste to any negative emotion her brain tried to feel.

Shuffling his feet, he moved closer, his arm wrapping around her waist to pull her flush against his body. Tingles broke out all over her as he bent his head until he was within a hairsbreadth of kissing her.

Standing on tiptoe, she grasped his head and pulled him down, closing the gap. Fireworks exploded behind her eyelids the second their mouths touched. Her entire body went on instant alert, screaming for more. Instinctively, she pressed against him, seeking closer contact.

He didn't disappoint her. Bending at the knee, he tightened his arm around her and lifted her off her feet, his other hand sliding into her hair to hold her head steady. She wound her arms around his neck, his jacket falling heedlessly to the ground.

Never in her entire life had she been kissed like this. It was exciting and mind-boggling.

Earth-shattering.

Suddenly, down to the marrow of her bones, she knew this was how it was supposed to be. That this was what all the books and movies were about. She'd never had that before. Hadn't really believed such passion existed outside of fiction.

But it was real, and it was happening to her right here in Tristan Mabley's arms.

Breathing hard, he pulled back, his eyes glittering like blue diamonds. He stared at her hard for several seconds, his thumb brushing her cheek. "This is insane."

"Agreed. But it's nice." She laid a hand on his jaw. "Do it again?"

The words were barely out of her mouth before he swooped in to kiss her hard. The intensity of the pleasure racing through her made her dizzy. She swayed into him, clinging tight.

With a groan, he pulled back abruptly. "We need to stop."

Chest heaving, she frowned. "Why?"

His eyes widened. "You know where this is leading if we don't, right?"

She nodded. "Yes. And I'm okay with that."

She was? Her mind raced as she mulled over the words that had popped free before she could stop them. Would it be so bad to let this play out? She had never just jumped into bed with a man before. But the heat Tristan evoked was completely foreign to her. She'd never had that with any other man.

Laurel knew she was throwing caution to the wind, but dammit, she was tired of being a wallflower. She had worked hard to make something of herself. She needed to stop letting her shyness and fear hold her back from the things she wanted. Avoiding Tristan the last several months had been a mistake, but she hadn't been able to overcome those two emotions to take a chance on something that could be life-changing.

Well, no more. Spine stiffening in resolve, she held Tristan's gaze as he stared down at her incredulously.

"An hour ago, you acted like I was going to attack you. What changed?"

"I realized I was being an idiot. That I can't keep letting fear get in the way of my life."

"Whoa." He lowered her to her feet, her words putting an effective kibosh on his ardor. "You're going to have to explain that."

Laurel sighed. She was making such a mess of this. There was a reason she avoided relationships. People in general, really. They were not her forte. "Just that my experiences with men haven't really been positive. What you make me feel— well, it's the opposite of that. I want to know that I *can* have something positive with a man."

He continued to scrutinize her. Laurel was sure he was going to call a halt to things. She had been too honest and scared him off. Dammit! If she had just kept her mouth shut and given some generic answer, they would be on their way back to his room at the lodge and she wouldn't be worrying about how to politely excuse herself.

Just as she was about to mutter something and walk away, he framed her face in his hands and bent down to her level.

"Someday soon, you're going to tell me all about those experiences. But not tonight." He kissed her quick and hard. "Let's go say goodbye to the bride and groom." Tugging on her hand, he led her back inside. They made quick work of finding Gemma and Ben. She prayed her face wasn't flaming red as they said goodbye. Thankfully, they were distracted by other guests and barely acknowledged their farewell.

Formalities out of the way, they left the barn. The wedding venue was part of an inn, and the bridal party all had rooms. Nerves fluttered in Laurel's belly as they navigated the path to the main building and went inside. Tristan paused in front of a door on the second floor and unlocked it. She still wanted to go through with this, but it had been a long time since she was with a man, and her previous experiences hadn't been the best.

Standing in the middle of the room, she clasped her hands in front of herself and tried not to fidget. Tristan walked up and stood in front of her, larger than life.

God, he was so big.

But he's nice, she reminded herself. Big didn't always mean bad.

"Nervous?"

She nodded shakily. "A little."

He reached out with one finger and traced her cheekbone. "We don't have to do anything. I will take you down to your car right now and kiss you goodnight."

It was that simple offer that made her relax. He was leaving this entire thing up to her, giving her control, and she appreciated it.

Sliding her hands up his chest, she linked them behind his neck. "I don't want to go home, Tristan."

He stared at her hard for several moments, assessing the

truthfulness of her statement, before he swooped down and took her mouth in a fierce kiss.

Laurel's entire being responded. She was instantly flush with heat. Arousal pooled low in her belly, making her ache. Oh, how she wanted this man. Her need pushed away any remaining doubts she had about what she was doing or why. All that mattered was Tristan and the way he made her feel.

He felt the need too. They didn't stand there long before he pulled her close and lifted her off her feet, carrying her to the bed. He laid her down and settled next to her. Continuing to kiss her, he ran one hand up and down her torso, leaving a trail of fire wherever he touched. Wrapping a hand around his tie, she pulled him closer and kissed him back for all she was worth, getting a groan in response.

His hand slid beneath her and found the zipper on her dress, pulling it down. Cool air whispered over her skin as he skimmed the material down her arms. The fabric pooled around her waist, baring her to his view with only her lacy bra still covering her.

He sat back to look down at her and trailed a hand lightly over the skin he had exposed. Her nipples peaked beneath her bra, rubbing tantalizingly against the fabric. Laurel bit her bottom lip to hold back the loud moan that wanted to break free. He had barely touched her and she was ready to pop like a champagne cork.

Hooking a finger in her bra, he pulled the cup down, completely exposing the rosy tip. He bent and sucked it into his mouth. This time, she couldn't hold back the moan. It just felt too good.

She felt him smile against her chest. "Feel good?"

Unable to speak, she gave a jerky nod.

Reaching beneath her again, he unfastened her bra and pulled it off. He filled his hands with her generous breasts, kneading her flesh with his strong fingers.

"God, you're beautiful," he murmured softly.

She had never really felt pretty. Her whole life, she had been told that she was plain. Too many freckles on her face to be pretty. Too short. But looking at Tristan and seeing the look in his eyes and the way his body responded to her, she believed that she was beautiful. A man like him wouldn't look at a woman with such need and desire if he didn't believe it was true.

Ready for more, she attacked the knot in his tie, quickly freeing it from his collar. He helped her with the buttons on his shirt and it quickly joined her bra on the floor, exposing his muscular torso.

She looked her fill. The man was beautiful. All hard planes and golden skin. Tattoos covered his upper arms. A military patch of some kind on one and an intricate map and compass design on the other. She wondered at the story behind them briefly before his mouth on her breasts short-circuited her brain. When he slowly ran his hands down her sides to grasp her dress, she lifted her hips so that he could pull it off, then kicked off her heels, leaving her in her lace panties and garter belt.

Tristan froze, his eyes raking down her legs. "God almighty. Do you have any idea how sexy a garter and stockings are? I am a firm believer that pantyhose should be outlawed and only stockings should ever be worn."

She didn't, but was glad that she opted for the stocking set instead of the pantyhose she normally wore for special occasions. She would never buy another pair of pantyhose ever again.

He drew his fingers up her leg, trailing fire in his wake, until they met the tabs at the tops of the stockings. With a flick of his fingers, he had the first fastener open, freeing the stocking. In moments, he had them all undone and was pulling the silky material off her legs. She felt very naked compared to him.

Sitting up, she picked at his belt buckle. Her hand brushed the hard ridge behind his fly.

A strangled groan got caught in his throat. "Christ, woman." He brushed her hands out of the way and quickly unfastened his pants himself. She helped him pull them down over his hips, taking his black boxer briefs with them. He kicked free of the material and knelt next to her on the bed, his hard body aroused and ready.

Laurel gulped nervously. He was big everywhere, and she was not.

"Your turn." He put two fingers in the waistband of her panties and garter and tugged, pulling the lacy material down. The fabric barely cleared her feet before he was moving between her legs, his shoulders spreading them wide.

"Tristan?" Was he doing what she thought he was? She'd never had a man do that before.

He glanced up at her, his blue eyes glittering. A lock of his chestnut hair fell over his forehead. He looked like he could be Prince Charming's doppelgänger. Except tattooed. "I am fully aware of how tiny you are compared to me. I want to make sure I don't hurt you."

Before she could do more than nod, he swiped his tongue through her folds, sending her hips rocketing off the bed and startling a cry from her.

Holy crap, that felt good.

He slid one finger inside her channel, slowly moving it in and out. Fire spread out from her center to make her limbs hot and languid. Coils of heat tightened in her belly. He added a second finger and then a third, stretching her. Just when she didn't think she could take anymore, the dam broke, and she came with a whimpering cry. Wave after wave of pleasure rolled over her until she was limp and boneless. Her legs fell open as she lost all muscle tone.

Breathing hard, she laid there savoring the languorous feeling of the aftermath. She didn't think it could get any better than that. It had certainly never been anywhere close to that before.

The bed dipped as Tristan moved, and the sound of crinkling reached her ears. She opened her eyes to see him rolling a condom on over his erection.

He crawled over her, the tip of him poised at her entrance. "I think you're ready now."

She grinned up at him lazily. "Ready? I'm a boneless pile of mush."

"Good. That's what I was aiming for." Slowly, he started to push inside. Her muscles were still melty, but his sheer size compared to her tiny frame made for a tight fit. She tensed slightly at the intrusion and he withdrew partially before pushing back in. Bit by bit, her body relaxed until he was seated fully within her. Flames spread outward from their intimate contact to engulf her, threatening to send her rocketing back over the precipice before they had even really gotten started.

He buried his face in the crook of her neck, lines of tension evident in every inch of his muscular frame as he held himself still above her.

"Are you good?" He nipped at her ear.

Shivering at all the delicious sensations flowing through her, she nodded.

"Thank God." Withdrawing, he pushed back inside in one fluid motion. They both groaned.

She clutched at his head and shoulders as he moved, the pleasure so incredibly intense. Never had it been like this. So electrifying. So powerful.

He increased the pace until she was panting in his arms,

her entire body strung tight as a bowstring. When the thread finally broke, she tumbled into the abyss headfirst. Tristan was right beside her as they fell through the sea of pleasure. Slowly, they reached the bottom where they settled, limbs tangled and bodies sated.

Trying to control her breathing, Laurel let her body melt into the mattress. She had been wrong. It could get better.

Two

Two months later...

Laurel sat on the closed toilet seat and tried hard not to stare at the timer on her phone as it counted down. She couldn't believe she was doing this. This morning she had been looking for more makeup sponges under her bathroom sink when her eyes had landed on the box of tampons.

The hadn't-been-used-in-two-months box of tampons.

She had immediately dropped onto her butt on the floor and stared at the offending item, shock and disbelief rendering her immobile.

As soon as the shock had worn off, she'd rocketed to her feet and made a mad dash for her car, trying not to drive like a crazy person as she made her way to one of the big box stores to buy a pregnancy test.

She glanced down at the timer. Another minute to go.

There was no way she could be pregnant. They had used protection. The entire night had been an impulse and completely out of character for her. But he had smelled and felt so good, and he was so nice. Combined with the magic woven by the cold, still, winter night, she hadn't been able to resist the urge to see how it felt to be loved by a man who wanted her for her and not by one who simply wanted to use her.

She glanced at the timer again. Thirty seconds.

It was just stress, she told herself. Work had been crazy. They were a paramedic short after Tim had quit abruptly to care for his ailing mother in Charlotte. She had picked up a lot of extra hours and hadn't been sleeping as much as she should.

Or eating as well. She had chalked up her recent food aversion to just being too busy and to a lack of sleep.

And her tender breasts were because her cycle was about to start. *Not* because she was pregnant.

The phone beeped in her hand, making her jump. She silenced it, nearly shoving her thumb through the phone. Inhaling a shaky breath, she reached out with one unsteady hand to pick up the test.

The word "Pregnant" glared back at her in bold, black letters.

Holy shit!

Body going boneless, she slid off the toilet to sit on the floor. Back against the vanity, she leaned her head back and closed her eyes, silent tears coursing down her cheeks.

This couldn't be happening.

Fear like she had never known hit her square in the gut as memories of days long past rushed to the surface. Of what should have been a happy time, turning tragic and frightening.

She tried to tell herself that Tristan wouldn't be angry, but truthfully, she had no idea how he would react. They hadn't seen much of each other over the last couple of months. He had drawn a new case right after the wedding and she had been working extra shifts.

There had been a bit of avoidance on her part too. That night had been magical, but she had been overwhelmed by the feelings he aroused in her and had needed time to process everything. They had lunch together a few times and dinner once, but there had been no more hot and steamy interludes. He'd kissed her after dinner, but she put a halt to things, telling him she wanted to slow things down. He'd respected her wishes and left shortly after.

That had been two weeks ago. She hadn't seen him since, only talked to him on the phone a few times.

She rested a hand on her belly, a fierce protectiveness stealing over her. No matter how Tristan reacted, she would love and protect this baby. It was a gift that she did not intend to give up.

Laurel just hoped its daddy felt the same way.

Just as Tristan stepped into the station after a long morning running down leads, his phone beeped, signaling a text message. Absently, he pulled it out and stopped in his tracks as he saw who it was from. Laurel had been silent for several days. Their last conversation had been short and rather awkward, so it was a surprise that she was texting him. He wished he knew where they'd gone wrong. After their night together at Gemma and Ben's wedding, he thought it was the start of something lasting. It sure hadn't turned out that way.

"Problems?"

Tristan's head jerked up at the sound of his boss and brand-new brother-in-law's voice. Two months after they stopped Derek Sutton from trying to kill Gemma, the previous sheriff, John Raymond, had a mild heart attack. His doctor had advised him to retire. John had agreed and nominated Ben to replace him until the next election. Ben had jumped at the chance, knowing that Gemma would rather stay in Foggy Mountain than follow him to Richmond or to Charlotte if he should transfer to the FBI office there.

Arms and ankles crossed, Ben leaned against the doorjamb of his office.

Tristan shoved his phone back into his pocket. "No. Why?"

Ben shrugged. "You were just frowning rather intensely. Are you sure everything is okay?"

Sighing, Tristan walked into Ben's office and closed the door. He paced to the window, staring out at the snowy parking lot. "It's Laurel."

"Laurel? Hunt?"

Tristan nodded.

"What about her?"

"You know we left your wedding together." It was a statement, not a question.

Ben nodded.

"She's been distant since and I don't know why. That night was—well, unlike any other, honestly. But she backed way off afterwards. It's been nothing but awkward lunch dates and short, stilted conversations ever since—mostly started by me. Now, she's sending me a text asking to meet me." He turned to look at Ben. "I just have no idea what the hell is going on or how to fix things."

"And she's said nothing about why she backed off?"

Tristan shook his head. "Not directly. But I get the feeling I make her nervous. Not even so much me, personally, but because I'm a man."

Ben walked closer, a concerned expression on his face. "You think she's been abused?"

Reluctantly, Tristan nodded. "It's the only thing I can think of to explain any of her behavior. I just wish she would talk to me about it."

"Maybe that's what the text is about. Maybe she's ready to talk."

Hope lit Tristan's eyes. "Maybe."

Ben gestured to the door. "Go. Text her back. Find out what's going on and do your damnedest to show her that you're nothing like the man in her past."

Tristan laid a hand on Ben's shoulder. "Thanks, Ben."

Ben grinned. "You knocked some sense into me when I was being an idiot about your sister. I think it's only fair to return the favor."

Tristan laughed. "Touché." He headed for the door.

"Oh, hey. Before you go, how's the investigation into that kidnap victim going?"

Smile vanishing, Tristan shrugged. "I don't have much. It's been months since she was seen and the people she normally associated with aren't the most reliable witnesses. I'm amazed any of them came out of their drug fog long enough to realize she hadn't been around in a while. I'm even more amazed that one of them thought to report her missing."

Ben frowned and gave a small nod. "Keep digging as best you can. I've got a bad feeling about this one."

It was Tristan's turn to frown. "Why?"

"It just reeks of human trafficking. Young female junkie goes missing. No one around to miss her. Makes her easy pickings. I worked more of those cases with the FBI than I care to admit."

"Did you ever find the girls?"

"Some. More often, they turned up dead or were never heard from again."

Tristan made a face of disgust. "I hate to think that filth has landed in our backyard."

"Unfortunately, it's becoming more common everywhere, especially as drugs spread."

"Yeah. Okay. I'll keep my ears open. Jake and I are going to go talk to the homeless community down by the river in Asheville later. Her friend who reported her missing said they spent a lot of time down there."

"Sounds good. Keep me posted."

Tristan nodded and left Ben's office, his mind switching gears from the missing woman to the one sending him cryptic text messages. He hoped that he could solve at least one mystery today.

Car loaded, Laurel climbed into the driver's seat, ready to pay a visit to Mrs. Preston before she had to meet Tristan later. She still wasn't sure how she was going to tell him about the baby, or how he would react to the news, but she couldn't not tell him. Even though she lived fifteen miles to the north, they were destined to run into each other at some point. The first responder community in their area was small and tight knit. She wouldn't be able to keep her condition a secret from him once she started showing.

Glancing back to make sure that the boxes of food and other items for the older woman were secure, she turned out of her driveway and headed into the mountains. Josephine Preston lived alone in a one-room cabin high up in the hills. She had been a widow for thirty years and a shut-in for the last five. Twice a month, Laurel made the trek up the mountain to deliver food and other goods to the elderly woman and to offer a little companionship. They made a lot fewer squad runs to the isolated cabin since Laurel started visiting.

Cruising around a bend in the road, preoccupied with what she was going to say to Tristan, Laurel was jerked from her thoughts as she came upon a car sitting perpendicular on the road. She slammed on her brakes and turned the wheel sharply to avoid colliding with the other car. The boxes in the back went flying, sending items all over the backseat.

She came to a halt inches from the black SUV.

Placing a hand over her belly, she inhaled deeply, taking stock of herself. "We're okay. No harm done." She glanced out the windshield to see debris on the highway near the edge of the road. This particular section plunged seventy feet before it leveled out.

Alarmed, she climbed out of her car, scanning the area for anyone who could be hurt before hurrying to the SUV and peering inside. It was empty.

Turning, she surveyed the area again. "Hello?"

When no one answered, she quickly made her way to the damaged foliage at the edge of the road and peered over the embankment. Forty feet down, she could just make out a small red car in the trees.

Alarmed, her training immediately kicked in and she scrambled over the edge. As fast as she dared to move, she slid/walked down the snow-covered hillside to check on the occupants of the other car. Ducking under a branch, she looked up just in time to see a man standing next to the driver's door of the car.

Pointing a gun at the window.

Before she could react, he pulled the trigger.

She must have made a noise, because he spun in her direction. He shouted at some unseen person in the trees before taking aim and firing his weapon in her direction.

The bullet struck a tree two feet away. With a shriek, Laurel didn't think; she just took off, running down the hill. Another bullet whizzed past her to hit the ground, snow spraying up and hitting her in the legs.

She ran harder and started weaving. That was what all the books and movies said to do when being chased by a madman with a gun, right? A glance behind her showed the man, dressed in black pants and a navy parka, only ten yards back. He took another shot, and it slammed into a tree to her right.

She yelped and ran faster, her mind spinning. She would never be able to outrun him. At barely five feet, she just couldn't outpace a man a foot taller than she was.

She needed to outsmart him if she was going to get away. A large outcropping just ahead gave her an idea. Legs pumping, she headed for the rocks. Skirting around them, she was briefly hidden from view. She headed for the nearest large pine tree and started climbing. Having grown up in the wilds of West Virginia, she had climbed many, many trees in her day. In seconds, she was twenty feet off the ground, buried deep in the pine boughs, out of sight.

Laurel took several deep breaths, trying to calm her breathing. It wouldn't do her any good to give away her position because she was breathing hard. Closing her eyes, she pictured the most tranquil scene that she could think of. The snowy landscape outside the barn at Gemma's wedding popped into her head. The cold, quiet scene, the memory of Tristan's warmth at her back, helped to give her a sense of peace and to calm her racing heart.

As silent as a church mouse, she clung to the tree branch, her legs and arms pulled up as far as she dared. Peering over the edge of the limb, she saw the man chasing her dash around the rocks. He skittered to a stop, looking for any sign of where she went. Laurel was thankful that the snow cover in the forest was light. It meant that there were large patches of bare ground, which had enabled her to climb the tree without giving him a trail to her location.

She held her breath and froze as he walked right underneath her, praying he wouldn't look up. She was tiny, but even the branch she laid on couldn't completely conceal her.

After a moment, he moved on, running deeper into the

trees. Laurel let out a long breath and rested her forehead against the branch. That was close.

She stayed in the tree several more minutes before she climbed down to make sure the man didn't double back. Once on the ground, she eyed the forest in trepidation. She couldn't go back the way she came. More than likely, the man's companion was long gone, but she couldn't take the chance of heading back that way and getting caught. Her only choice was to go deeper into the woods and hike until she came to a road or a house.

Huddling deeper into her coat and wishing she had worn better shoes and heavier pants, she took off into the trees.

Three

"What have we got?" Tristan walked up to the deputy in charge at the scene. He and his new partner, Jake Maxwell, had been called to a homicide up on County Road 146.

"Looks like the vehicle in the ravine may have been forced off the road," the deputy replied, leading Tristan and Jake to the edge of the road. "We found paint transfer on the bumper of the car down the hill. The driver of that car—a young woman in her early twenties—has been shot point-blank in the head."

Christ. "Okay. You get info on the occupants of that SUV yet?" He looked at the blue Honda behind him sitting sideways across the road.

"We're actually not quite sure what's up with it. It doesn't have a scratch on it and the paint transfer on the other car is black, not blue. We think whoever was in it was a witness. It's registered to a Laurel Hunt out of Northridge."

Tristan spun and stared at the deputy, his heart leaping into his throat. "Laurel Hunt?" He looked around the site for her blonde head. "What's she doing here? Where is she?"

The deputy frowned. "You know Miss Hunt?"

Tristan nodded, swallowing around the lump in his throat. "Yes. Where is she?"

"We don't know. The accident scene was called in by a passing motorist." He pointed to a young man standing next to an old pickup just outside the crime scene tape. "He was the only one here when we arrived."

Alarm bells went off in Tristan's head. He pulled his phone out and immediately dialed Laurel's number. The muted trill of a cell phone broke the quiet. It was coming from inside her SUV.

Sliding his thumb to end the call, he cursed violently. He had a very bad feeling about this. There was no way that Laurel had run that other car off the road. She certainly hadn't murdered the young driver.

"Sir?" the deputy said.

"Tristan? What's going on? Why are you freaking out?" Jake asked.

He held up a finger to silence them both and dialed Ben, who picked up on the second ring.

"We have a problem," he said in lieu of greeting.

"What?"

"Laurel's missing."

"What?" Tristan could hear the frown in Ben's voice. "I sent you up to a murder scene. How is your girlfriend involved?"

"Her car is here, but she isn't. I'm guessing she came up on the accident. She probably got out to help and saw something she shouldn't have." He just hoped that she managed to get away and hadn't been abducted.

Ben cursed. "Okay. I'll send a dog team up to help search."

"I'm not waiting around, Ben. If there's a trail to follow, I'm going."

"I wouldn't expect otherwise. Be careful." Ben hung up.

Tristan pocketed the phone and started down the hill to assess the scene below, his mind locked on finding Laurel.

"Whoa, Tris." Jake grabbed his arm and pulled him to a stop. "What's going on? You're getting a little crazy."

Tristan took a deep breath and forced himself to slow down and think. Jake was right. He would have better luck finding her if he wasn't half-crazed with worry.

"Who's Laurel?"

"The paramedic who saved my life. We've also been sort of seeing each other the last couple of months."

"And that's her car up there?"

Tristan nodded.

Jake cursed softly. "No one's seen her?" he asked the deputy who had followed them.

The man shook his head solemnly.

"Okay. I get it now. Let's go."

Tristan didn't have to be told twice. He started back down the hill, Jake and the deputy on his heels.

"Dr. Tate!"

The coroner, Cullen Tate, looked up at Tristan's shout. "Hello, detectives. Jake, congratulations on your promotion. Is Detective Mabley treating you well?"

"Like the newbie I am," Jake quipped. "What have you got?"

Cullen grinned in response, then turned to the victim still sitting in her car. "Caucasian female, late teens or very early twenties. Single gunshot wound to the head. She died instantly."

The deputy, who had been silently prowling around, looked in the car. "Um, detectives?" He straightened to look at them. "There's an infant seat base in the backseat."

All three men bent to see what the deputy was talking about. A plastic frame sat strapped to the rear seat.

"You're sure that's what that is?" Tristan asked, frowning.

The deputy nodded. "I have a nine-month-old at home. I'm sure."

"This just keeps getting better and better," Tristan muttered, switching gears. He still wanted to start searching for Laurel, but a small baby in the wilderness took precedence. "There's a search dog coming, but let's start looking. Hopefully, the baby wasn't in the car."

Radioing up for assistance, they fanned out and started looking. Tristan prayed he wasn't going to find an injured or dead baby in the woods. This case was turning out to be beyond complicated and he had only been on scene a few minutes.

Thirty yards from the car, he found the first bullet lodged in a tree. His heart leapt into his throat, then tried to race right out of his chest. He looked down at the ground for signs of blood, but didn't see any. One tiny footprint in the snow stood out, though, just to the left of the tree.

Laurel.

It was the perfect size for a woman of her stature.

He lifted his radio, calling for someone to come take over his search quadrant to look for the baby, then headed back to the road to gather some supplies. There was no telling how far she had run to get away or whether she was injured. He wanted to be prepared.

Jake met him at the back of their cruiser as he was shrugging into a backpack and strapping a rifle over his Kevlar-clad chest.

"You need to wait for the dog. He'll have better luck."

Tristan loaded a magazine into the rifle. "She's out there being chased by some psycho with a gun. I'm not going to leave her alone any longer than necessary. The dog can catch up." Walking around his partner, he started back down the hill.

"Tristan, the snow is spotty under the tree cover. You're going to lose her trail." Jake followed behind.

He spun around, worry making him snap. "I have to try, Jake. I can't just sit back and wait while she's out there."

Muscles twitching in his jaw under his dark beard, Jake stared hard at him. "Okay, fine," he finally relented. "Hang on while I suit up. I'll go with you."

"No." Tristan laid a hand on Jake's arm. "I'll move faster and quieter alone. I know what I'm doing. You stay on top of the investigation here. Find that baby." He appreciated his partner's willingness to help, but he needed Jake here to run the investigation. Tristan would concentrate better on finding Laurel, knowing that the scene was in good hands. Jake might not have been a detective long, but he had quickly shown his aptitude for it and Tristan trusted him to handle the situation.

Reluctantly, Jake nodded. "Be careful. Try to stay in radio contact. I know reception can be spotty, but there's a weather system moving in tonight. You don't want to get caught out in it if at all possible."

Tristan had read the weather report that morning. For March, it was cold, and they were expecting several inches of snow tonight. More up here in the mountains.

Nodding and giving Jake a grateful look, he set off down the hill, following Laurel's trail through the woods.

Four

Sides aching like she'd been stabbed, Laurel ran as far as she was physically capable before the pain finally forced her to stop. Leaning against a tree, her breath sawed in and out as she pulled air into her burning lungs. She was in good shape, but her body was not conditioned for an all-out run over the rocky, branch laden ground of Pisgah National Forest.

Once the pain was manageable, she set off again. She couldn't afford to rest for long. She had no idea if the man after her had doubled back and stumbled upon her path or not.

Slower this time, she picked her way over the rocky ground, trying to continue heading north. She thanked her lucky stars once again for her hillbilly upbringing. There may not be any love lost between her and her family, but she couldn't fault growing up in the back of beyond. Not when it was currently saving her life and that of her unborn baby.

Tears burned her eyes as she thought about the life growing inside her. Would she ever get to see her baby's face? Would she even get to tell Tristan he was going to be a daddy?

Or would he find out when they found her body and the medical examiner did an autopsy? *If* they found her. She was about as far into the middle of nowhere as a person could get. If she died out here, the wildlife would probably eat her before she was ever discovered.

Suppressing a shiver, she shoved the maudlin thoughts from her mind, focusing instead on her footing. If she twisted an ankle, she was doomed for sure.

Huddling deeper into her coat, she trudged on.

The sound of the river reached his ears as darkness began to creep in around him. Softly falling snow muffled the noise, but the sound of water tumbling over boulders was still unmistakable. He couldn't believe how far Laurel had managed to go. He was a good seven miles from the accident site now. She must have really been moving, especially since he hadn't caught up to her yet.

Eyes peeled, looking for signs of where she went, he prayed she hadn't crossed the river. Even if she found a shallow place to cross, she would still get soaked. Hypothermia would set in within minutes in temperatures like this if she were wet.

In the mud along the river bank, he found her footprints. She was getting tired if she was leaving such an obvious trail. She had done a good job of hiding it up until now, but he was a trained tracker and had been able to follow the more subtle signs of her movements. She'd been heading almost due north.

He followed the trail along the river to the east, where it completely disappeared. The mud gave way to rock. Any wet or muddy footprints that she may have left on the granite had been covered by the falling snow.

Feeling like he was close, Tristan took a chance that her pursuer was nowhere near and called out.

"Laurel!"

Rustling from his right, back in the forest, had him moving.

"Laurel? Honey, if you're out here, answer me."

Eyes straining in the growing darkness, he tried to pinpoint where he heard the noise.

"Laurel?"

"Tristan?"

At the sound of his name, he spun left. Nothing but the dark outlines of the trees met him. "Sweetheart, where are you?"

One of the shapes shook and then suddenly she was in front of it, her blonde hair gleaming bright in the low light.

In several long strides, he reached her and scooped her straight into his arms, cradling her against his body. Relief like he had never known flooded his system, making his hands shake. He pressed a kiss against her head and held on tight.

She sobbed against him. Huge, wracking cries that shook her small frame. Tristan murmured soothingly to her while she cried, stroking her hair. He felt like crying too, but held the tears in check. Barely.

"Honey, are you hurt?" He tipped her head back far enough to get a good look at her. Tears and dirt streaked her face, but there was no blood.

She swallowed hard and took a shaky breath. "No. I'm fine. Just cold and tired."

Her lip wobbled. "The man after me—he shot the driver of that car, Tristan. I watched him. He just stood there and pulled the trigger without saying a word." She dissolved into tears again.

He tucked her close once more. "I know, honey. I'm so sorry you had to see that. But you're safe now. I've got you."

She nodded into his chest and sniffed hard.

"Come on. We need to get someplace warm. This snow is

ramping up." And it was. The tracks he made just a few minutes ago were gone, covered by fresh powder.

"Where are we? I just ran and tried to keep going the same way, so I didn't walk in circles. I think I went north."

"You did. Almost due north, in fact. We're not far from Hot Springs. If we follow the river to the northwest another few miles, we'll walk right into town."

She squirmed to be let down, so he lowered her feet back to the ground. "Okay. I think I can make it that far."

He was shaking his head before she finished speaking. "Not tonight. Tomorrow, we'll go there."

She frowned. "But you said we needed to get out of the cold."

"We do. But, with the darkness, it's getting too dangerous to continue. There's a hunting cabin near here." He pointed southwest. "We can ride out the snowstorm there and either hike out tomorrow, or, if I can get a signal, have someone ride in and pick us up."

"That sounds good. Let's go. I'm freezing." She stepped back and turned in the direction he pointed.

Tristan grabbed her hand, bringing her to a halt. "Hang on there, sweetheart." He shrugged out of his pack and opened it. Reaching in, he pulled out a bottle of water and a protein bar.

"Here. You've been out here all day without any food or water. Finish those and then we'll go."

She took both from him, twisting the cap off of the water, immediately chugging half its contents.

Tristan took a second bottle from his pack and took a drink. She tore into the protein bar. While he waited on her to eat, he tried to call Ben, but he didn't have enough of a signal for either his phone or the radio.

Putting them both away, he glanced up to see that Laurel looked a little green around the gills. She had only eaten about half of the protein bar. He hoped she wasn't getting sick. There was no way that he could get her to a doctor before mid-morning at least if she fell ill.

"Here, I'm done." She held the half-eaten bar out to him.

He tried to make her take it back. "You need to eat the rest, Laurel."

She shook her head and took another sip of water. "I'm good. Really," she added when he lifted an eyebrow.

"Are you feeling all right?"

She nodded, sipping on her water again.

Still unsure, he eyed her speculatively before taking the bar and stuffing it into his pack. He was going to take her at her word for now. They needed to get moving. Slinging the straps of the pack over his shoulders, he readjusted the rifle before taking her hand and leading her in the direction of the cabin.

Thankful that he'd grown up in these woods and had a good map and compass with him, they soon found the cabin. It had been winterized against bears and other assorted vermin, but with the help of his tactical knife, Tristan was able to pry the boards off of the front door and let them inside.

Laurel stood in the middle of the room, hopping and rubbing her arms to stay warm. The temperature had plummeted rapidly once night completely fell. They were both frozen to the bone now.

Dumping his pack and the rifle on the table, he turned to her. "I'm going to gather some firewood. There's a pile out by the shed. Why don't you see if you can find some newspaper or kindling in one of the wood boxes over there and lay the beginnings for a fire?"

She nodded, and he headed out.

∽

Laurel made quick work of building the base for a fire in the woodstove. She couldn't wait to be warm. Her leggings and tall boots, while fashionable, didn't offer much warmth. As a result, her legs felt like solid blocks of ice. It was going to take a hot bath to completely warm her up, but such an amenity was not available here. She'd noticed an outhouse behind the cabin as they walked up. No indoor plumbing for them tonight.

The door banged open, and she jumped a foot. Tristan walked inside, his arms laden with pieces of split wood. He dumped them into the larger wood box, then dug a lighter out of the front pocket of his backpack. Tossing it to her, he disappeared outside again to get another load.

When he returned a few minutes later, Laurel had a fire burning and was parked as close to it as she dared, trying to thaw her frozen body.

Tristan dumped the wood and took off his coat, snuggling up behind her. She leaned back into him and took her first relaxed breath since she had almost t-boned that SUV.

He wrapped an arm around her, holding her close. They sat that way without speaking for several minutes, just soaking up the warmth from the fire and from each other.

Once she wasn't frozen solid anymore, Laurel turned in his arms, looking up at him. "Thank you for coming after me."

He brushed a lock of hair away from her face. "Always." He kissed her forehead and hugged her head to his chest. "I'm just so glad that you're safe."

Clinging to him, her eyes burned with unshed tears. She was glad too. Now she could tell him her news. She just hoped he wouldn't be mad.

Her eyes drifted to her stocking-clad feet. Maybe she should have left her boots on so she could run if she had to.

Mentally, she slapped herself. Whether he was happy or not, he would never hurt her. She had figured out that much about him in the last couple of months. That knowledge was the only reason she was telling him about the baby now, instead of waiting until they were back amongst civilization and more people.

Pulling back, she looked up at him. "Tristan, I need to tell you something."

He looked at her quizzically. "Does this have anything to do with that text you sent me asking me to meet you?"

She nodded. Pushing away, she sat up. He was muddling her senses with his warmth and yummy smell. She needed a clear head for this conversation.

He frowned at the distance she put between them. "What is it?" he asked, his voice full of concern. "Is everything okay?"

She shrugged. "I guess it's all in how you look at it. I don't know how to say this gently, so I'm just going to come right out and say it." She took a deep breath, fixing her eyes on his. "I'm pregnant."

Disbelief rendered Tristan momentarily speechless. His eyes widened so far they hurt.

"Pregnant?"

He looked down at her still flat stomach, then back into her warm brown eyes. No deceit shone there. All he saw was truth and fear.

It was the fear that galvanized his brain back into motion. He framed her face in his hands and looked down at her in wonder.

"You're seriously pregnant?"

She nodded.

"With my baby?"

Again, she nodded.

His eyes widened again. He was going to be a daddy! "Oh

my God!" he breathed, his face breaking out into a grin. This was totally not the way he planned on having children, but he couldn't think of another woman with whom he wanted to have them more than Laurel. From the moment he opened his eyes in the helicopter the day he was shot, he knew she was someone special.

"You're not upset?" she asked warily.

"Upset?" He kissed her fiercely, trying to convey just how un-upset he was. "No, I'm not upset."

She frowned, throwing Tristan for a loop. "Why aren't you upset? We barely know each other."

He frowned back at her. "Are you upset?" It suddenly occurred to him that she might not want this baby. That the fear he saw in her eyes was because she didn't want a child. Swallowing hard, he picked her up and deposited her on his lap. "Please don't tell me that you want to get rid of it. If you don't want the baby, I'll take him or her after it's born. I—" she laid a hand over his mouth, stopping the tumble of words.

"I don't want to get rid of it, Tristan. I fully intend to raise it and love it more than I've ever loved anything in my life. And in answer to your question, no, I'm not upset. It was a shock, but I have loved this baby from the moment the test turned out positive. Children change everything, though, and in my experience, a lot of men find that upsetting, especially when it's unexpected."

Hands shaking, he cupped her face. "Well, I'm not like those men. Children change life in a wonderful and fantastic way. I swear by everything that is holy, I will be there through all of it. The good and the bad. I want to support you and watch our child grow up. To be a dad like mine is to me."

Tears welled in her eyes, and she kissed him gently. "Thank you." The words came out as a broken whisper. A sob ripped itself free and then she was bawling in his arms again.

He had heard that pregnant women could be emotional,

but had never experienced it for himself. He was going to have to invest in industrial-strength handkerchiefs if she kept this up.

Sniffing hard, she swiped at her eyes with her sleeve and sat back. "Sorry," she mumbled.

He wiped away a stray tear with his thumb. "You don't have anything to be sorry for. I can only imagine how you feel. Women get the short end of the stick when it comes to pregnancy, I think. Especially when it isn't planned. You're the one who can't escape it, and if you don't have a partner there to support you, you face the whole terrifying experience all by yourself."

Laurel nodded. Sighing, she snuggled back into his chest. Tristan leaned against the chair beside him, enjoying the warmth from the fire while trying to wrap his head around the fact that he was going to be a dad. It was a lot to take in.

Gradually, he felt Laurel's body relax and her breathing slow as she fell asleep. A huge, jaw-cracking yawn took him by surprise. His adrenaline had completely worn off. Coupled with the relief that he found her safe, he was feeling a bit sleepy himself.

Knowing he would be unable to move in the morning if he slept in his current position, he stood with Laurel in his arms and moved to the lone bed in the cabin. Removing the dust cover, he laid her on the bare mattress. She barely twitched at the change in position.

Stoking the fire in the stove, he added a few more logs so that it would burn for a good portion of the night. He chucked his boots, then grabbed some blankets from the chest at the foot of the bed, spreading them over Laurel, before climbing in beside her.

His last thought before he drifted off, Laurel snug in his arms, was that he could get used to falling asleep like this.

Five

The morning dawned bright and clear. Laurel stretched languidly. She was warm and toasty. Except for her nose. It felt like a block of ice.

It was that last thought that snapped her awake. Rolling over, she realized she was alone in the cabin. A quick glance around the room revealed that Tristan's boots were gone, but his backpack and his long rifle were still on the table where he put them last night.

Reluctantly, she crawled out of bed. Her bladder was screaming at her that she needed to use the facilities.

She scurried over to the woodstove to pull on her boots. They were still warm from the stove's residual heat and felt wonderful sliding onto her feet. Pulling her coat on next, she traipsed to the door and pulled it open.

The blast of cold air was enough to make her wince. This was going to be one cold bathroom trip.

Scurrying off the porch and around the back of the cabin, Laurel located the outhouse. She closed herself inside the dingy building and quickly did her business, only to realize that there wasn't any toilet paper.

She cursed silently before rummaging in her coat pockets, hoping she had a tissue handy.

Her fingers closed around the soft ball stuffed into the bottom of her right pocket.

"Aha! Victory!" she muttered softly.

Finishing up, she stood from the freezing cold seat and pulled up her leggings. She would never take her tiny bathroom for granted again. At least it was warm.

Opening the door, she stepped out into the snow. Tristan stood near the shed, looking at the ground.

She called to him as she approached.

He turned to look at her. "Hey. What are you doing out here? You should be inside soaking up what little warmth is left before we set out."

She hooked a thumb over her shoulder toward the outhouse. "I had to pee. Why were you staring at the ground?"

Glancing back, he pulled her closer and pointed. "Bear tracks. We had a visitor last night."

Laurel's eyes widened. She looked around warily at the forest surrounding them. Bears had never crossed her mind yesterday as she had run pell-mell into the woods. "Shouldn't they all still be sleeping?"

"We're not that far from spring, so it's not unheard of that one would be out already. I know it's cold now, but a couple of weeks ago it wasn't. We'll just need to keep an eye out."

He pulled her back toward the cabin. "Come on. Let's get something to eat and then get going. I tried calling Ben and Jake again, but there's still no signal. We're on our own to get out of here, and in this snow it'll be slow going."

"You have something other than protein bars in that pack, right? Even as hungry as I am, my stomach is going to reject those bars." The memory of how she had very nearly thrown up yesterday after eating one made her shudder in revulsion.

She was sure they were very good, but her pregnancy stomach believed otherwise.

"I think there's some granola bars and trail mix in there. Have you been getting sick a lot?"

She shook her head. "No. The smell of some foods will turn me off to eating, but that's been about the extent of it. I'm sure it'll get worse, though. I'm not very far along."

Tristan held the door open for her, then followed her inside, shutting the door behind them. He crossed to the table and rummaged in his backpack, pulling out a protein bar for himself and a bag of trail mix for her.

"Eat as much as you can," he said, handing her the bag. "You're going to need the energy."

Thankful that it wasn't a protein bar, Laurel dug into the bag. The nuts and sweet, dried fruit tasted delicious. She had polished off half the bag before she realized it.

"I take it that tastes better than my protein bars?" he said, grinning.

She smiled sheepishly and traded him the bag for a bottle of water. "Definitely. I will be glad to get back to civilization, though. I want a big, juicy cheeseburger and fries. Preferably from Daisy's."

He laughed and pulled her in for a hug. "I will make sure you get one as soon as possible."

She looked up at him, sobering. "Thank you, Tristan. For not being a jerk."

He cupped her face and rubbed her bottom lip with his thumb, a searching look in his eyes. "One day, I hope you tell me about the man who hurt you. But until then, just remember that I will never do anything to intentionally cause you harm."

Shock made her eyes widen. "How did you know?" she whispered. Her mind whirled. No one in her new life knew about her past. Had she let something slip while they slept?

"I see abused women every day in my job. You try to hide it, but I see the way you react to me sometimes." He shrugged. "It just makes sense."

She bit her lip and looked away. "There's a lot about me you don't know. Things I can't easily talk about." Looking back up at him, she offered him a small smile. "Just be patient with me?"

He nodded, his eyes glittering. "You'll tell me when you're ready," he said, confidence ringing in his deep voice.

She wished she shared that confidence. Laurel was terrified that when she finally did tell him all about her past, he wouldn't want her anymore.

But they needed a future before she could talk about the past, and that meant getting the hell out of the wilderness.

Rising up on her toes, she pulled his head down and kissed him tenderly before stepping back. "Come on. Let's go get me that cheeseburger."

Cold permeated every single part of Laurel's body, from the top of her head—covered with the stocking cap Tristan gave her—to the tips of her toes. The storm system that came through brought bitterly cold temperatures with it, so today's hike was much more miserable than yesterday's.

The only saving grace in all of this was that Hot Springs was only a few miles away from the cabin. According to Tristan's map, they had gone about halfway since they started out.

She clenched her teeth to stop them from chattering. This had been the longest two hours of her life, and they had at least two more to go. Ice was warmer than she was right now. She had snow inside her boots, and her gloves were soaking wet and useless from all the times she'd stumbled over a fallen branch or rock hidden beneath the snow.

Ducking under a tree branch, she winced as some of the snow piled on it dropped down into her collar. She pulled at her coat and shirt, trying to make it fall through. Not paying attention, her foot hit a rock, and she went flying.

On her hands and knees, she took a deep breath and just stayed there for a moment, fatigue starting to wear on her.

"Laurel! Are you all right?" She could hear Tristan doubling back toward her.

"Yeah," she called out. Huffing out a breath, she looked up.

And immediately froze. Twenty feet away, partially hidden by a bush, was a black bear. It watched her warily through the bare branches.

Her survival instinct kicked in and she scrambled to her feet just as Tristan reached her. She grabbed his arm and pointed. "Bear!"

He pushed her behind him at the same time he swung the rifle up. "We're going to back away slowly."

Laurel clutched fistfuls of the backpack's straps and backed up, pulling him with her.

The bear rose up on his hind legs, watching them. His nose twitched in the air as he tried to get their scent.

Just when she thought they were going to be in the clear, her foot hit another damn rock in the snow. She lurched backward, still hanging onto Tristan's pack. It pulled him off balance, which tipped her past the point of no return. She crashed into the snow. Tristan twisted at the last second to keep from falling on her. He landed next to her, letting out a grunt of pain as he came down hard on his hip.

The bear bellowed and charged forward. Laurel screamed.

It skittered to a stop just feet away and swiped at Tristan's leg, just missing him.

Backpedaling, Tristan ran a hand through the snow, coming up with a rock. He threw it, hitting the animal square on the nose. It let out an angry cry and swiped at its face, but backed up several steps.

"Go away, bear!" Tristan threw another rock, hitting his mark again. Getting to his feet, he found the larger rock that Laurel tripped over and threw it with all his might. It struck the bear in the side. This time, the skinny bear ran back several yards before it turned to look at them. Finally, he decided they weren't worth the effort and ran off into the trees.

Laurel flopped back into the snow and closed her eyes, heedless of the fact she was now covered in the fluffy precipitation. She was already wet and cold. What was a little more?

When she opened her eyes, Tristan loomed over her, concern etched all over his handsome face. "Honey, are you okay?"

Nodding, she huffed again and sat up. She groaned as she rose to her feet. Her legs hurt.

"You look like a snowman." He started to brush the snow off of her backside. "God, Laurel. These pants are soaked. Why do women wear leggings? They're useless."

She grinned up at him. "They're cute. Besides, they're usually fairly warm. These are lined."

"Yeah, well, they're still not meant for you to wear hiking in the middle of a snowstorm."

Slapping at his arm, she mock-glared at him. "It's not like I planned on that. And you need to get used to them, because they're going to be my favorite thing to wear once I can't fit into anything else." She was both looking forward to and dreading that. Her belly was going to be huge. Between her short stature and Tristan's genes, there was going to be very little room in her stomach for anything but their baby by the time it arrived.

He scooped her up, lifting her so that her face was level with his. "You will look beautiful in anything you wear," he said earnestly and kissed her soundly.

She was never going to get tired of that.

When he finally set her back on her feet, she wasn't feeling the cold as much anymore.

"Come on, let's go find you some dry leggings."

Giggling, she took his hand and followed him through the snow.

Six

A mile outside of town, Tristan spotted the first cell phone tower. Pulling his phone from his pocket, he powered it up and prayed he would have a signal. Laurel was shivering and pale now. He had stopped an hour ago and made her put on his flannel shirt under her coat, but it hadn't helped much. Her bottom half was soaked, the pants nearly frozen to her skin. Until he could get her out of those clothes and into dry ones, he would never be able to get her warm.

The phone finished powering up and showed two bars of service. Elated, he opened the phone app. "Finally."

"D-did you get s-service?" Her teeth chattered like castanets.

He nodded and quickly punched the speed dial for his brother-in-law, who picked up immediately.

"Tristan? Thank God! We were starting to get worried. Your sister slept with the phone in her hand all night. Where are you? Did you find Laurel?"

"I did. We're about a mile or so outside of Hot Springs. Can you send an ambulance to meet us at the edge of town?

Laurel's hypothermic. We're hiking up the western side of the river."

"How hypothermic are we talking?"

"She's still mobile and alert, but she's shivering and getting clumsy. Did you guys find that baby?"

"No, so we don't think it was with her. There's been some other more interesting developments in the case, though."

A fierce frown dipped his eyebrows. "Like what?"

"A mess, that's what. We'll get into it later. Jake's on top of it. You just get yourself and Laurel to Hot Springs. I'll alert their EMS." He paused and Tristan could hear him take a deep breath. "I'm glad you two are safe, Tris."

"Me too. Okay, I'll see you soon." He ended the call.

Looking up, he saw Laurel sway. She was barely on her feet now. He was debating carrying her the rest of the way, but she seemed to read his mind and shook a finger at him, straightening.

"N-no. I w-will walk out of here. M-moving will keep me warmer. Even if you c-can move faster carrying me, I'll still cool d-down quicker if I'm n-not m-moving."

Knowing she was right, he nodded reluctantly. Silently, he took her hand and started walking as fast as he thought she could keep up—which was probably faster than what she actually could. But she needed to get out of the cold. Her wet clothes in this wind were not doing her any favors. He didn't know what the cold would do to the baby, so the sooner he could get them all out of the wilderness, the better.

His mind drifted as they walked. A warm glow lit him from within as he thought about the life growing inside Laurel.

A baby.

At thirty-five, he had almost given up hope of ever finding a woman with whom he could share his life and have children. While he didn't know what the future would bring for him and Laurel, he knew that no matter what happened with them, he would always be there for their child. That tiny life didn't know it yet, but it was already loved beyond measure.

He glanced back to check on Laurel. She had her blonde head bent against the wind, the collar of her coat clutched around her neck with her free hand, trying to keep some of the warmth in. Tristan was grateful that her jacket was good quality and warm even if her choice of pants sucked. She would be in much worse shape without the warm, cold-weather coat.

It was killing him to not just pick her up and carry her the rest of the way. His protective instincts were screaming that she shouldn't be walking. He kept having to overrule the urge to grab her and run. Only the knowledge that she was right about the need to keep moving to stay warm stopped him.

Facing forward again, he lengthened his stride just a little more.

By the time they reached the outskirts of Hot Springs, Laurel had tunnel vision. She had gotten so clumsy from the cold, she now had to focus on putting one foot in front of the other so she didn't fall flat on her face.

The ground whirled beneath her, jolting her back to awareness. Her hands shot out to brace her fall, but she soon realized that Tristan had picked her up and was carrying her.

"I can walk," she mumbled, struggling clumsily in his arms to get him to put her down.

"Baby, I can see the ambulance. Stop squirming."

Turning her head, she did indeed see an ambulance just up ahead. She sagged against him in relief. They were safe.

Another violent shiver shuddered through her. The crew

better have the heat on full-blast in the back of the truck, she thought absently.

Tristan's long legs ate up the remaining yards, and he was soon stepping up into the back of the ambulance, placing her on the gurney.

The paramedics immediately spread a space blanket over her while Tristan pulled off her boots and socks. Her feet were completely white and felt like bricks. He tackled her leggings next, reaching up under the crinkly blanket to find the waistband and pull the wet fabric down her legs. She couldn't even appreciate that he was undressing her. She was too busy shivering and couldn't feel his fingers touching her, anyway.

One of the paramedics put a thermometer in her mouth. She knew the reading was going to be low.

"Ninety-three point six."

Yep, that was low. Worry for her baby set in. Her eyes caught Tristan's and she could see it in his eyes too.

"She's pregnant," he told the team working on her.

The paramedic with the thermometer froze momentarily. "How far along are you?"

"T-ten weeks."

He nodded before pulling out an IV insertion kit. "Our doppler isn't sensitive enough to pick up a heartbeat at that stage of gestation, but they'll check at the hospital with the ultrasound." Cleaning the inside of her elbow, he opened the kit. "I'm going to put in an IV. We brought some warm saline with us."

She nodded, the movement shaky.

With quick, deft hands, he put in the IV and hooked up the saline drip. Immediately, she could feel the warmth flooding into her. It felt so very, very good.

The paramedic turned to his partner. "We're good, let's go."

The other man nodded and hopped out, closing the doors behind him.

Tristan sat down on the jump seat and took her free hand in his. Her eyelids felt heavy, and she blinked up at him slowly.

"Everything is going to be fine." He brushed a lock of hair away from her face.

Sleepy, she nodded. She was having a hard time staying awake. The adrenaline crash coupled with the hypothermia was catching up to her.

Tristan stroked her hair. "Sleep, honey."

That sounded like a wonderful idea to her. Closing her eyes, she let her mind drift and quickly fell asleep.

Seven

Hurried footsteps sounded in the hallway outside of the emergency room cubicle moments before the door swished open. Tristan looked up from watching Laurel sleep, expecting to see the doctor coming back to finish Laurel's exam. She had needed to get some other equipment. Instead, it was Ben and Gemma.

Immediately, he could tell how worried his sister had been. Her eyes were red-rimmed, with dark circles visible even through her makeup. She looked frazzled.

He rose as she rushed toward him, catching her as she enveloped him in a hug.

She pulled back and smacked him on the arm. "Don't you ever run off like that again. What were you thinking going off into the wilderness without backup? We had no idea where you were or even if you were okay."

"Gemma." He cupped her face to still her. "I'm fine. And you know why I went." He looked at Laurel where she lay on the bed, slowly rousing at the commotion.

Pulling her face away, she turned to look at Laurel too.

Some of the fight leached out of her shoulders. "Yeah. But you still scared me."

Ben walked up behind his wife and wrapped an arm around her waist. "She's a little on edge. This whole ordeal brought back some bad memories."

Concerned, Tristan frowned down at her. "Are you okay? I'm sorry I worried you. I just couldn't leave Laurel out there alone."

Gemma smiled up at him softly. "I'm fine now that I know you're fine." She tipped her head toward Laurel and walked to the bedside. "How are you doing?"

Laurel yawned widely and rubbed the sleep from her eyes. Some of the color had come back into her cheeks as she warmed up on the ride to the hospital. Even dirt-streaked and exhausted, she was beautiful.

"I'm fine. Just tired and cold."

The curtain rattled behind them as the fiftyish female doctor who had done the initial exam came in, pushing a cart with a monitor on it.

"Hi. I'm Dr. Kessler," she greeted the newcomers. Ben and Gemma introduced themselves.

"It's nice to meet you all," the doctor replied. "But I'm going to have to ask everyone except Dad to step out while I examine my patient."

"Dad?" Gemma asked, confused. "Her dad isn't here."

Tristan knew there was a goofy grin on his face, but he was powerless to stop it. "Not Laurel's dad, Gemma," he said, touching his sister's arm. His grin grew, knowing he was about to rock her world. "The baby's dad. Me."

Her eyes widened comically. "Baby?" She looked at Laurel, who smiled shyly, then back to Tristan. "When did this happen? I didn't even know you two were dating."

"It's complicated," he replied, taking Laurel's hand. He looked to Ben imploringly for help, wanting to let the doctor get on with making sure the baby was all right. Not knowing was starting to wear thin for both him and Laurel.

"Honey, let's go out to the waiting room," Ben said, taking the hint. "I'm sure there will be plenty of time for you to ask Tristan and Laurel questions later."

Gemma sputtered for a second before reluctantly nodding. "Fine." She shook a finger in Tristan's face, making him smile. She was still a brat even if she was all grown up. "But you are going to explain things later."

He offered her a mock-salute, at which she glared, making his grin widen.

"Don't poke the bear," Ben muttered to him as he guided his wife from the room.

Tristan's smile turned into a soft laugh. Where was the fun in that?

As soon as the door snicked shut, the doctor smiled and wheeled the ultrasound machine next to the bed. "Okay. Let's take a look at this baby of yours, shall we?"

"Please," Laurel said. Her hand tightened around Tristan's. "We just want to know that everything is all right."

Rolling a stool up in front of the machine, Dr. Kessler sat and picked up the wand. "I think everything should be fine. Being too hot is a bigger risk than being too cold, and you're only mildly hypothermic." She squirted some gel on the wand. "Can you lift your shirt for me, please?"

Laurel let go of his hand to push the blanket down to her hips and lift her top.

"This is going to be a little cold," the doctor said, holding the wand just above her stomach.

Laurel chuckled. "Can't be any worse than what I've already been."

Dr. Kessler smiled. "True."

Placing the wand on Laurel's belly, grainy images immediately popped up on the screen. After several moments of adjusting, a small human form emerged out of the static. Tristan watched amazed as it moved, tumbling about in its watery world.

"There we go." The doctor pressed a button on the machine's console and a quick swish-swish filled the room.

Emotions so intense they threatened to bring him to his knees hit Tristan square in the chest. Love, so pure and unconditional, unfolded inside him as he watched the baby move on the monitor. It was unlike anything he had ever felt before. He looked down at Laurel and saw the same feelings written all over her face. Their baby may not have been planned, but it was most definitely loved.

Taking her hand in his, he turned back to the squirming figure on the monitor.

"Everything looks good," Dr. Kessler said. "The heart rate is normal, and the baby is measuring right on for its gestational age. Your placenta looks to be forming nicely, and I don't see any bleeding." She pulled a calendar wheel from a pocket on the side of the machine, turning the dials, and gave them a due date in late October.

Laurel blew out a rough breath, her relief palpable. Tristan bent and pressed a gentle but fierce kiss to her forehead, his own relief that all was well, choking him up.

Dr. Kessler slid back on her stool, handing Laurel a handful of tissues so that she could wipe off the goop from the scan.

"I think you and the baby will be just fine. Your temperature at last check was coming up nicely, but I still want to keep you until you're back to normal."

She bent to reach the bottom shelf of the ultrasound cart, then handed them a handful of glossy pictures from the printer housed there. "Here you go. Baby photos." With a bright smile, she left them alone.

Laurel stared at the black and white pictures in her hand in complete awe. It was hard to believe that two days ago she hadn't even realized she was pregnant and now she was holding photographs of the wiggling, flipping, living baby growing inside her.

"This is crazy," she whispered.

Tristan perched one hip on the bed and looked over her shoulder at the pictures. "Yep." Peering down at her, his expression turned serious. "We have some things to figure out. But I meant what I said last night. I'm not going anywhere. No matter what happens between us, this child will have both parents."

She reached up and wrapped her arms around his neck, pulling him down into a tight hug, completely overcome with emotion. No one had ever cared about her the way this man did. He made her believe that she deserved more. That she was worth more, which was something she had never felt before.

The door swished again, and the curtain skated open. Ben and Gemma stood in the doorway.

"The nurse came out and said the doctor was done." Immediately, Gemma noticed the ultrasound pictures in Laurel's hand. With a squeal, she ran forward. "Let me see."

Laurel laughed at her enthusiasm and held out the pictures. Tristan just rolled his eyes.

"Oh my God! This is amazing." Gemma looked up at her brother. "The way you were going, I never thought you would have any children." Her gaze dropped to Laurel. "Thank you for that. I hope you're prepared to have one spoiled child. I already have a ton of cute things in my head that your baby needs." Her expression turned introspective. "When do you get to find out the gender?"

They all laughed at Gemma's rapid-fire speech.

"Ben, you need to work on giving her a baby of her own before you don't have any money left to spend on one," Tristan quipped.

"Working on it," Ben replied.

Gemma glared at her husband before slapping at her brother's arm lightly. "That is none of your business."

Tristan made a face. "Trust me. It's not something I want to think about."

Laurel smiled at the exchange. It was so nice to see a normal sibling relationship at play. She hoped Tristan and Gemma knew how lucky they were.

Tears welled in her eyes as she thought of her own childhood. She didn't know why she was crying. She had put the past behind her when she left West Virginia. Her family was a non-entity, as far as she was concerned.

So, why did it bother her so much that her child would never know her side of its family?

"Laurel?"

She looked up at Tristan through her watery eyes. The concern on his handsome face just made the tears come faster.

The bed dipped as he sat. "Honey, what's wrong?"

She sniffed and took a deep breath, trying to bring her emotions back under control. This was ridiculous. She felt so out of control.

Waving her hand at him, she tried to make light of her reaction. "Hormones. Ignore me."

He frowned down at her, clearly wanting to say more, but she was thankfully saved from the inquisition by Ben's phone.

The call was brief, but the quick conversation had a furrow forming between Tristan's eyebrows as he listened.

When Ben hung up, he looked over at Tristan. "You need to call Jake."

Laurel tried not to let her relief show. She was not ready to delve into the reasons behind her crying jag. He was going to have to accept the half-truth she gave him.

Tristan nodded. Turning to her, he leaned close and placed a soft kiss on her forehead. "I'll be back. You can tell me what's bothering you after you've had a chance to rest."

Her heart sank at the determination glittering in his eyes. The urge to slip away while he was out of the room hit her hard, but she quashed it. She had quit running away from her problems a long time ago. Avoiding Tristan wouldn't solve anything and it wouldn't help their relationship. While he scared the bejesus out of her, she wanted them to at least be cordial to one another for the baby's sake. Running away from him at every turn to avoid uncomfortable conversations would only make things difficult.

So she nodded and offered him a small smile.

He pressed another kiss to her forehead, then stood and ambled out of the room.

Laurel sighed and closed her eyes when he disappeared from view, sagging in relief at the respite.

The bed sagged again, making her eyes snap open. Gemma sat where Tristan had been moments before. The same look of concern her brother had worn was etched on her pretty face.

She laid a hand over Laurel's and gave it a gentle squeeze. "He means well," Gemma said softly. "Don't let him run roughshod over you, though. He likes to fix things and can get tunnel vision when he's on a mission."

Laurel felt the tears welling again and quickly blinked them away. She had never had an ally against a man before. Or even a best friend. She had a feeling Gemma was going to be both.

"Thank you," she whispered.

Gemma patted her hand. "You're welcome. Now, I need some details. How long have you been dating my brother?

And what on earth made you do that?" She made a face of utter disgust, making Laurel laugh.

"He's sweet."

Gemma's eyebrows skyrocketed in surprise. "Sweet? Are we talking about the same man who has lived to torture me my entire life?" She looked up at her husband. "Have you ever seen him be sweet?"

Ben's mouth twitched. "He did advocate for us to get together so you would be happy."

She glared at him. "You're not helping." Spinning back around, she pinned Laurel with her bright blue gaze that was so much like Tristan's. "So, he's sweet. Occasionally. How long have you been seeing him?"

Laurel's mouth quirked. "Just since your wedding."

Gemma's eyes widened. "My wedding? That was two months ago. And to think of all the crap he used to give me for hiding my relationships from him." She shook her head.

Laurel just stared at Gemma, beginning to feel slightly overwhelmed. The woman was a whirlwind of energy.

Gemma seemed to notice Laurel looked a little dazed. With a small laugh at herself, she stood. "We're going to let you rest. If you need anything, just holler. We'll be out in the waiting area." Bending, she wrapped Laurel in a quick but firm hug. "Remember what I said," she whispered. "Make sure he hears you."

Pulling back, Laurel nodded, grateful for the support. She already knew that Tristan could be dogged and pushy, both things that she was not. She was going to have to learn to be a little bit more stubborn, and he was going to have to learn to compromise if they were going to succeed.

Ben and Gemma left, leaving Laurel alone with her thoughts. Her eyes landed on the glossy ultrasound pictures sitting on the bed. A wave of love knocked into her. She cupped her hands over her belly, wondering at the new life growing inside of her.

"Are you going to be as much of a handful as your daddy and your aunt?" A smile quirked her mouth as the image of a little boy who looked just like Tristan, ornery smile and all, filled her mind. She had a feeling she was going to have to learn how to push back or Tristan wasn't the only one who would run roughshod over her.

Sighing, she leaned back against the pillow and closed her eyes, giving in to the fatigue. She fell asleep to the image of that little boy holding his daddy's hand, twin twinkles in their matching eyes.

Eight

Rolling his shoulders to relieve the stiffness, Tristan walked into the station a few hours later alongside Ben. His muscles were sore from his trek through the wilderness, and he wanted nothing more than to stretch out on the sofa with a beer cuddled up with Laurel. That would have to wait, however. He had a case to catch up on. Jake had given him the cliff notes version of things on the phone earlier, but there was a lot more to go over yet.

Once Laurel had warmed up enough to be discharged, Ben and Gemma had taken them back to their house. Laurel still needed to rest, and Tristan didn't want her to be alone. She was their only witness to a murder. A witness the murderer had seen. Until he caught the bastard, Laurel was going to be under a round-the-clock guard. Ben had posted uniforms outside his house to keep watch, then he and Tristan headed into work.

Walking into the squad room, Tristan made a beeline for his desk and his new partner, Jake Maxwell. Ben was right on his heels.

"Hey, Jake. Fill me in. Where are we on the dead woman and the missing baby?"

Jake's head snapped up, and he stood. "I told you to stay home. I can handle this."

Tristan shrugged. "I know. But you don't need to. Laurel's safe and doing fine. I'm fine. Now fill me in."

Jake sighed as he turned to the papers strewn across his desk. "This case blew up in my face after you took off. Like I told you on the phone, our murder victim is also our kidnapping victim." He pulled an info sheet with their kidnapping victim's face on it from the mess on his desk. "Dr. Tate confirmed it early this morning. Her prints match the ones on file."

That same uneasy feeling he had when he heard the news earlier punched Tristan in the stomach again as he looked down at the paper Jake handed him. Veronica Chapman was indeed their kidnapping victim and their dead woman.

He looked up at Jake. "What about the baby?"

"Dr. Tate confirmed she had recently given birth. We're looking for an infant no older than three weeks. Our killer took her purse, if she had it with her, but we found her phone buried in the center console. The techs are working on getting it unlocked. I'm hoping there will be some information about the baby on there. A picture and hopefully something to indicate its gender. I put out a BOLO on the infant, but it was very vague."

Tristan's mind spun. That was a tiny baby. It wouldn't survive long without proper care. "There was no sign of the infant at the crash site?"

"No." Jake shook his head. "We combed the woods a hundred yards in every direction from the location of the car, as well as up and down the road. Nothing. The baby either wasn't with her or the killer took the baby with him."

"We also found this." Jake picked up an evidence bag from his desk. "It's a receipt for a local hotel. She paid cash for a room for a week. There's still two days left on her reservation according to this."

"Nice. Have you searched her room yet?"

"No. I just got the warrant. I'm not sure we'll find much, though. We found her suitcase in her car full of clothing for her and the baby."

Tristan scowled. Jake was right, that didn't sound promising. "Okay. Did you find anything on her killer?"

Jake's mouth flattened. "No. The crime scene techs pulled two bullets out of the trees. They're a match to the one that killed Ms. Chapman, but there were no prints on them."

Damn. It was looking like Laurel was their only lead. He didn't like that. This guy had gone to great lengths to hide his identity. The fact that Laurel could identify him was going to make him eager to silence her.

"All right. Let's go search her room. We also need to go down to that homeless community and talk to the people there. See if we can find someone who knew her. They might know who she had been talking to. Maybe even who the baby's father is."

Jake nodded. "We need Laurel's statement too. I take it from the fact she ran, she witnessed the whole thing?"

Tristan grimaced. "Yep. She said she watched the guy shoot our victim through the window."

"She give you a description at all?"

He shook his head. "No, not yet." He had been focused on getting her out of the cold and then she'd dropped her bombshell on him. Nothing else mattered after that except getting her to safety.

Jake frowned, looking slightly confused that Tristan wouldn't have asked Laurel for details, but didn't say anything. "Okay. Well, the sooner we can get a description of the killer, the sooner we can put out the BOLO."

Tristan nodded in agreement, but was unwilling to sacrifice her welfare and the baby's welfare for their case. "She needs to rest first. We can talk to her after we search Ms. Chapman's room and talk to her acquaintances." Tristan looked to Ben for confirmation, who nodded.

Ben pulled out his phone. "You two go investigate. I'm going to let Gemma know to be extra vigilant. Laurel's the key to all of this right now."

If that wasn't a punch to the gut, Tristan didn't know what was. Now he understood better how Ben had felt last year when that serial killer targeted Gemma.

Jake tossed everything back onto the mess that was his desk and picked up the warrant before following Tristan out to the parking lot. They quickly climbed into the cruiser Jake checked out earlier and pulled out of the lot.

Tristan stared out the window as Jake drove, his brain a jumble of thoughts. Now that he'd had time to process the last twenty-four hours, it was hitting him how lucky he had been to find Laurel in the vast wilderness. She'd done an exceptional job of covering her tracks by avoiding the snow until she couldn't. If it hadn't been for his experience as a tracker, he would have missed the tiny clues her passage left behind. It bothered him to think how differently things could have turned out if he hadn't found her last night.

It also bothered him to know that this whole ordeal was far from over. Until they found Veronica Chapman's killer, Laurel and their baby weren't safe. And that terrified him. He had just learned about the child, but fatherly instincts were already kicking in. There wasn't anything he wouldn't do to protect that life growing inside Laurel.

The car slowing brought Tristan out of his thoughts. He

perused the motel as they pulled in. It and the area around it were about as rundown as a place could get and still be habitable. This part of Asheville was the definition of pay-by-the-hour.

Eyes searching for anything out of place or anyone paying them too much attention, Tristan headed for the motel office, Jake on his heels. Reaching the building, he pulled open the plexiglass door and stepped inside. The smell of stale cigarette smoke and microwave burritos immediately slapped him in the face. A glance at Jake revealed that he had noticed it as well.

"Can I help you boys?" A man who had to be eighty or more stepped out from the door behind the counter marked "office." His thin, wispy, white hair was sticking up in every direction, and the gray cardigan he had on over his dingy white shirt had seen better days.

Tristan and Jake held up their shields. "We have a warrant to search one of your rooms," Tristan told him. Jake held up the paper signed by the judge.

Warily, the man eyed the document. "We ain't had no trouble here. I haven't had to call the cops in days."

"That's good. We're still going to need to see the room registered to Veronica Chapman, though."

The old man lifted an eyebrow. "Who?"

Tristan pulled out his phone and brought up the picture from the missing person's report and showed it to the man.

The old man leaned over the counter and peered at the phone before he straightened. "That girl checked out yesterday morning. Don't know why. She paid through the weekend."

Tristan shared a look with Jake. It was beginning to seem like the girl had been on the run. But from whom?

"Did she say where she was going?" Jake asked.

The old man shook his head. "Nope. Just packed up that itty-bitty baby of hers, turned in her key and left."

Dread filled Tristan's gut. "What time was that?"

"Oh, well, it was in the morning." The man scratched his head absently in thought. "Let me see if I can find the receipt. I felt bad for her with that tiny baby, so I refunded her the extra days she already paid for." He walked back into the office and opened the file drawer against the back wall, removing a folder. Shuffling back out to the counter, he laid it open and began flipping through the handful of receipts.

"Here. This one." He handed it to Tristan. "Time stamp says ten-oh-seven."

The dread started to churn. He looked up at Jake. The call from the passerby had come just after eleven. The area where she had been forced off the road was nearly an hour from Asheville. If she had dropped her baby off somewhere along the way, she had done so quickly.

"Why are you asking about that sweet girl, anyway? She in some kind of trouble?"

Tristan handed the man back the receipt. "She's dead. Murdered shortly after she left here yesterday."

The old man took a few deep breaths and rubbed at his jaw. "Murdered. Ain't that something?" His eyes suddenly snapped up to meet Tristan's. "What about her little one? Is she okay?"

"The baby was a girl? Sir, anything you can tell us about Ms. Chapman would be very helpful. Did she ever mention a friend? Someone she might have trusted her baby with?"

"No. The only thing she told me was the name of her baby. Haley. Is she all right?"

Well, at least they had a name now to go with the missing infant. "She's missing. Did you get a good look at the baby?"

The man nodded. "Pretty little thing. Head full of dark hair."

"Was she white, or did she look mixed?"

"White."

"What was the baby wearing when Ms. Chapman checked out?"

"I'm not sure. She had her all bundled up. All I could see was her face. Everything else was covered by one of those silky pink blankets."

Tristan nodded, then glanced at Jake, who pulled out his phone and stepped outside to call in the new information.

"I'm going to guess you've already cleaned her room?"

The old man nodded.

Trying not to let his frustration show, he nodded. "I still need to see the room. Did she leave anything behind?"

"Not that I know of. The maid is out now, cleaning. You could ask her." He handed Tristan a key to room twelve.

He handed the man a business card. "If you think of anything else, please call."

Nodding, the old man tucked the card into the pocket of his cardigan. "I hope you find that baby, detective."

So did Tristan. With a nod, he walked outside. Jake hung up as he stepped through the door.

"The BOLO's been updated. You get the key to her room?"

Tristan held up the key chain. "The manager said it's already been cleaned."

Jake grimaced, following Tristan down the sidewalk. "Great."

"We need to talk to the maid." Tristan pointed at the maid cart several doors down from the one he had stopped in front of. "Go turn your charm on her and I'll start looking in here."

His partner grinned, dimples flashing and icy blue eyes twinkling. "On it." He jogged away, leaving Tristan just shaking his head. Jake was a good cop, but he was a flirt. The maid had no idea what was headed her way.

Thrusting the key in the lock, Tristan unlocked the door

to Veronica's room and pushed it open. Just as he had expected, it was neat as a pin. The threadbare comforter was pulled taught over the queen-size mattress, the dingy carpet swept of all debris. Peering into the trashcan as he entered the room, he noted that it had been emptied.

Sighing, he set about opening drawers and peering under the bed, looking for anything that might tell him where she had been headed or with whom she might have had contact. What he came up with was a big, fat nothing.

Frustrated, he relocked the door and tracked down Jake, who he found leaning against the door jamb of the room three doors down, grinning flirtatiously at the young woman holding the handle of a vacuum.

Her shy smile disappeared when she noticed him in the doorway. She straightened, her hand clenching on the vacuum. Tristan stopped and tried to put a pleasant expression on his face, not wanting to frighten the woman. He was pissed they had so little evidence, but it wouldn't do them any good if he scared off a potential witness.

Jake pushed away from the wall, smile still in place. "Shay, this is my partner, Detective Mabley."

She offered him a slight nod.

Tristan smiled politely. "Ma'am."

"Shay was just telling me that she talked to Veronica the day before yesterday when she brought her some clean towels."

Hope lit in Tristan's chest. "Did she happen to say where she was headed? Or why she was camped out in this motel with a brand-new baby?"

The young woman shrugged and looked down before glancing up at Jake through her lashes. "She said she was thinking about going home. To Virginia. But she wasn't sure that her parents would welcome her back, especially since she had Haley now. She seemed real scared too. Always looking out the window like she expected someone to show up."

"Did she happen to leave anything behind when she left yesterday?" Jake asked.

Shay shook her head. "No. She was pretty neat. She made her bed every day and never left trash lying around. It was easy to get the room ready after she left. I just had to wipe it down and change the sheets."

"You ever notice any visitors?"

"No. She kept to herself the few days that she was here."

Jake took a card from his wallet. "Call me if you think of anything else, okay?"

The young woman took the card and nodded. "I hope you find her baby." She sniffed and blinked away some tears. "That poor thing," she murmured.

Tristan and Jake bid the woman goodbye and stepped out.

"Well, at least we got a name and a description of the kid," Jake commented on the way back to the cruiser.

They got more than that. "We need to contact her family. Find out why she was estranged in the first place and see if they've heard from her recently. Maybe they can shed some light on who might have wanted to hurt her and take Haley."

Settling into the passenger seat once again, Tristan contemplated little Haley's fate as Jake drove them the few blocks to the homeless encampment where Veronica had previously lived.

Why had the killer taken the baby and not left her in the car? Could it have been the baby's father? Or did the killer have a soft spot and didn't want to leave such a small baby exposed to the elements? If that was the case, what did he do with the infant? They would have heard by now if she had been turned over anonymously to the authorities.

There was always the chance Veronica had dropped the baby off with a friend, but Tristan didn't think so. She had been headed north, her car packed with what meager belongings she had. He had a feeling she'd been on her way to her family in Virginia.

Jake parked the cruiser at the curb close to the alley where the girl who reported Veronica missing said they camped. Box shelters lined the sides of the brick buildings, tarps covering the tops to keep out the snow and rain. Various items, from coolers to lawn chairs to broken televisions, surrounded the box houses. The stench of unwashed bodies and urine was heavy even from the street.

Jake stared into the mouth of the alley, a frown on his face. "You think we'll find anyone sober enough to tell us anything?"

Tristan shrugged. "Probably not, but we have to try. What was the name of her friend again? The one who reported her missing?"

Pulling out his phone, Jake looked up the case notes. "Miranda Benning." He showed Tristan the picture—a mug shot from when she had been arrested for prostitution. Her dishwater blonde hair was piled haphazardly on her head. The drug-induced acne all over her face and her gaunt appearance all made her look much closer to Tristan's thirty-five than her twenty.

With a nod, Tristan stepped over the curb and headed for the alley. "Let's see what we can find out."

Pulling up Veronica's picture on his phone, Tristan lifted the flap on the first shelter and peered inside. The stench was almost enough to bowl him over.

Trying not to breathe, he nudged the man sleeping inside with his foot. "Hey."

The man snorted and kept sleeping.

Tristan nudged him again. "Hey!"

This time the guy startled awake. He glared up at Tristan through glassy eyes. "What?"

"You know this girl?" Tristan held out his phone.

The guy barely glanced at it. "No. Go away." He turned on his side and closed his eyes again.

Letting the tarp flap back over the shelter's opening, Tristan straightened and gulped in a breath of slightly less foul air. Jake just arched a brow, and they moved on to the next shelter.

They made it half way down the alley before someone took the time to actually look at the picture of Veronica.

An older woman huddled around a small fire smiled softly at the image Tristan showed her. "Yeah, I remember her. Sweet girl when she was sober. She got in with some guy who comes around here and offers us work sometimes. She was pretty, so he took a quick shine to her."

Anticipation that they might have their first real lead made Tristan crouch down beside the woman. "Do you know this man's name?"

"Called himself Adam. I got a card around here somewhere." She pushed out of her lawn chair to go rummage through a pile of her belongings. "He handed them out to all of us. Told us if we ever wanted to work to call the number and he would send someone for us and that he'd pay cash at the end of the day."

"Did you ever go?" Jake asked.

She shook her head, still rooting through her stuff. "No. I can't do no manual labor and I'm not much for lying around on my back neither. I'm too old for that."

Tristan frowned. "You think he was prostituting the women who came to work for him?"

"I know he was. Them girls would come back with a wad of cash or new clothes. They said for a few hours of letting him or his friends do what they wanted, he fed them and threw money around like it was confetti."

"How often did Veronica go with him?"

"Oh, once a week or so. She never called him, but anytime he showed up, he managed to convince her to go with him. Then one week she didn't come back. We thought she had decided to stay. Randi, though, she wasn't so sure. Aha! I knew I had it still." Straightening, she held up a little white card.

"Here. It's probably not his real name, but the number works and someone always comes."

Tristan took the card. Adam Richland. Like the woman said, it was probably an alias. He hoped they would get lucky and it would pop up in their system.

"One more question. Is Randi here? We wanted to talk to her some more. She's the one who reported Veronica missing."

The old woman shook her head. "No. I ain't seen her in quite a while now. She just up and disappeared like Veronica did."

"Why is a woman like you out here, if you don't mind me asking?" Jake enquired. "I know this is going to sound terrible, but you don't fit the mold of a homeless person."

The old lady grinned. "Oh, trust me, honey. I have my vices just like everyone else here. I just have a little more control. And, I like the freedom of being out here without anyone to answer to. No bills. No connections. It suits me."

"Can we buy you dinner?" The words were out of Tristan's mouth before he knew what he was saying.

She eyed him speculatively. "I wouldn't turn down a hot meal."

"Good. How about we find you a place in a shelter, too? It's supposed to snow again."

She immediately shook her head. "No. I'll lose my spot here if I'm gone too long, and a shelter won't let me bring my stuff."

"You're sure?" Jake asked, leading the woman to their cruiser.

"Yep. Dinner with two handsome men is enough for me."

As they helped the woman into the car, Tristan's mind churned with the new information. This case had taken a dramatic twist. He was beginning to wonder if they hadn't stumbled into something much bigger than a simple murder.

NINE

When Tristan finally pulled into his sister's driveway, it was dark. He stayed at work much longer than he intended. After they took the homeless woman, Debbie, back to her camp, he and Jake went back to the station and started a search for Adam Richland as well as Miranda Benning. Tristan had a bad feeling they were going to find her in a similar state to her friend.

Muscles protesting all the activity of the last thirty-six hours, he trudged up the stairs, vowing to find a bottle of ibuprofen as soon as possible. Pulling open the door, feminine laughter assaulted him the moment he stepped inside. He followed the sound to the kitchen, where he found Laurel and Gemma elbow-deep in flour, pans of cookies spread around them. Laurel's blonde hair was pulled back, highlighting her pretty face. Her cinnamon eyes sparkled as she laughed at something Gemma said.

God, she was beautiful. He really hoped they could work things out. He wanted to come home to that smile every night.

His stomach growled as the scent of the cookies invaded his brain. He loved Gemma's cookies. Even though he'd eaten not long ago, he could never resist her baking. Stepping into the room, he snagged a chocolate chip cookie off of one of the pans, rolling his eyes in ecstasy. He was a cookie junkie, and he knew it.

"Hey, Tris. It's about time you got back. Ben's been home over an hour." She gestured to her husband, who sat at the end of the island, sneaking cookies and watching the women bake.

Tristan swallowed his cookie and slanted a glance at his brother-in-law. "Yeah, well, my case blew up in my face. Again." He'd filled Ben in earlier on everything they learned. Tristan hoped it was nothing, but it didn't sit well that the guy whom Debbie mentioned was using the homeless and they were then turning up missing.

"Everything okay?" Laurel asked softly.

"Yeah. It's just complicated." He walked around the island to her side. Lifting a hand, he brushed some flour off her cheekbone. "How are you feeling?"

"I'm okay. My legs are still a little weak and sore from running so far, but I'm warm again." She smiled and laid her hands against his cheeks to demonstrate.

He covered them with his own and held them there, staring down at her.

"Good."

She was so very tiny. It still amazed him that she had run so far over such rough terrain in her condition. And in those boots of hers that weren't made for anything except making the wearer look good.

Leaning down, he pressed a kiss to her forehead, inhaling her sweet scent. "We need to talk," he murmured against her hair.

She pulled back to frown up at him. "About what?"

"About what you saw that made you run."

Her mouth tightened into a thin line, but she nodded.

"Just let me help Gemma finish up in here, and then I'll answer any questions you have."

"You go on," Gemma said, having overheard their conversation. "I'm just going to throw these dishes in the dishwasher."

"What about all the cookies?" Laurel frowned and gestured to the still full pans and those cooling on racks.

Gemma waved a hand. "Tristan will eat a pan before he leaves, and I'll send a bunch home with him. The rest Ben can help me throw in bags. He'll take them to work in the morning. Trust me, I have this down to an art form. You go. We can handle cookie clean up."

After a moment, Laurel nodded.

Taking her hand, Tristan gave his sister and brother-in-law a quick nod of thanks and led Laurel from the room. But not before snagging a couple more cookies on his way out.

Laurel giggled when she saw his loot. "You really will eat a whole pan, won't you?"

He grinned, taking a bite. "One thing you will learn about me is that I have an extraordinary weakness for chocolate chip cookies."

"That's good to know. Gives me leverage if I ever need to sweet talk you." She tossed him a saucy grin.

He polished off his cookie and stared down at her, fire in his eyes. His gaze roved over her pretty face and lower. "You have many ways to talk me into things and none of them involve food."

She bit her lip and blushed, making Tristan hungry for more than Gemma's cookies. Leaning down, he kissed her soundly, unable to help himself. He wrapped his arms around her and lifted her off her feet, pulling her close. She was a welcome weight in his arms after the long day he'd had. He'd missed her and hadn't realized just how much until now.

When he begged entrance to her mouth, she wound her

arms around his neck and opened for him. Losing himself in her delicious heat, he let go of the stress of his day. She washed it all away and left him feeling new again.

Slowly, he pulled back and lowered her to her feet. She smiled up at him softly, her cinnamon eyes warm and inviting.

"You taste like chocolate," she said softly.

He laughed and gave her another quick kiss. "I guarantee that you taste sweeter. Come on. Not to ruin the moment, but let's go get this over with. I want to be done with this case for the day."

Nodding, she followed him into Ben's office. He pulled her down next to him on the old leather couch shoved against one wall. "Okay. Start from the beginning. What happened?"

She took a deep breath and clutched his hands, staring at a point over his shoulder as she talked. "I was headed up to Mrs. Preston's. She's a shut-in we used to get a lot of calls for. I noticed that a lot of the time she was just lonely, so I started taking food and other necessities to her every couple of weeks and spending an afternoon visiting. Anyway, I rounded the bend and nearly hit the SUV that was sitting across the road."

"What SUV?" Tristan interrupted. Only Laurel's car and Veronica Chapman's car had been at the scene when he and Jake arrived.

"There was a black SUV, a Ford I think, parked perpendicular on the road. I managed to avoid colliding with it, then got out to check on everyone. I saw the damage to the rail, and when I looked over the edge I could see the red car." She looked at him then. "I didn't think. I just ran down the hill, wanting to get to whoever could be injured."

"You didn't see the man standing outside the car before you ran down?"

She shook her head. "There were too many trees. The car was wedged, and he was standing behind the one on the driver's side. I was only a few yards away before I saw him. He came into view just as he lifted the gun and shot her." Her voice trailed off into a choked whisper as she remembered.

Taking several deep breaths, she blinked hard before continuing. "He saw me then and took a shot, but I moved as soon as we made eye contact and he missed. I just ran and tried to make myself as hard to shoot as possible until I got to a place where I could hide. I climbed a tree behind some rocks. He didn't see me and kept going."

Tristan frowned. "Why didn't you come back to the road when he didn't spot you?"

"There was someone else with him."

He leaned forward at the new bit of information. "You're sure?"

She nodded. "He yelled back at whoever it was that I was there. I didn't stick around, though, to see who it was."

A second suspect changed things. It made it less likely that it was just a scorned baby daddy bent on revenge. It also explained why the SUV was missing.

"What did the man you saw look like?"

"Brown hair, dark eyes. Probably about six feet tall. I only got glimpses of him as I looked back while I ran. I got a really good look at his face, though. He looked right at me after he shot that girl."

Which meant that the killer had gotten a good look at Laurel. Tristan's concern for her safety rose tenfold, and he cursed. Standing, he paced to the window and looked out. The night was still. Snow fell lightly, giving the world a dreamy quality. The peacefulness of the scene outside was in direct contrast to his churning gut.

A small hand on his back had him turning around to look down into Laurel's warm eyes.

"This is bad, isn't it? That I saw him and he saw me?"

"Yeah." He framed her face in his hands. "But I'm not going to let anything happen to you. Ben already agreed to post a guard on you at all times. If I'm not there, someone else will be."

She frowned up at him. "What about when I'm at work? There isn't room in the ambulance for an extra person all the time."

Déjà vu slapped Tristan in the face. It was Gemma all over again. He let his hands drift down to hold hers. "How about you take some time off? Just until we catch this guy."

She was shaking her head before he had even finished. "I can't. We're already down a paramedic. Besides, I can't take a bunch of time off now if I want to take more than the six weeks of maternity leave I get when the baby comes. I'd really like to not have to turn my newborn over to daycare because I can't take an extended leave."

He resisted the urge to growl in frustration. Leave it to him to find a woman with the same stubbornness as his sister. "You do realize that I can support us without you ever having to work again, don't you? I spent years in the back of beyond fighting terrorists and got paid well for it. And I never spent much of it because I was always in a war zone or living on base. I invested it all. Between that and my detective's salary, we wouldn't be hurting if you wanted to stay home and raise our baby."

A flash of pain crossed her face. "I have no right to any of that, Tristan. I'm not your wife."

The urge to change that hit him square in the chest. "Maybe you should be."

Ten

Laurel's eyes widened until they seemed to take over her face. "You can't be serious. We barely know each other." She was not doing that again. As nice as Tristan was, she was not marrying someone she barely knew. No matter how good his touch made her feel.

"So, let's change that. Come home with me. Nothing has to happen. There's a guest room. But you're right. We need time to get to know each other. With our schedules, the best way to do that is going to be to come home to each other. By spending our evenings together and finding out how grumpy the other one is first thing in the morning."

His hands framed her face again. "I know I make you nervous. But I'm hoping I can change that by showing you I'm nothing like the monster in your past. I promise not to pressure you into anything. I just want to give us a chance. What do you say?"

Covering his hands with her own, her mind whirled as she thought about it. He did make her nervous, but he wasn't going anywhere. They were going to have to deal with each other in some capacity for the next two decades, at least, and she didn't want their relationship to be strained. It wouldn't be good for their child. She wanted this baby to grow up knowing that his or her parents could get along, whether they were married or not. Her own upbringing had been lacking in that department. Her father wasn't a nice man.

But could she trust Tristan to treat her the way she had finally come to realize she should be treated? She'd heard Gemma's stories tonight about how bossy he could be. Laurel couldn't live like that. Not again.

She owed it to her child to try to make things work, though. Tristan was a good man and would make a great father. She couldn't justify keeping him at arm's length when it was within her ability to give her child a two-parent home. If he got too bossy, well, they would cross that bridge if and when they came to it. They would just have to learn to compromise for their child's sake.

"Okay," she finally answered. The smile that lit his face could have powered the sun. "I will stay with you, but we're staying at my house. I'm sorry, but I'm not up to living with your parents too." Gemma had mentioned that Tristan was living in their childhood home at the moment.

His smile quickly turned down. "In my defense, they're not normally there. Gemma and I have been the caretakers of their house while they run around the country. Mom's been a little more—clingy since I was shot. She was my nurse while I recuperated and then she got involved in Gemma's wedding. Dad just went along with whatever she wanted and suddenly I've found myself living with my parents again."

She giggled at the look of consternation on his face. "I think it's nice that your family is so close. I never had that growing up. My mom died when I was young and my dad and brothers weren't exactly sure what to do with me, so I got ignored a lot." *When her dad wasn't beating her, anyway.*

"Well, you have it now. Once my mom finds out you're

carrying my baby, she's going to be all over you like squirrels on a bird feeder."

Nerves assaulted her in a wave. She wasn't comfortable being the center of attention on a good day, and while she liked Caroline Mabley, the thought of being her sole focus was scary. She could be every bit as overbearing as her son, according to Gemma.

Apparently, he saw her eyes widen, because he grinned. "I promise to run interference anytime she gets too pushy, or you get overwhelmed. I'm used to it after Gemma's wedding. I have refereed many arguments between the two in the last few months."

She bit her lip, still peering up at him anxiously. "Can we wait a while yet to tell her and your dad? I just need some time to adjust to all of this. I took the test the morning of the murder. I don't think I've processed any of the last thirty-six hours yet."

He nodded. "I wouldn't even have said anything to Gemma yet if she hadn't been in the room."

Laurel worried her lip. "She won't tell anyone, will she?"

He shook his head. "No. As excited as she is, she knows it's not her news to tell. Until we say otherwise, she'll keep it a secret." He brushed a few wisps of her hair back that had come loose from her ponytail. "Now, are you ready to go? I don't know about you, but I'm ready for bed. It's been a long-ass day."

She knew her cheeks flushed bright red, but she was powerless to stop it. Images of Tristan in the hotel bed flooded her mind and made every cell in her body turn up the heat.

He groaned, and she knew that the hunger she felt was reflected in her eyes. His jaw worked as he stared down at her, his eyes heating. "I promised I would leave you alone, but you make it damn hard."

His words didn't help the desire now running rampant

through her body. She didn't want him to leave her alone, even though she knew she should. He muddled her brain and made it hard for her to make rational decisions.

With a growl, he took her hand and towed her toward the kitchen. "Come on. Let's get my cookies and say goodbye before I lock us in Ben's office and say to hell with it."

Suppressing a whimper at the idea of putting that leather couch to use, Laurel followed him down the hallway. What the hell was wrong with her? She had never craved sex before, but suddenly it was all she could think about. It had to be the hormones talking.

Her eyes drifted to Tristan's tight butt outlined by his jeans.

Or maybe it was just the man. God, he was gorgeous.

Eyes still glued to his rear, she nearly slammed into his back when he came to an abrupt halt in the kitchen doorway.

"Really? I thought I got away from this when you moved out."

Laurel peered around him to see what he was talking about just in time to watch Gemma glare at her brother. A wicked slant curled Ben's mouth, his arms wrapped around his wife.

"Go home and you will," Ben said.

Tristan pulled her into the room. "That's my intention. I just want my cookies and to say bye."

Gemma untangled herself from her husband and picked up a plastic container from the counter, thrusting it at Tristan. "Here. Love you. Bye."

Laurel couldn't stop the laugh that bubbled out. Gemma's exasperation was palpable. And it was understandable. She kinda wanted to do the same thing to Tristan that they had just caught Ben and Gemma doing.

Rolling his eyes, Tristan looked at Ben. "I'll be at Laurel's if you need me."

Ben's expression turned serious. "Keep your eyes and ears open. Anything weird happens, you call."

"I will."

The short exchange effectively doused her mirth. Much more somber, she waved at the couple, who were already turning back to each other and followed Tristan out of the kitchen.

She stuffed her feet into her boots, then Tristan helped her into her coat. When she picked up her purse, her keys jangled, reminding her that she had her car again.

"Some of your colleagues dropped off my car." It had been delivered that afternoon, its load of supplies for Mrs. Preston taken to the elderly woman by one of the other paramedics. "Do you just want to follow me home?"

He hesitated only momentarily at the suggestion before nodding. "So long as you're sure you're okay to drive."

"I'm fine."

He nodded. Hand on her back, he guided her outside and helped her into her vehicle. She smiled up at him tentatively as he stood in the door to her car while she got settled. It was a little weird having a man be so chivalrous. No one had ever bothered before.

He asked for her address in case they got separated. She rattled it off. With a long, heated look, he finally closed her door to get into his truck. Laurel expelled a breath, willing her heart rate back under control before she shifted the car into reverse.

What the hell was she thinking, inviting him to stay with her? Vowing to give him a chance and moving him into her house before she really knew him were two very different things.

So was sleeping with him after one dance, her subconscious reminded her.

But that was just all the more reason why she should have

politely told him she would be fine on her own. Ben had agreed to allocate manpower to protect her. There would be someone there to keep her safe. It didn't have to be Tristan *in her house*. A deputy parked outside would be just as good. Maybe even better, because he could see what was coming. Tristan would be inside with her and wouldn't know that anything was amiss until the killer broke in.

Nearly talking herself into rescinding her invitation, she looked in the rearview mirror to see his headlights behind her. The sight oddly calmed her. She huffed out a sigh, knowing she was an idiot to even be wasting the brain power on considering someone else protecting her. No one would make her feel as safe as Tristan. It wasn't just because he was big and tough. His partner was big and tough. But Tristan had come after her in a snowstorm, even after the way she'd treated him the last couple of months. He hadn't been willing to wait for search and rescue. Laurel knew without a shadow of a doubt that he would do anything to keep her safe. Not because of the baby she carried, but because of *her*. No one had ever done anything to keep her safe except her younger brother and that had been too little too late.

So, she was going to welcome Tristan into her house with open arms and pray that she wasn't making the biggest mistake of her life by trusting a man. This time, she had far more to lose.

∼

Tristan's headlights lit up the white siding façade of Laurel's tiny house as he pulled in behind her SUV. Small as it was, the house and yard were tidy. The fresh snowfall sparkled in the light given off by the decorative pole light in the yard, while her porch light shone brightly over the dark red door. It was the only pop of color on the house in the dark winter night.

Shutting off the engine, Tristan grabbed his container of cookies and climbed out of the truck, locking it before walking into the garage. Laurel pushed the button on her remote to close it behind him and got out of her vehicle.

Silently, she led him to the interior garage door. He was pleased to see that she had to unlock it with her keys to get inside. So many people thought that the overhead garage door meant security. He had seen more than one home invasion where the burglars spoofed the garage door frequency and gained entry to the house through an unlocked interior door.

Once inside, she flipped on the light and tossed her purse and keys onto the kitchen counter. The creamy formica counters were uncluttered except for a few pieces of mail. He didn't know how she did it. The counters at his house were always covered in stuff. Mail, work files, dishes—it all collected, even with his parents home. His dad was one of the main contributors to the mess. But Laurel's kitchen was spotless.

"There's some leftovers in the fridge if you're hungry," she told him, taking off her coat. She tossed it over a kitchen chair. Tristan set the cookies down and shucked his own outerwear, putting it next to hers.

"I'm good. I ate earlier. I'll stick to my cookies," he said, a grin spreading over his handsome face. "You should eat something, though. Keep your energy levels up."

She laughed softly. "I'm going to bed soon, Tristan. I don't need any energy right now."

Heat flared at the reminder of how she had looked lying on his bed. First, flush with passion, her body ripe for the taking, and second, all soft and sleepy after he slaked her lust.

He cleared his throat. "You did eat, though, right? I didn't get you that cheeseburger from Daisy's like I promised."

Her face broke into a broad grin. "Gemma did. You had no sooner left than she was asking me if I was hungry. She made Ben bring us food."

Tristan just shook his head. His brother-in-law was so whipped. "Did it stay down okay? No queasiness?"

She shook her head. "Nope. It tasted fantastic. I ate the whole thing, which is probably why I'm not too hungry now."

Forgetting his vow to keep his distance, he walked closer until he could brush that flyaway strand of hair back again. "You should still try to eat something. Dinner was hours ago."

She shook her head. "No, I'm good."

He retreated to the table, picking up the cookies. Opening the lid, he offered it to her. "Not even one cookie?"

Rolling her eyes, she took one from the container and sat down at the table. He sat across from her, appeased. Unlacing his boots, he toed them off. After everything he had walked through in the last couple of days, he didn't want to track that filth through her house.

Grabbing a cookie of his own, he ate silently, trying not to stare at her as she nibbled on her own. By the time he had finished three cookies, she was only halfway through her first one.

He frowned at her. "You sure you're feeling all right?"

"Yes," she replied testily. "I already told you I was fine."

Tristan held up his hands. "I just wanted to make sure you were okay."

She sighed and sat back in her chair, abandoning the rest of her cookie. "I'm sorry, Tristan. I just—the overprotective stuff gets to me. I don't like people hovering and watching over everything I do. It brings back bad memories."

Fury sparked in Tristan's chest at the reminder of her past, but he tamped it down. Getting angry at a long ago, unseen enemy wouldn't help. "I'm sorry. I know I can be overbearing, as I'm sure Gemma has already told you, but I don't do it to be mean or controlling. Making sure that you're taken care of and safe is important to me. I want you to be happy. I'll try to back off, but you're going to have to bear with me."

Surprising him, she reached across the table and covered his hand with her own. "I know, and I understand. Just please try not to hover. Trust that I can take care of myself?"

He nodded. "So long as you promise me that if you need something or if you're not feeling well, you'll let me know."

"I will."

"Good." Giving her hand a squeeze, he rose, snatching one last cookie from the container.

She laughed, shaking her head. "How do you have room?"

One corner of his mouth tilted up. "There's always room for cookies," he quipped before taking a huge bite.

She just shook her head at him again, an amused grin on her face.

After tossing her half-eaten cookie in the trash, Laurel led Tristan to the back of the house to a linen closet. "I only have one bedroom, so you'll have to sleep on the sofa. It pulls out." She bit her lip again, sending his blood pressure higher. "I hope that's okay?"

Accepting the blanket and sheets she handed him, he nodded, holding the linens tight so he wouldn't touch her. Her skittishness was back. "I've slept in worse places. The sofa bed will be fine."

She worried that lip between her teeth again. "Let me grab you a pillow." She ducked into the room across the hall.

Tristan stood in the doorway, taking in her bedroom. The walls were a soft gray, the bed underneath the window was a creamy iron frame, its mattress covered in a bright floral quilt. A maple dresser was pushed against the wall to his right while her closet covered the left wall. What caught his eye, though, were the paintings on the walls. They were landscapes, and the colors were so vibrant, the scenes practically leapt off the canvas.

He walked into the room to take a closer look at one. "These are amazing. Where'd you get them?" He glanced back at her to see her cheeks flushing bright red, her lip tucked between her teeth again.

"I painted them."

Eyes wide, his head whipped back around to stare at the beautiful lake scene. Water shimmered in bright sunlight, the foliage on the trees on the bank the lush green of summertime. The most striking part was the eagle, wings spread wide, talons open, as it went for a fish in the water.

Unable to help himself, he wandered further into the room to look at the one over the dresser. She had captured the fog over the rolling hills that gave the Smokies their name.

He looked over at her in awe. "Why are you a paramedic and not some famous artist living in a trendy apartment in New York? These are incredible."

She shrugged shyly. "It's just a hobby. It helps me —escape."

The slight hesitation spoke volumes. Tristan felt that fury well up again.

"Well, I think they're beautiful and you shouldn't hide them in your bedroom where no one ever sees them." His eyes roved over the painting again. He felt like he was there, watching the sunrise over the foggy mountain.

She came to stand beside him, a pillow clutched against her belly. "I have a bunch more in the basement."

He looked down at her. She looked up at him, her eyes hesitant.

Tristan swallowed hard as he realized she was offering him a glimpse of her inner self. It felt like she had given him a precious gift. Every time he turned around, he learned something new about this woman that amazed him.

"I'd love to see them."

Nodding, she smiled softly. "Tomorrow. There are a lot, and we're both tired."

Wordlessly, he nodded and followed her back into the hallway. She passed him the pillow.

"Good night, Tristan."

Leaning in, he placed a soft kiss on her cheek, the scent of her skin filling his nose. He knew he would dream about that creamy goodness all night. "Good night, Laurel."

Turning on his heel, he forced his feet to walk away before he couldn't.

Eleven

Laurel stared at the multitude of canvases lining her basement walls, worrying her lip between her teeth. She couldn't believe she'd offered to show Tristan her paintings. When he followed her into her bedroom last night, she hadn't even given the artwork on her walls a second thought. Her bedroom was her sanctuary. She had created it to be a place of peace. Often, when she got home from a shift, she would curl up on her bed and watch TV or read. When she decorated the room, she had done it with the idea of having a soothing place to help her relax at the end of a long day. Her art represented a release of emotions for her, and it gave her almost as much peace to look at the two paintings on her walls as it had to create them.

Sighing, she flipped through the canvases that were several deep on pallets to keep them off the floor. She knew the chilly, damp basement wasn't the best place for them, but she didn't have anywhere upstairs to store them. She barely had room in her closet to store her easel and paints.

She paused on a painting she did shortly after she moved to Northridge. It had been a beautiful summer day and she had gone out hiking. The scenery had been breathtaking. When she got home, she stayed up all night to get the bones of the painting on canvas, then refined it over several days.

Moving to the next pallet, a darker one caught her eye. This one she did shortly after she left West Virginia. While she'd been elated to be away from the turmoil there, part of her had been terrified her father or brothers would show up and force her to go back. One night, she had been so scared of that very thing, she had painted her family homestead, trying to expel it from her brain. It was a bleak, stark painting full of pain.

God. She had lost her mind by agreeing to let Tristan see these. They were like a diary of her life. All her ups and downs were right here for anyone to see.

Anxiety made her stomach churn. Maybe she should just tell him she changed her mind. Or bring up a few that were acceptable. That didn't delve too deeply into her emotional state at the time she painted them.

The front door slammed, causing her to jump. A quick glance at her watch told her she had been downstairs far longer than she had intended. Tristan was home.

"Laurel?"

His voice carried down the stairs from the living room.

Cursing herself for not paying better attention to the time, she went to the bottom of the stairs. There was no hiding them now.

"I'm down here, Tristan."

His large frame loomed in the doorway seconds later. Boots clomping on the stairs, he walked down, stopping just above her.

"Can I come down?"

The look in his eyes told her that he was asking for more than just permission to enter the basement. He wanted to see her work. Wanted to see her.

Taking a deep breath and reminding herself that she had promised to try to cultivate a relationship with this man, she pulled her courage around herself like a cloak and nodded, stepping back.

He descended the last couple of steps, hunching slightly in the cramped space.

"Wow. You weren't kidding." He spun, looking at the years' worth of art lining the walls.

She pointed to the far end of the basement. "Start down there. Those are the earliest ones I did."

He didn't wait for her to change her mind. Shoulders still slightly bent in deference to the low ceiling, he strode down the line of paintings to the furthest pallet.

Laurel hovered near the stairs, her arms wrapped around her middle. As he neared the back of the first stack, she sucked her lip between her teeth, then immediately let it go. She was going to wear a hole in her bottom lip before the day was out at this rate.

Suddenly, he froze, then took the painting she'd just been looking at out of the stack. He held it higher to look at it more closely before glancing over at her. "Where is this?"

Apprehensive about all that it revealed, she looked away before answering. "My family's home in West Virginia."

His chest heaved as he took a deep, steadying breath. Jaw clenched, he replaced the painting. "I think I'm glad you escaped that place."

She was too.

Moving on to the next pallet, she stood back as he looked through her art. She had been right. It was like letting him read her diary. Every extreme emotion she'd felt over the last few years—both good and bad—was chronicled through the paintings.

Silently, she watched as he moved from pallet to pallet, sometimes stopping to look closer at a few or to ask questions.

The newer ones were more joyful, she realized. As the years went by and she settled in here, she had put her past behind her and started living again. Looking at her work through Tristan's eyes had allowed her to see that.

A lightness filled her as she let go of some of the fear she hadn't realized still remained. Sometime over the last several years, she had healed.

"You should give this one to Gemma and Ben."

Startled out of her thoughts at his voice, she looked at the painting he held. It was of the snowy scene outside the barn where Gemma and Ben got married. The place where she had started to fall for the handsome man in her basement.

She walked closer, studying the painting. The peace and wonder of that evening leapt off the canvas. She smiled up at him, a flirty smile teasing her lips. "I didn't paint it because of them."

His eyes lit with that familiar fire. "Never mind, then. This one is just for us." He put the painting back, then turned to her, wrapping his arms around her waist to hold her close.

Brushing back that wayward lock of hair, he looked down at her softly. "Thank you for sharing these with me. I can tell it wasn't easy for you. Your work—I understand now why you keep it to yourself. You pour your heart out into each and every one." He looked back down at her. "I'm honored you let me see it."

She looked away briefly, gathering herself. "I promised myself I'd let you in," she said simply. She waved a hand at the canvases around them. "All this is a diary of my life since I moved here. It's the first step to that vow."

Tenderly, he placed a kiss on her forehead. Laurel closed her eyes, savoring the contact. Sharing this part of herself had loosened some of her reservations around him. He could have scoffed at or quickly perused her work, barely glancing at the art. But he hadn't. He had seen what she had put into them. Had seen *her* and respected her.

Hugging him back briefly, she shifted away before she gave into the urge to haul him upstairs to her bedroom. She might be softening toward him, but she didn't want to muck everything up by sleeping with him yet. It would just mess with her feelings too much. She was having enough trouble sorting them out as it was.

"Come on." She pulled him toward the stairs. "I made dinner."

Accepting the change of subject, he followed her up the stairs. "I smelled it when I came in. Lasagna?"

She looked back, laughing at the boyish light in his eyes. "Yes, Garfield."

A sardonic tilt slanted his mouth. "Haven't heard that one before. Gemma calls me Cookie Monster a lot, though."

Laurel's laughter increased. "After last evening, I can understand why."

He shrugged. "Can't deny it."

She just grinned, her heart lighter than it had ever been.

Twelve

Unable to sleep, her mind still wired from her revelations earlier, Laurel tiptoed her way into the kitchen to get a glass of water and one of Gemma's cookies. Tristan had surprisingly not eaten them all yet. It probably helped that she'd kept him distracted after dinner. Having broken through a barrier, the conversation had flowed much more easily between them and they sat in the living room talking about a myriad of subjects before parting for the night.

She had learned a lot about him in those few hours, including what his tattoos meant. One was his Army Ranger insignia, and the other—a map and compass—was an artist's rendering of a map of Foggy Mountain. He had told her that it was to remind him that no matter where he was in the world, the Smokies were home. Laurel loved the sentiment behind it and it only endeared him to her more.

As quietly as she could, so that she didn't wake Tristan, she filled a glass with tap water and leaned against the counter, staring out at her dark lawn and munching on her cookie.

Movement near her table on the patio caught her attention.

What was that? A coyote?

Leaning closer to the glass, she stared hard, trying to make out the shape. It was the wrong size for a coyote. A bear maybe? They'd been known to scrounge for food in town on occasion. This early in the year, there wouldn't be much for them to forage in the woods. Maybe one had wandered in looking for an easy meal. She didn't need it trying to get into her trashcans, though. That had happened once when she still lived at home. It had strewn trash from one end of the yard to another. Her dad had been so mad.

Moving to the door, she flipped on the back porch light, hoping to startle it into running away. But it wasn't a bear that startled. It was a man.

Laurel screamed.

∼

Tristan came awake with a start at the sound of Laurel screaming from the kitchen. Sitting bolt upright, he reached for his gun and launched himself off the couch toward the sound, thankful he left his jeans on.

"What? What's wrong?" He skidded to a stop just inside the doorway. She stood by the back door, staring out at the yard.

"There was a man out there by the table!"

Stuffing his feet into the tennis shoes he had brought over to her house and grabbing his handcuffs off the counter, he unlocked the back door.

"Call 911 and stay inside."

She nodded, her eyes wide. He pushed past her through the door.

The early March wind chilled him to the bone as soon as he stepped outside. He wished he'd left his shirt on to sleep now, too.

Scanning the yard, he saw footprints leading away from the house toward the shed and the fence that surrounded the backyard. Cautiously, he crept around the small building, clearing the area at the back of the structure. It was empty. Laurel's house backed up to a wooded area. Tristan shined the flashlight attached to his gun into the trees. A flash of red flannel caught his attention ten yards past the fence.

"Freeze! Sheriff's department!"

The partially concealed figure took off running at Tristan's shout.

With a curse, Tristan leapt the fence and took off after the man, his longer legs quickly eating up the distance. In moments, he caught up and tackled the guy to the ground. Pinning his arms, he handcuffed the guy with a couple of quick flicks of his wrists, then hauled him to his feet.

"All right, who the hell are you, and what are you doing here?" This man was blonde, a far cry from the description Laurel gave of the killer. Maybe this was the partner.

Silent, the man just stared straight ahead.

"Okay. Fine. You don't want to talk, we'll just sort it out at the station." Getting more than a little cold now, Tristan towed the man back to the house. The first sirens broke through the quiet night.

Heading for the gate at the side of the house to meet the officers out front, the sound of the back door opening stopped him.

Laurel stepped out snuggled in her coat, her feet stuffed into those ridiculous boots she traipsed through the wilderness in.

"Honey, go back inside where it's warm. This guy doesn't match the description of the man you saw."

But she ignored him, instead staring intently at the young man cuffed at his side. Frowning fiercely, she moved forward.

"Laurel—"

A wave of her hand silenced him.

Curious now about her behavior, he watched as she came around to stand in front of him and the young man he'd caught, still staring hard at his captive.

The man raised his eyes to look at Laurel and she gasped, her own eyes going wide in shock.

"Bobby?"

The young man smiled sadly. "Hi, Sis."

Thirteen

Stunned didn't even start to describe how Laurel felt. Flabbergasted, stupefied, utterly shocked—those came closer. Her little brother was the last person she had ever expected to find prowling outside her house.

"Sis? What's he talking about?" Tristan's gaze bounced back and forth between her and the man he held onto. "Laurel? What's going on? Do you know this man?"

Still shocked, she nodded. "He's my brother—my younger brother, Bobby." Coming back to herself a bit as the questions started popping into her head, she put her hands on her hips and frowned at her brother. "What the hell are you doing here? How did you even find me?" Another scarier question presented itself. She swallowed hard. "Do Dad and the others know where I am?" Her eyes darted around the yard, half expecting her older brothers to leap out and ambush them all.

"No!" he vehemently denied. "They have no idea I'm here. I haven't talked to any of them since I graduated high school. I packed up and left in the middle of the night right after graduation."

She frowned harder, her mind spinning. "So, what are you

doing here?"

His shoulders sagged. "I've been trying to find you since I left. I finally had the means to hire a private investigator. He found you for me a few weeks ago." He shrugged as she glared at him. "I just wanted to make sure you were okay." He glanced up at Tristan, who still held his arm. "I'm guessing by the fact that this guy came charging half-naked out of your house that you've done just fine for yourself."

She glared at him, her tiny hands balled into fists that she propped on her hips. "What the hell do you care? My welfare never concerned you before."

"I helped you get out of Womack, remember? Brought you—" he broke off and shot a glance at Tristan.

"After I nearly *died*!" After she had lost everything.

Bobby hung his head. "I know," he said softly. "I should have done more, but I didn't know how." He lifted his eyes to hers. "I was just a kid. I couldn't stand up to Dad and our brothers. And Johnny. I'm sorry, Laurel. I just wanted you to know that."

Exasperated, she threw her arms wide. "Then why didn't you just knock on the front door and tell me? Why sneak around my house in the middle of the night? You're lucky Tristan didn't shoot you."

Eyeing the bigger man again, who continued to frown down at them both, Bobby shifted his weight. "I didn't think you'd talk to me. I just wanted to make sure you were doing okay. I know I should have approached you during the day, but I didn't know what to say."

"Sorry would have been a really good start."

The sirens wailed louder, pulling up out front. Tristan's voice rose over the cacophony. "Laurel, what do you want me to do with him? I can arrest him for trespassing and criminal mischief."

Closing her eyes, she muttered a few swear words. Why

was it that she had lived such a normal, boring existence these last few years, but now, in the span of two months, her entire life had turned into a freaking soap opera?

Sighing, she opened her eyes and shook her head. "No. Let him go."

Tristan quirked an eyebrow at her, silently asking if she was sure. She nodded.

An officer for Northridge's police department came running around the side of the house and hopped the fence.

Tristan immediately identified himself and asked the officer for his handcuff key, explaining that it had all been a misunderstanding.

Bobby rubbed his wrists as Tristan released him.

Eyeing the younger and smaller man warily, Tristan bent his head closer to hers. "Will you be okay with him while I go put on a shirt and talk to the officers? I need to make a report and cancel the cavalcade of deputies that are likely coming our way."

She nodded. "We'll be fine."

He kissed her quick before casting a glare at her brother and stepping into the house. The officer followed him.

Bobby spared a glance at Tristan's back before training his eyes on her. "You look good, Laurel. Happy."

She crossed her arms, still ticked, and still not trusting his reason for lurking in her backyard. "I am happy. What are you really doing here?"

He held up his hands, his expression open. "Exactly what I said. I just wanted to make sure you were doing all right. It's bothered me ever since the day you left that I didn't have a way to check on you. I know you were the one always taking care of me, but it doesn't change the fact that I wanted you to be safe. Like I said, I wish now that I would have done more."

So did Laurel. Maybe her nightmare would have ended a little sooner and with a lot less heartbreak. But the past was exactly that—the past. Wallowing in it and wishing it were different wouldn't change anything. She was finally beginning to see that.

"Does he know about—everything?" Bobby motioned toward the house where Tristan had disappeared.

Laurel bit her lip. "He's guessed a lot of it, but no, he doesn't know everything. We haven't really been together all that long, and I'm still working up the courage to tell him."

One eyebrow, so similar to her own, lifted over Bobby's brown eyes. "Yeah? Well, considering the way he looked at you, I don't think he's going anywhere."

Laurel tamped down the hysterical laugh that threatened to erupt, her emotions close to the surface. Oh, if he only knew.

Taking a deep breath to get herself under control, she motioned Bobby toward the house. "Come on. Let's get you warmed up." His clothes were wet from where Tristan had obviously tackled him into the snow.

Removing her coat and draping it over a chair, she turned on the coffeepot and busied herself adding grounds and water to the machine. "So, where are you living now if you've left Womack?"

"I actually just moved to Asheville. I joined the Navy when I left home. Did a few tours on an aircraft carrier, then got out. I'm an airplane mechanic and a hobby pilot now."

Impressed with what he had accomplished, she turned and rested against the counter, more interested in the conversation. "I'm glad you left. You were never like them."

He smiled. "No. Because I had you. You showed me what it meant to be kind. That there were ways to solve problems and conduct yourself without using your fists. Or lying."

She smiled despite herself. "I did do plenty of that, though."

"Only to protect yourself. Or me. You were always trying

to shield me from them."

The coffee gurgled as it finished brewing. She poured Bobby a cup and left the rest for Tristan. Pouring herself another glass of water, she sat down across the table from her brother.

"I truly am sorry, Sis."

She waved a hand. "It's in the past, Bobby. If you really want to make amends, let's try to start again. Just don't expect me to trust you right off the bat. You may have never laid a hand on me, but you did plenty of squealing and sticking your head in the sand. You're going to have to convince me you've changed."

He nodded eagerly. "I have, Laurel. I know that being such a coward was wrong. The Navy helped me to recognize that and to change. I want us to start over and to get to know each other as adults." He held out a hand for her to shake. "Hi. I'm Rob."

With a small smile, amusement lighting her eyes, she took his hand. "Rob, huh?"

He grinned. "When I decided to make a new life for myself, I decided I needed to see myself in a new light." He shrugged. "Going by Rob seemed like a good way to put who I was as 'Bobby' and the life I'd led in Womack behind me."

Laurel's smile broadened. "Well, it's nice to meet you, Rob."

He squeezed her hand before letting it go and turning his gaze to the window, where the Northridge police car sat, its lights still blinking red and blue.

Laurel stifled a groan. Her neighbors were going to hate her.

"So, what's the story with the mountain who tackled me in the woods? You said he hasn't been around long, but it sure looked otherwise."

She shrugged, unwilling to discuss her budding relationship with this brother she barely knew anymore. "There isn't much to know. He's a detective with the sheriff's department. We met on the job. He's nice."

Rob quirked his brow again, but didn't comment on her lack of information. "He treats you well. Not like—" He stopped, a sheepish expression crossing his face. "Sorry. I don't want to drudge up bad memories."

Laurel couldn't stop her short laugh. "If that were the case, you would never have come here."

His smile took on a hint of irony. "Okay, I don't want to drudge up the really bad ones."

She smiled back. "It's okay. Like I said. I've put a lot of it behind me."

The front door opened, letting in an icy blast of air, making Laurel shiver. She could hear Tristan stomp the snow off his shoes before he made his way across the hardwood floors to the kitchen and dining area.

When he appeared in the kitchen doorway, her breath caught. He had removed his coat and was wearing just a t-shirt stretched tight across his chest and arms, tendrils of his tattoos showing beneath the short sleeves. His face, though, was what truly had her searching for air. Concern drew his mouth into a tight line, and the fine lines around his eyes seemed sharper as he took in the atmosphere in the room. As soon as he realized she was okay and not in tears or worse, his features softened and he smiled tenderly at her. If she hadn't already been putty in his hands, that concern and his tender look would have done it in a heartbeat.

"There's coffee if you want some to warm you up," she managed to say around the lump in her throat. She pointed at the pot.

He nodded his thanks, quickly pouring himself a mug. Dragging a chair around to sit right next to her, he sat, his thigh pressed against hers.

"So, Bobby," Tristan began after taking a sip of the warm brew. "You always scare your sister half to death in the middle of the night?"

"Tristan," she admonished. She didn't want to argue anymore tonight. The hour was beginning to wear on her and she just wanted a peaceful ending to this situation so she could go back to bed.

"It's okay, Sis," Rob said, gently laying a hand on her arm. He turned his gaze to Tristan. "It's Rob now, and I'm sorry for the trouble. I never meant to startle her. She wasn't even supposed to see me. I was just making sure everything was okay."

Tristan frowned. "Why wouldn't it be? Didn't you know that she wasn't alone? My truck is hard to miss."

"I saw it. But you aren't the only visitor she's had lately."

Alarm bells clanged loudly in Laurel's head. "Wait. What are you talking about? No one ever comes here. When did you see someone?"

"Yesterday evening. I was sitting out in my car, trying to work up the nerve to knock, when a car pulled up down the street. Some guy got out and walked back this way. I thought it was weird, because there was plenty of parking right out front. He walked up the side of your house and disappeared. I got out to follow him, but he quickly came back out and left."

"Why didn't you call the police?"

Rob's eyebrows shot up. "And say what? Hey, while I was staking out my sister's house—who I haven't seen in nine years and parted on terrible terms with—waiting for her to come home, I saw someone prowling? Yeah. *That* would go over well."

Tristan scowled but didn't contradict him. "What'd the guy look like?"

Rob shrugged. "Dark hair, average build, average height, I guess. It was dark, so I didn't get a very good look."

Fear made Laurel's hands begin to shake. That sounded a lot like the man who had chased her through the forest.

Noticing her sudden change in demeanor, Tristan covered her hands with one of his, swallowing them in his grip. She sucked in a breath, letting his touch ground her. For the moment, she was safe.

"What kind of car did he drive?"

"A sedan of some kind. Silver, I think. I didn't pay too much attention to it. I was more focused on him."

"Did you notice anything tonight while you were prowling around?"

He shook his head. "Nope. It was just me tonight." He frowned, looking back and forth between them both. "What's going on, anyway? When you brought me up to the house, you told her I didn't match the description of the man she saw. What man? Has she seen this prowler before?"

"Your sister witnessed a murder a few days ago. She got a good look at the guy's face. Unfortunately, he got a good look at hers too."

Rob's eyes widened, and he frowned at her. "Only you. You're such a trouble magnet."

Tristan scowled. Laurel could see the angry reply building in his eyes. While she loved that he was so quick to rise to her defense, Rob wasn't wrong.

She put a hand on Tristan's arm, attempting to quell his ire. "No. He's right. Trouble has a way of finding me. Not lately, but it used to all the time."

Turning toward her, his eyes softened, as did his fierce frown. "I don't care if all the shit in the world lands on you. It's not your fault, and he needs to remember that." His blue eyes glittered like cold diamonds as he glared at Rob. They promised retribution if he didn't change his tune.

Rob had the grace to look chagrined and nodded. "I'm sorry, Laurel. I didn't mean anything bad by it."

"Thank you, Rob. I know you didn't." She cast a glance at the big man at her side. He was still frowning, but had relaxed slightly. "You'll have to forgive Tristan. He's a little overprotective." She tossed a smile up at his scowling face. "We're working on it."

"Baby, until we catch this guy, my overprotective side isn't going anywhere."

"Good," Rob stated firmly, surprising Laurel. "You need someone looking out for you. Not because you can't look out for yourself," he rushed to assure her, "but because you shouldn't have to. I wish I'd had the courage to do it when we were younger. Maybe things would have been different."

Laurel felt her heart constrict at the look of regret on his face. "Or maybe it would have been you instead."

"Better me than you. At least as I got older, I could defend myself."

"Not against all of them. And you know they would have ganged up on you. Aaron and Justin, especially." Their two oldest brothers were ruthless. No one dared cross them. If they did, there were painful consequences. She hated to think what they would have done to Rob if he had tried to defend her against them or their dad.

"Regardless, I still should have."

"Yes, you should have," Tristan grumbled, his voice low. "But rehashing the past won't change anything. I hope you're ready to prove yourself. If it were up to me, I'd tell you to get lost and slam the door in your face. But Laurel's got a soft heart, so you'll likely get a second chance. I highly suggest you don't blow it." He leaned forward, his look so menacing it made Laurel shiver. "And if you lay one finger on her or say anything to upset her, I will make what your dad and brothers are capable of look like a paper cut."

Rob held up his hands. "I won't, I swear." He turned pleading eyes on Laurel. "I just want a relationship with you again. I have never hit a woman, and I never will. The Navy taught me what real respect is. I won't go back to the kind of respect Dad tried to teach me."

Laurel studied her brother's face, looking for any signs of deceit. Her older brothers tricked her so many times she had a hard time trusting Rob, even though he'd never hit her. She didn't know what went on after she left home. But what Rob did to help her back then carried a lot of weight. He was the only other man besides Tristan who had ever given a damn about her.

"Just promise me there will be no more sneaking around my backyard in the dark. You want to talk to me, you use the phone or come to the front door like a normal person."

He nodded. "Okay." Draining his coffee mug, he pushed back his chair. "I'm going to head out if that's all right?" He looked to Tristan, who nodded. "It's late, and I never intended to wake you."

"Leave some contact info." Tristan's tone brooked no argument.

Laurel fetched some sticky notes and a pen, so Rob could write down his phone number and address.

"You need a ride?" Tristan asked.

Rob shook his head. "My car is parked down the street."

Laurel followed her brother to the front door, Tristan trailing silently behind.

"Thank you, Laurel. For not immediately throwing me out. Or letting your boyfriend arrest me."

Laurel merely nodded, beginning to feel a bit overwhelmed.

With a small smile, Rob let himself out.

Locking the door behind him, Laurel leaned her forehead against the wood. Her emotions felt like they were in a blender.

When Tristan curled his hands over her shoulders, the

lid popped off. The first sob felt like it had been pulled straight from her soul. He turned her around and tucked her into his chest, his strong arms surrounding her like a shield.

She clung to him as she cried. Her heart breaking all over again for the childhood she and Rob never had. For all the pain her family had caused her. For the lost time with the one family member who had ever cared about her.

Through it all, Tristan just held her, murmuring nonsense into her hair and placing gentle kisses on her head. His hands stroked up and down her back, trying to soothe her shredded emotions.

When she was finally able to take a breath without sobbing, she leaned back and sniffed, wiping her eyes with the back of her hand. "I'm sorry."

His thumb swiped at a tear. "Don't be. Knowing what you went through just makes me admire you more. I've seen a lot of abused people not come out the other side of a crappy situation with even a tenth of the strength you have, Laurel. Even your brother, who seems to have escaped the cycle of abuse, can't hold a candle to you."

He framed her face, the earnestness in his eyes freeing something inside of her. Taking away some of the hurt she had carried for so long.

"You amaze me. Every day. I'm sorry you had such a miserable childhood, but I can guarantee that so long as I'm around, no one will ever lay a hand on you again."

She stared up at him. His admiration of her and the promise that he would never hurt her gave her the courage to tell him the rest of her story.

"There's still a lot about me you don't know. About my life before I moved here," she said quietly.

"Are you ready to tell me?" He swiped at another tear.

Hesitantly, she nodded. "I think so."

He stepped back, taking her hand. "Come on. Let's sit. I have a feeling this might take a while."

Leading her into the living room, he sat in the recliner, pulling her down onto his lap. Laurel tucked her head into the crook of his neck and shoulder, letting her hand rest on his jaw. She ran her fingers over the rough stubble. It helped ground her to the present as her mind drifted into the past.

"It started when I was young. My mama died about a year after Rob was born. Pneumonia. I was four. Daddy was already mean, but he got meaner after she passed—at least to us. Mama wasn't there to take the brunt of it anymore. Anyway, from then on, I was the lady of the house and expected to do all the things that Mama had done, never mind that I couldn't even reach the stove or the kitchen sink, let alone knew how to cook a meal. If I didn't do something or did something wrong, he'd beat me. My older brothers finally started to help out when he broke my arm because I burnt dinner for the third time. He told them to help me until I was better or they'd suffer the same fate. Once I healed, though, they only helped when I couldn't reach something. I think I was seven when Aaron built me a stool so he didn't have to stir the pots on the stove anymore or pull the wet laundry out of the bottom of the washing machine.

"After that they treated me like a servant, because that's how Daddy treated me. I was just there to cook and clean and make sure Rob wasn't filthy all the time and got to school. I was so happy when I turned eighteen. I thought I could get out of there. Go to college. Make something of myself, you know? I wanted to study art. Daddy, he had other ideas."

She stiffened as she remembered. Tristan stroked her back and turned his head to place a kiss on her palm, reminding her that he was here and that she was far away from that place that had caused her so much pain.

Fourteen

Tristan fought to stay calm as she related the horrors of her youth. He had seen a lot of abuse as a cop, but being so personally attached to one of its victims was gut-wrenching. He better understood now why some people went after abusers with such vehemence. It was taking all he had not to plan a trip to West Virginia and track down the son-of-a-bitch.

Laurel got stiffer in his embrace as she continued her tale. Dread pooled in Tristan's stomach as he realized it was about to get much worse.

"He had a friend who had a son. Johnny was three years older than me and a heap of trouble. His daddy thought that if he got married and settled down he would mellow out, get a job and stop freeloading off of him."

Tristan closed his eyes and bit back a moan. He knew what was coming.

"Daddy forced me to marry him. Said he'd break my arm again, then tie me up in the woodshed and leave me out there until I agreed to marry Johnny. I didn't want to, but in my mind, it was a way out of that house, so I agreed. I thought it would be easier to deal with just one man who wanted to hurt me instead of four."

She looked up at him through her lashes, more tears shimmering in her pretty eyes. "It wasn't. Things weren't any better with Johnny. They were worse. On our wedding night, I was scared because I had never been with a man. I wanted to go slow, but Johnny backhanded me and told me that a real wife made love however her husband wanted. Suffice it to say, it was not a pleasurable experience."

Tristan growled and had to clench his fists to contain the rage. The thought of anyone hurting a woman like that, but especially Laurel, made his blood boil. He wanted to get that man alone in a room for five minutes and teach him what it truly meant to be cruel.

"Anyway, I got pretty sick the first winter we were married and had to take antibiotics. I didn't know then that it would affect my birth control, and I got pregnant."

Her watery brown eyes stabbed him straight through the heart. The sorrow there was deep. "He didn't react the way you did. After he threw me down the stairs, he beat me bloody, then left to get drunk. I managed to crawl to the phone and call for help. I broke five ribs, my wrist, both cheekbones, and sustained a severe concussion. And I lost the baby."

Tristan saw red. He didn't care that he was a cop and that he lived by the law. Laurel's ex-husband was lucky he wasn't in the room or Tristan would have been hard pressed to remember why murder was a bad thing. He was astonished she had told him about their baby at all now, knowing how things had turned out the last time she had tried to tell a man that she was pregnant with his child.

She wiped her face again. "The nurses at the hospital took me under their wing and helped me get a restraining order and a pro-bono lawyer so I could file for divorce."

"Please tell me the bastard is in prison," he said through gritted teeth.

"He's dead." She looked up at him warily, her expression tortured. "I killed him."

Shock rippled across Tristan's face and he sat a little straighter. "You what?"

"Killed him. It was self-defense." She wiggled until she was more upright and held his gaze as she explained. "You see, Johnny's dad was the chief of police of our little town. When he found out his son had beaten me to within an inch of my life, he got the responding officer to alter the police report so that things looked better than they were. All mention of the baby was removed and according to the documents, I fell down the stairs after he hit me once—his daddy made it sound like most of my injuries came from the fall. Johnny was still arrested, but on a much lesser charge, and he made bail within twelve hours."

She leaned into him again. "After I was released from the hospital, I rented a miniscule studio apartment using what meager savings I had managed to squirrel away from the money Johnny gave me for groceries. It wasn't much, but it was away from the abusive bastard.

"Three days after I moved in, Johnny found me and broke in. He was a big man, like you, and tried to manhandle me out of the apartment, telling me he was taking me home, where I belonged. He dragged me past the couch that doubled as my bed on the way out the door. I had a pistol stuffed between the cushions that Rob had taken from our dad's collection and brought to me after he heard what Johnny did. Said that he'd never agreed with the kind of punishment Daddy meted out."

She took a shaky breath. "Anyway, I somehow managed to twist away long enough to grab the gun, and I shot him in the leg. Just to make him stop. But he didn't leave. Shooting him just made him angrier. He came at me again, and I just reacted. The bullet went straight through his heart. He died instantly."

"That's a pity," Tristan muttered. "The bastard should have writhed in agony for all the pain he caused you." He hoped the man was rotting in hell at the hands of the devil. "How did you get past the police chief? After what he did to help his son, didn't he charge you with murder?"

"He tried. I called my lawyer right after I called the police. He called the state troopers and explained the situation. They had been aware of all the corruption in the town and were just trying to gather enough evidence to prove it. My attorney convinced them to take over my case, and their investigators proved I acted in self-defense.

"As soon as I was cleared, I left. Rob had an after-school job working for a local mechanic and he gave me enough money to get a bus ticket and a hotel room for a few nights. I headed to Asheville and got a job cleaning the first day I was there. It wasn't easy, but I worked my way out of the gutter to a better life."

Fierce admiration for this woman burned through his veins. "I am so damn proud of you. Moving past a nightmare like that couldn't have been easy. You could have fallen so far down to the bottom of the barrel, but you didn't. You rose above it all and became such an amazing woman. I'm amazed you even had the guts to tell me about our baby after hearing what you went through." He framed her face, staring down at her intently. "Thank you for sharing all of that with me. I can't imagine how hard it was or where you found the courage."

She shrugged. "The last few months with you have helped me realize how much I've healed since I left Womack. You still make me nervous, but not because I'm worried you're going to hurt me. I've learned you're a good man who will do whatever it takes to keep me safe and happy."

She swallowed hard. "I'm more worried I'll give up the autonomy I've fought so hard for to you. You're such an overwhelming presence at times, and it would be easy to let you take over and take care of everything for me."

Running a hand tenderly up and down her back, he was surprised to see his hands were shaking. His emotions were a jumble of awe and residual rage, as well as something that felt stronger than just mere adoration for the woman in his arms. He rested his cheek against her hair and inhaled the scent unique to her, letting the fact that she was here and safe settle him. "I'm sorry you had to go through all of that, but I'm not sorry it brought you to me. You saved my life and you've given me a reason to look forward to the future. I understand your fear. I am a very take-charge kind of man, but I will try to work on that."

He pulled back and tipped her face up to look at him. He wanted her to see that he meant what he said. "I don't want you to ever feel like you've lost yourself."

Tears flowed over her eyelids, and she nodded, tucking her face back into his neck. "Thank you. I'm glad it brought me here too," she whispered.

Tristan didn't know what the future would hold for them, but he damn sure knew what he wanted it to be. It was going to take a friggin' nuke to make him leave her now. He just had to convince her she could always trust him. That he was never going to turn into her father or her bastard of a husband.

Fifteen

Laurel went back to work the next day, much to Tristan's displeasure. His scowl had only softened long enough for him to kiss her goodbye when he dropped her off at the firehouse for her shift. He made it abundantly clear to her boss and her partner that they were to be on the lookout for anything or anyone out of the ordinary while she was on duty. It had only been her fierce glare and the knowledge he had a case to investigate that made him leave. She was sure if he'd been able to and hadn't promised her he would try to curb some of the overprotectiveness, he would have been climbing into her ambulance and refusing to go anywhere.

Trying to put the danger out of her mind, Laurel checked the stock on the truck as they waited on their first call, concentrating on her task. Her partner Wade Carpenter thumbed through their paperwork file, making sure they had all the forms they needed.

Despite her desire to empty her mind, thoughts of last night crept in. She couldn't believe Rob had tracked her down. And hid in her backyard. He had scared ten years off her life when she flipped on the porch light and saw him crouched out there.

She had mixed feelings about him being back. In a way, she had missed him. Of all her family, he was the nicest. He hadn't ever hit her, but he could be mean. Mostly, though, he had ignored her.

Now, he was back, saying he was a changed man. She really hoped that was true. Time would tell, she supposed.

She wasn't scared to be around him now, though. Having Tristan at her back made all the difference. If Rob even looked at her funny, Tristan would be there to set him straight. She couldn't help but wonder what all her brothers would have been like if he had been around when they were growing up. He would have made sure they walked the straight and narrow.

Placing her hand on her stomach briefly, she couldn't help but be glad her child would have such a kind, strong, honorable man for a father. This baby would grow up knowing how to treat others the right way. That was something she had never dared hope for before. The baby she lost certainly wouldn't have.

The emergency tones sounded, and Laurel immediately shoved all thoughts from her head as she listened.

The dispatcher's voice boomed over the loudspeaker. *"Unit 4. Possible MI. Please respond."*

"That's us," Wade said, stuffing the files back into the cabinet and climbing up front. She could hear him confirm the call as she quickly locked all the cupboards. Following him upfront, she buckled her seatbelt as he rolled out of the ambulance bay.

"You sure you're up for this?" Wade asked, glancing over at her as he drove.

"Of course. Why wouldn't I be?" She fought the urge to cover her stomach again. No one except Gemma and Ben knew about the baby, and she wanted to keep it that way a little longer. Until she figured out what she was going to do about its father.

He shrugged. "That was quite a hike you took and hypothermia is no joke."

"I'm fine now, Wade. I was completely warmed up within a few hours, and I had all day yesterday to rest." *Sort of*, she amended. She *had* rested quite a bit while Tristan ran down a few leads where he could on a Sunday, but last night's sleep had been broken thanks to her churning thoughts and her brother's reappearance. Not to mention, pregnancy fatigue was starting to kick in. She was going to crash so hard tonight.

He frowned, but didn't say anything, for which Laurel was grateful. She was done rehashing the weekend's events.

The site of their first call wasn't far, and they were on scene within a few minutes. A frantic man in his seventies ran out to meet them.

"Please! My wife. Something's wrong. She can't catch her breath, and she's very sleepy."

Recognizing the signs of a possible heart attack, Laurel grabbed her med kit and the defibrillator, throwing them onto the stretcher. Swinging open the back doors, she grabbed the end of the gurney. Wade had climbed through the cab and was unlatching the bed from the floor locks.

Pulling it forward, she lowered it to the ground while Wade guided it and jumped out. They followed the man back into his house.

What greeted them inside was nothing short of chaos. Two women in their forties hovered over an older woman who was flat on the floor, convulsing. With a cry, the husband rushed forward.

"Rose! Oh my God, what's happening? Rose?"

"Sir, we need you to move back so that we can work on her," Wade stated, gently pushing on the man's shoulder.

Laurel caught the eye of one of the women and motioned toward the husband with a quick jerk of her head. The woman wiped a few tears off her cheeks and nodded. With one last long look at the woman lying on the floor, she stood and turned her attention to the man who was sobbing next to Wade.

"Dad, let's give them some room." She walked around behind him and pulled on his shoulders. The other woman moved to help.

Laurel quickly moved into the space they vacated and began pulling items from her bag. With swift, efficient movements she attached EKG leads to the woman's chest.

"You said you thought she was having a heart attack?"

The man, who had composed himself slightly, nodded. "She complained it was hard to breathe and then she just got very tired."

"Does your wife have any health problems, sir?" Wade asked.

"High blood pressure."

Wrapping a blood pressure cuff around her arm, Laurel quickly took her pressure. It was normal. So was the tracing coming off the EKG.

Suspicious, Laurel pricked the woman's finger and checked her glucose level as she listened to the conversation. The number that appeared on the monitor had her eyes widening.

"Wade." She turned the monitor around. "I need the dex," she told him, referring to dextrose 50, a sugar solution they used to bring up blood sugar in severely hypoglycemic patients.

"What's happening?" one of the daughters asked.

"Your mother's blood sugar level is thirty. It should be nearly three times that," Laurel explained, moving quickly. She uncapped a needle and plunged it into the top of the vial Wade handed her, then injected it into a bag of saline.

While she had readied the medicine, Wade had started an IV. Laurel handed him the bag, and he quickly hooked it up, opening the line as wide as it would go.

"Why would her blood sugar be low?" the husband asked. "She's not diabetic."

"It's possible that she is and just didn't know it," Laurel explained. "There are also other illnesses and medications that can cause the blood sugar to drop. Once she's stable, we'll get her to the hospital and hopefully they can figure out what caused it."

As they waited, the medicine began to take effect, and the woman started to come around. She flailed wildly, and one of her arms connected with Laurel's face.

Immediately, her eyes watered, and she tasted blood.

"Laurel, are you okay?" Wade struggled to hold down the woman's arms as she came out of the hypoglycemia.

Shucking her gloves, she grabbed a gauze pad from her bag and pressed it against her lip. "Yeah," she mumbled around the pad. "She split my lip, but I'll be fine. You got her?"

Wade nodded. "She's starting to calm down." He looked up at the husband and daughters kneeling nearby. "She should wake up very soon."

Gradually, the woman's jerky movements calmed, and her breathing slowed. Her eyes opened, and she blinked, confused.

"Rose? My name's Wade and this is my partner, Laurel. We're with Northridge Fire Rescue. Your blood sugar was very low, and that's what caused your issues today. How are you feeling now?"

The woman brought a shaky hand up to her face. "Dizzy."

"That's normal. You just rest for now. We're going to get you packaged up and take you to the hospital in Asheville."

Laurel kept the gauze stuffed between her lip and teeth as

she worked. It was still bleeding, and she hoped that she didn't need a stitch or two. Tristan was going to have a conniption as it was.

Quickly loading the woman and her husband into the back of the ambulance, Wade passed her the keys. "You drive since you're still bleeding."

She nodded and climbed through into the front, hoping the rest of her day was uneventful.

By the time her shift ended that evening, Laurel was beat. Every bone in her body felt like it was made of lead. Tristan took one look at her and scooped her up, carrying her out to his truck.

Other than a squeak of surprise, she couldn't even muster up the energy to protest. She laid her head against his strong chest and closed her eyes, wishing she could ride home like this. All too soon, though, he was depositing her onto the seat and buckling her in. He climbed into the driver's seat and pulled out of the parking lot without a word.

When she finally mustered up the energy to open her eyes and look at him, she saw that his jaw was set and his fingers were tight around the steering wheel. He looked angry.

"I'm okay," she said softly.

He glanced over at her, his blue eyes glittering. "Don't. I'm trying really hard right now not to go into caveman mode and demand you quit today, but seeing you hurt and so utterly exhausted is really testing my self-control."

"If it helps, it was an accident. I had a patient in a hypoglycemic emergency. She jerked reflexively, and I was in the way." She lightly touched her swollen lip. It thankfully hadn't needed any stitches, just a little skin glue.

He sighed and rubbed the back of his neck before looking

at her again. His eyes were softer this time. He took her hand and threaded his fingers through hers. "It doesn't address the exhaustion, though. You can't come home like this every day. It's not healthy. Especially not in your condition."

Weakly, Laurel threw up her hands. She knew he was right, but she didn't have a choice. Not if she wanted to keep a roof over her head and food in her fridge. "What else am I supposed to do, Tristan? I have to work."

The muscles in his jaw worked until suddenly, he jerked the wheel and pulled them over onto the shoulder. Laurel's hand shot out to steady herself as the truck bumped over the rough ground.

He put the truck in park and turned in his seat to face her. His eyes sparkled like sapphires in the glow from the dashboard.

"Marry me."

Laurel's eyes widened, and her brain froze. Fatigue made her thought processes sluggish, and it took her a few seconds to make her mouth work. Even then, what came out wasn't genius.

"I can't."

His frown was immediate. "Laurel, I have never been more serious about a woman. And this has nothing to do with the baby, if that's what you're worried about. When I pulled up on that crime scene the other day and realized you were missing, the murder I was there to investigate became an afterthought. I left Jake in charge because I *had* to find you. I couldn't imagine a life without you then, and I still can't. I don't even want to try."

His big hands covered hers, his expression earnest. "Marry me, Laurel. I promise you will never want for anything. I will spend the rest of my days trying to make you happy."

Tears welled in her eyes at the picture he painted. He was offering her nearly everything she had ever wanted. A home filled with happiness and warmth. A family. Every dream she'd ever had and given up on, he was offering to her on a silver platter. All but one.

"But do you love me?"

His eyes widened at her question, and he seemed to withdraw slightly. Laurel's heart sank, and she pulled her hands back.

Heart heavy, she shook her head. "I can't marry you, Tristan. I want to, but I won't marry again without love. I promised myself that when I left Womack. It doesn't matter that we would have a good life. I want to know that my husband loves me as much as I love him. That the only way I will ever lose him is to God. I'm sorry, but I just can't." Her words ended on a broken whisper, and she pressed the back of her hand against her mouth to hold back the tears.

Tristan looked out the windshield, staring silently for several moments before he spoke. "Truthfully, Laurel, I don't know what I feel for you. I haven't had a chance to process it all. It's certainly more than just a strong case of lust or like. But love? Hell, I don't know. I've never been in love. I do know I care more about you than anyone I've ever been with. You've brought a light and a joy to my life I didn't even know was possible."

He turned to look at her again. "I know I'm asking a lot of you—and I do understand where you're coming from—but I just want what's best for you and the baby." He took her hands again. "If you won't marry me, will you at least move in with me and let me support you while you're pregnant? If you want to go back to work after the baby comes, that's fine. And if you don't, that's fine too." A corner of his mouth crooked up. "You'll be helping me and my caveman urges if you take it easy."

That made Laurel laugh softly. "Keeping me barefoot and

pregnant in the kitchen isn't exactly what I'd call non-cavemanish."

His grin widened. "But there will be a lot less of the yelling and teeth gnashing variety of caveman if you agree."

Their shared laughter helped to break some of the tension. With his thumb, he swiped away the few tears that had managed to escape and trickle down her cheeks. "You know, you could use this as an opportunity to try a new career."

Her eyebrows dipped quizzically.

"Your art."

Immediately, she started to protest. Those paintings were personal, many of them too painful to share.

He cut her off. "I don't mean the ones you showed me. At least, not all of them. But new ones that you would have time to create if you quit your job. Laurel, your talent is amazing. People would line up at your door to get one if they knew what you could do with a paintbrush."

Her mind spun. Could she really do that? Throw away everything she had worked so hard to accomplish—the life that she'd built for herself—and start fresh with something new? Her mind whirled with the possibility. She had always loved to paint, but once she'd been forced to marry, she never considered doing it for a living again. It had been her escape for nearly a decade. Could she really bring it out into the light again?

She looked into the blue, blue eyes across from her and began to wonder if, with Tristan by her side, it just might be possible.

He leaned over and pressed a kiss to her forehead, his lips lingering in the softest caress. Pulling back, he stayed close, looking down at her. "Think about it?"

Brain full of the new possibilities their conversation had opened for her, she could only nod. It seemed she had a lot to consider. So much for sleeping tonight.

Sixteen

For the second night in a row, Laurel found herself staring out the kitchen window in the middle of the night. Despite the turmoil Tristan's proposal caused her, she had fallen asleep soon after they arrived home. She even managed to get several hours of sleep before her bladder awakened her. Now, having gotten a modicum of rest, her thoughts were running rampant again and keeping her awake.

She didn't know what to do. Being an artist—a real artist—was something she hadn't let herself dream about in years. For so long, she had been focused on what needed to be done to survive that she hadn't allowed herself to think about what she really wanted. Her art had always been so personal—a way to deal with emotions she couldn't otherwise handle. But sometime over the last couple of years, it had turned into more of an expression of what she saw in the world. The wonder and beauty. Those paintings she could definitely share.

She just wasn't sure she could give up her job, though. Laurel liked being a paramedic and enjoyed helping people when they needed it most. And she was good at it. The man sleeping on her pull-out was a testament to that. But it didn't give her the satisfaction that she got from taking a scene in her mind and bringing it to life on canvas.

Art wasn't a guaranteed income, though. If she didn't sell any paintings, she wouldn't earn a paycheck.

Her mind catapulted to Tristan's proposal. It had been so tempting to say yes when he asked her to marry him. She knew she could have a good life with him. He would always treat her well and would support her in whatever she wanted to do. Now that she'd had time to think about it, she wondered if she was doing herself and her baby a disservice by turning him down.

Her vow not to marry again without love seemed a little silly now that she was thinking more clearly. She was tied to him, whether she married him or not because of the life they'd created. Wouldn't it be better for their child if his or her parents were committed to each other?

It certainly wouldn't be a hardship to call Tristan her husband. But she was terrified of falling into a loveless marriage that would stagnate and fall apart. She wanted her next marriage to last the rest of her life.

But would it really be loveless? It wouldn't for her. She had realized in the truck that she was head over heels for the gorgeous man who had barreled into her life. Could she love him enough for the both of them? Would he eventually feel the same way? And what happened if he didn't? One thing she did know was that if he never loved her the way she loved him and he found some other woman to love, it would shatter her heart into a million pieces. It wouldn't matter if they were married or not.

So why couldn't she say yes to him? Unless he fell in love with her, she was almost guaranteed a broken heart—a wedding ring wouldn't make a lick of difference. And marrying Tristan could offer her and their child a stability that apart they could not. It would also let Laurel spread her wings in ways she had only dreamed of before her father and Johnny dashed those dreams into teeny tiny pieces.

"Laurel?"

She let out a shriek and whirled at the sound of Tristan's voice. He stood in the doorway to the kitchen, bare-chested, his jeans hanging low on his hips and staring at her through sleepy but concerned eyes.

She laid a hand over her hammering heart. "You scared me to death."

"Sorry," he mumbled, moving closer. "I saw the light on. Is everything okay?" He peered through the window. "Your brother isn't out there again, is he?"

"No. It's all clear. I just couldn't sleep. Too much on my mind."

"Want to share?"

Fright clearing, her brain registered his half-naked body radiating heat from just a couple of feet away. Stark desire skated down her nerve endings and short-circuited the path from her brain to her tongue.

"Laurel?"

Her eyes snapped to his. In the low light, they were midnight pools, tempting her to take a dip. Would she ever not feel this way around him?

"Yes." That was not what she had intended to say. Not at all.

"Yes, what?" he asked with a confused frown.

Swallowing hard, and realizing whether she had intended to say it or not, she meant it, Laurel stepped forward until she was close enough to smell the heady mix of man and laundry detergent wafting off of him.

"Yes. I'll marry you."

∾

Tristan stared down at Laurel, confusion etched all over his face. "What? You said—"

She laid a finger over his lips. "I know what I said. But I've had some sleep and a chance to think. Saying no was ridiculous. I realized that no matter what happens—and no matter what society says these days—its best if we're married. That we do our best to make things work between us for our baby's sake. This isn't about us anymore. Do I hope you love me one day? Of course. But I can't be selfish and say no because of a vow I made after my husband nearly killed me."

Hardly believing what he was hearing, he grasped her face in his hands and stared down at her. "You're sure? I meant what I said in the truck. I will support you whether we're married or not. You don't have to marry me to get that."

"I know. But it feels weird to just move in with you and not be married. We might as well be if I do that. I'm already tied to you—and that's not a bad thing. I just agree, now that I've had some rest and time to think, that we should make the tie official."

He searched her eyes, looking for any hesitation or fear on her part. All he saw was honesty and something deeper he couldn't quite put his finger on.

Heart stuttering in his chest, he gathered her close. "We're not waiting. As soon as we can arrange it, I want to put my ring on your finger. Call me a caveman, but I want the world to know you're mine." He laid his hand low on her belly. "You and this little one."

She smiled shyly and nodded. "I'd like that."

Mindful of her injured lip, he kissed her gently, joy infusing his soul that this tiny, amazing woman had agreed to marry him. Lifting her off her feet, he swung her around, smiling against her mouth.

He pulled back to look down into her delicate face. "Thank you, Laurel. For trusting me."

She ran her hands through his hair, her fingers sifting through the thick strands and making his toes curl. "You make it easy. I've never known a man like you. I don't think I could find another like you, even if I spent the rest of my life looking." Pulling his head down, she kissed him, harder this time.

Her fingers drifted down his neck and over his shoulders, leaving a trail of goosebumps in their wake and ratcheting up Tristan's need. He wanted nothing more than to carry her down the hall and make love to her all night, but part of their conversation last night pushed its way through the haze of want clouding his brain.

With a mighty effort, he pulled back. She moaned in disappointment and tried to draw him down to her again, but he resisted.

"As much as I want to take you to bed, I want us to wait more."

Her frown was quick and fierce. "Why?"

Stroking her silky hair, his eyes roved her face. "Because I want you to have the wedding night you deserve."

If possible, she frowned harder. "How will waiting make it more deserving?"

He smiled. "Anticipation. It'll make that night at the lodge pale in comparison."

She groaned and rested her forehead on his chest briefly before looking up at him again. "I hate you right now."

He bit back a groan of his own. The feel of her lush body pressed against his wasn't helping his resolve any. "I hate myself a bit right now. But I promise you it'll be worth it."

Reluctantly, she nodded, but sucked that lip between her teeth again to worry it.

"What?"

Her eyes snapped to his. "What?"

"You're worrying your lip again. You always do that when

there's something on your mind that you want to say, but don't know whether you should or how to say it."

Immediately, the lip popped out, and she huffed. "Stop going all cop on me," she admonished with an impish tilt to her mouth.

He smiled, but waited for her to explain.

"Will you sleep with me?"

"Sleep? Like sleep, sleep?"

She nodded.

He blew out a harsh breath, swallowing hard. Talk about testing his resolve. "I don't know if that's such a good idea, Laurel."

"Please? I just want to sleep. I keep waking up, hearing noises or just worried. I think having you there would help."

Tristan weighed her words. He knew he would sleep better —once his body got the message that it wouldn't be getting any play time—by having her close. He was normally a sound sleeper, but the last two nights on her pull-out, he'd been waking at the slightest noise. Knowing she was safe and slept soundly in his arms would let him get some much-needed rest.

In answer, he bent and picked her up. She was light as a feather and just as soft. "Sleep?"

She nodded. "Sleep."

Tamping down the hunger still racing through his body, he headed for the bedroom, his soon-to-be wife in his arms.

Seventeen

When Laurel woke the next morning, it took her a minute to realize why she felt like her blanket was weighted. Tristan was wrapped around her like a vine, his heavy limbs thrown over her protectively.

She savored the weight and the feel of being held by him and laid there quietly while he slept. Glancing at the clock, she realized it was still a bit early, so she closed her eyes and tried to go back to sleep for a little while longer. After a few minutes, though, she realized how futile that was. Her bladder insisted she get up. She had read online on a pregnancy forum that the urge to pee kicked in almost right away. The article wasn't kidding. She had been making several extra trips to the bathroom lately.

The urge getting more insistent, she tried to slide out from underneath Tristan's heavy frame, but he grumbled and pulled her closer.

"Tristan."

He shifted slightly, but didn't wake.

She rolled onto her back and tried again. "Tristan."

"Hmm?"

"Let me go. I need to use the bathroom."

His sapphire eyes blinked open to slowly focus on her and a smile curved his lush mouth. "Hi."

She smiled back and pressed her thighs together. "Hi. Can you let me up, please? I really have to pee."

His sleepy confusion was awfully cute. Laurel was sure she would appreciate it more *after she peed*.

He sucked in a deep breath, coming more fully awake, and rolled, releasing her.

She shot up and dashed for the bathroom. She could only imagine how this was going to feel when she had a seven pound, thrashing weight sitting on top of her full bladder.

Feeling much better after she relieved herself, she headed back to the bedroom and had to stop at the sight as she entered the room. Tristan was sprawled over her bed on his back, one arm thrown over his head, the sheet down to his waist, and one bare leg poking out from under the covers. A dusting of dark hair covered his chest and muscled calf and thigh. He was a sight to behold, and it made her weak in the knees. She hoped they could plan this wedding fast, because the interim was going to be torture.

His brilliant blue eyes opened into sleepy slits to look at her. He crooked a finger at her. "C'mere."

Slightly self-conscious—having a man in her bed who she wanted there and who was so completely masculine was a foreign concept to her—she edged forward and crawled up next to him.

She wasn't even settled when he rolled, pulling her beneath his large frame. His hips pressed into hers, the evidence of his desire for her prodding her belly. She dug her fingernails into his biceps, trying hard not to whimper in need. Their wedding needed to be soon. Really, really soon.

Brushing back her hair, he stared down at her. Laurel was

caught in the midnight sea of his eyes. They churned with emotions that moved too quickly for her to name.

"I think I'm going to like waking up like this every day," he said softly. His low voice rumbled through her, driving her need higher.

She bit back a moan. "Me too. I think I'll like it even better when you do something about this." Sliding her hand between their bodies, she circled his erection and squeezed gently.

His eyes rolled back and he moaned, burying his face in her neck. One of his large hands palmed her breast, kneading the soft flesh and eliciting a moan of her own.

He nipped at the tender skin behind her ear, then soothed the bite with his tongue. Laurel moaned again and clutched a handful of his thick hair. Her other hand clutched his hip, holding him against her. He was going to set her off without taking a stitch of clothing off of her.

With a growl of frustration, he pushed away from her, moving back to sit on his haunches down by her knees.

Laurel sank into the mattress, a quivering mass of need. Her lungs worked overtime trying to draw in air.

"We need to set a date." His voice was rough with unfulfilled desire.

She nodded. "Soon. It needs to be soon."

"Agreed."

The bed dipped as he got up. Fabric rustled as he pulled on his jeans. Laurel looked over in time to see his tight, boxer brief-clad butt disappear under the dark denim. He turned as he fastened his pants, giving her a full view of his beautiful chest and abs.

She bit her lip and just stared.

"Stop looking at me like that, Laurel."

She ignored him and let her eyes rove over the taut muscles and the intricate tattoos. Her fingers itched to touch him. She clutched the sheet beneath her to stop herself from sitting up and doing just that.

"Laurel." Her name was a growl that skated along her nerve endings. She squeezed her eyes shut to block out the sight and regain a modicum of control.

"Could you put on a shirt? Please?"

His quiet chuckle had her opening her eyes to glare at him, effectively dousing some of her hunger. "It's not funny. You worked me into a frenzy, then left me high and dry, only to stand there looking like—*that*." She waved her hand at his naked torso. "My hormones are going crazy right now." She covered her face and groaned. "You'd think my body would get that it's already pregnant and not go into overdrive at the sight of you."

He laughed again, and she glared at him through her fingers. "Go! Find a shirt." She tossed a pillow at him, which he dodged while still laughing.

Holding up his hands, he backed toward the door. "I'm going. You get dressed, too, and come out to the kitchen. We need to discuss what we're doing today."

She nodded and waved her hand at him, eyes still closed to block out the tempting sight. "Okay. Go!"

With another chuckle, he left.

Laurel lingered on the bed for several more moments before sitting up and padding to her closet for a change of clothes. Dressing quickly in jeans and a sweater, she pulled some warm socks on her feet and headed for the kitchen.

Tristan had started the coffeepot and thankfully pulled on a shirt.

Still not back on an even keel, Laurel poked her head in the fridge, blocking out the sight of his shoulders stretching the fabric of his t-shirt.

The coffee pot gurgled, and she heard the clank of ceramic on the counter as Tristan poured himself a cup.

"You want some coffee? Wait, can you have coffee?"

She shut the fridge door, her arms full of makings for omelets, and turned to look at him. His quizzical look was endearing, and she couldn't help but smile. "A cup of coffee is fine. I just can't drink a lot of it."

His head bobbed, and he picked up an empty mug, pouring her a cup.

Laurel grabbed a mixing bowl and a cutting board and began making breakfast.

He came to stand next to her while she worked, leaning one hip against the counter, facing her.

"You're off today, right?"

She nodded. Her normal schedule was two days on, two days off. Yesterday had been her second of two days on, but she had taken Sunday off to recuperate.

"How would you feel about spending the day with my parents?"

Laurel whipped her head around to stare at him wide-eyed. "What?"

He glanced away briefly, uncertainty shining in his eyes. "I know we talked about waiting to tell them about the baby—about us—but if we're getting married sooner rather than later, we need to tell them. My mom is already going to go nuts. The more notice we give her, the better."

She sucked in a breath, dipping her chin to her chest, then nodded. "Speaking of, when are we going to do this?"

He quirked a brow. "Saturday? That would give us the weekend to spend together unless something happens with my murder case."

She bit her lip, thinking. "Okay. Are we going to the courthouse?" She really didn't want to—that was what she and Johnny had done—but if that was what they had to do, then she would do it.

But he shook his head. "No. Not unless you want to. I

know several of the magistrates and judges. My dad used to be a judge. I'm sure one of them would come marry us wherever we wanted. What do you want?"

Surprised, Laurel looked up at him. She hadn't really thought about it. Her first wedding had been a quick affair planned by her father. He hadn't given her a choice in anything. He had even picked out her dress.

Long ago dreams about the kind of wedding she wanted surfaced. Soft colors and flowers drifted into her mind's eye. She knew that the summer wedding she had dreamed of as a girl was impossible, but there was no reason she couldn't bring some summer to the event.

"Flowers. Lots of flowers. And lace. Mostly, I want to feel pretty."

"You'll be beautiful even if you show up in your pajamas."

Laurel blushed at the intensity in his eyes. She looked back down at the vegetables on the cutting board in front of her. "So, where do we hold the ceremony? I don't want to get married at the courthouse. Not again." She peeked over at him to see his jaw muscles twitch at the reminder of her disastrous first marriage.

"Okay, then. When we go to my parents' house, I'll talk to my dad about getting Judge Huston to perform the ceremony. The weather is supposed to warm up some this weekend, so we could have it outside somewhere if you wanted. The yard at my parents' house is wooded. Or we could have it here."

"Outside," Laurel said immediately. In all her dreams of her wedding day, she had always been outside.

Tristan gave a short nod. "Outside it is. I'll help you with whatever I can, but I know next to nothing about wedding planning, even after helping Gemma. She just threw stuff at me and told me to do it. So, whatever you want, just tell me."

She smiled up at him. "Flowers. Pretty."

He grinned down at her, kissing her gently. "Then that's what we'll do."

Tristan's gut churned as he pulled into his parents' driveway a little while later. He called before they left Laurel's to make sure his mom and dad were awake. He didn't think his mother would appreciate him springing this kind of news on her before she had a cup of coffee. His second call had been to Jake to tell him he would be late.

He didn't know why he was so nervous. His parents knew Laurel and liked her. They would be over the moon that he was marrying her. Would be ecstatic about becoming grandparents.

But this was a major life change, and it was very sudden. He knew they were going to be shocked. His dad, especially, would question if Tristan was making the right decision or a rash one.

He wasn't worried that they wouldn't welcome Laurel with open arms; just whether they thought they were moving too fast, even with the baby on the way.

Putting the truck in park, he shut it off and climbed out. He met Laurel around front, taking her hand.

"Ready?"

She looked up at him. "Are you?"

He wasn't surprised she'd picked up on his hesitation. He'd been a little stiff on the way over.

Inhaling deeply, he nodded. "Let's go."

Using his keys, he unlocked the door and stepped inside. "Mom? Dad?"

"In the kitchen," his mother's voice rang out.

Taking Laurel's hand, he led her down the hall to the back of the house, where he found his parents seated at the table, eating breakfast.

"Hello, dear," Caroline said. She saw Laurel behind him and surprise made her eyes widen. "Laurel. Good morning." Her eyes flickered to Tristan briefly, and her smile wavered slightly in confusion before she looked back at Laurel. "How nice to see you."

The newspaper Will Mabley was reading rustled as he set it down. "Morning."

Tristan and Laurel murmured a greeting.

Will motioned to the two empty chairs. "Have a seat and tell us why you woke us up this morning."

Caroline noticed their entwined hands, and her eyes grew wide once more.

Tristan helped Laurel into a chair and sat next to her, taking her hand again. "So, Laurel and I have some news." He looked over at her, his eyes softening as she gave him a hesitant smile.

Squeezing her hand, he turned back to his parents. "We're having a baby."

Caroline let out a squawk and covered her mouth. Her hazel eyes were huge above her fingers. Will sat straighter in his chair, his expression rapt.

Tristan rushed ahead before either of them could recover. "We're also getting married. On Saturday."

He thought his mother was going to faint. She shrieked behind her hands and sagged against her chair. Will's hand shot out to grasp his wife's as he just stared at them through wide eyes.

"Why so quickly?" Will finally managed to ask.

Tristan tried to keep the heat out of his gaze as he glanced at Laurel. Her own eyes told him she was remembering this morning. Twin spots of color popped out on her cheeks.

"We just didn't see any reason to wait," Tristan replied.

"Are you sure this is what's best? I get that there's a child involved, but that doesn't mean you have to get married. Not in this day and age," Will countered.

Caroline, having recovered slightly, slapped a hand lightly against Will's chest. "Hush. If they want to get married and give their child a stable home, then we should be happy for them."

Will frowned at her. "I never said I wasn't happy for them. I just wondered if it was best. They don't know each other all that well. Marrying a virtual stranger isn't the best idea, especially if you're going to subject a child to the learning process that comes with getting to know someone."

"You're assuming we don't know each other, Mr. Mabley." Laurel's voice rang out clear and strong, surprising Tristan. She hadn't wanted to be part of this conversation, so the fact she was speaking out meant that some strong emotion had prompted her. He turned to her, curious as to what she had to say. His parents' eyes swung to her as well.

"I know I haven't been part of Tristan's life long, only a couple of months, but I do know him." Her eyes caught his and held as she talked. "I know that he's kind. And courageous. Fiercely protective and loyal. Impulsive, but thoughtful. He's a good man. The best I've ever known, in fact." She looked back at Will and Caroline. "The fact is, time isn't a factor. I don't need more time to know we're making the right decision. Whether we get married in a week or in a year, that will never change."

If his parents hadn't been sitting five feet away, he would have kissed her.

"She's not wrong," he echoed. "I don't need any more time, either, to know this is right. I've waited my entire adult life for someone like her to come along. I know all I need to know."

Laurel gave him a watery smile.

God, how he wished they were alone. His heart cracked

open and feelings foreign to him peeked out. He knew he was falling in love with her now. But sitting with his mom and dad was not the place to let her know that.

A sob from his mother had him breaking eye contact with Laurel. Turning his head, he saw his mom still covering her mouth, but now tears coursed down her cheeks.

She removed her hands and fanned her face. "Oh. You don't know how happy I am right now. I get a new daughter-in-law—which I thought would *never* happen—and a grandbaby. The only thing that could make life better would be for Gemma to give me a grandbaby too."

Tristan couldn't hold back the bark of laughter. Leave it to his mother to want a grandchild when she was already getting one.

Will threw up his hands. "I guess all I have to say, then, is congratulations." He smiled at Laurel. "And welcome to the family, my dear."

Laurel smiled back. "Thank you."

Caroline squealed and stood, running around the table to wrap them both in a hug. "Oh, this is so exciting." She pulled back to look down at them. "There's so much to do! Where are you getting married?" Stopping abruptly, she made a face. "Please don't tell me you're just going up to the courthouse."

Tristan couldn't help but smile. His mother reminded him where Gemma got her hyperactive personality. He shook his head. "No. We were hoping you'd let us do it in the backyard." He looked over at Will. "And that we could see if Steve Huston would be willing to perform the ceremony?"

Will nodded. "I'll call him and ask. I don't think he would have a problem with it, though."

"Oh! We could decorate the trellis and hold it there. Laurel, have you given any thought to what you want? We need to move quickly."

Tristan tuned his mother out as she peppered Laurel with

questions. They had started talking about flowers and tulle and all things wedding, none of which he had any idea about.

Will tipped his head toward the hall, silently asking Tristan to follow him.

Murmuring to Laurel that he would be back, he followed his dad out of the kitchen. Will led him to his study.

Tristan waited, knowing his dad had something on his mind.

"You've made your mother a happy woman."

One corner of Tristan's mouth tilted up. That was an understatement.

"I still think this is fast, but I won't stand in your way. I learned a long time ago that while you're impulsive, you always think things through. And I like Laurel. And not just because she saved your life." He motioned to the scar visible on Tristan's neck.

A sudden frown crossed Will's face. "That's not what this is about, is it? You don't think yourself in love with her because she saved you, do you?"

Tristan's reaction was immediate. "No. It's what brought us together last year, but it has nothing to do with how I feel about her. Dad, you have no idea how amazing she is. The things she's overcome to get where she is."

"And your case? That has nothing to do with the speed of this marriage?"

He shook his head. "Not at all. This is all about us and the baby. The pregnancy is taking its toll on her already. She can't continue to work twelve to fourteen-hour days and stay healthy. I want her to relax and focus on getting ready for our baby, not be so exhausted that she's comatose by the time she gets home at night. The sooner she can quit her job, the better."

"So, she's just going to stay home and do nothing? Son, that woman is used to being independent. She'll get so bored you're going to wish you hadn't pushed for her to quit."

"She won't be doing nothing. Dad, Laurel's an incredible artist. If she lets me, I'll bring a couple of her paintings over for you to see. She's going to focus on trying to make a career out of painting. I don't think she'll have a problem."

Will just quirked an eyebrow, clearly skeptical that Tristan had been blindsided by his feelings.

Tristan chuckled, able to read his dad's expression clearly. "I'm not exaggerating or seeing something that's not there because of my feelings for her. She really is quite talented."

"Then why is she a paramedic?"

Tristan hesitated. Laurel's story was not his to tell. "She hid it for years. Her family—they're not the most supportive. One day, I hope she'll be comfortable enough with you and with her past to tell you about them. I had to convince her that her work wasn't just mediocre. She's got nearly ten years' worth of art in her basement that no one except me has ever seen, and it's a damn shame. They don't deserve to be shut up in some dark, dingy place where no one gets to enjoy them."

Still looking slightly skeptical, Tristan knew it would take seeing them to make his dad truly believe him, but he now at least looked open to the possibility.

"I just don't want to see you hurt. If she's using you—"

"She's not. Like I said, if you knew her story, you would understand."

Will regarded him for several moments before nodding. "I'm not going to like her story when I hear it, am I?"

Tristan just shook his head.

Will's eyes narrowed. "You'll let me know if there's anything I can do? I may be out of the game, but that doesn't mean I don't still have contacts."

Tristan hesitated. Laurel would kill him if she found out what he was contemplating. But that overprotective, caveman side of him was yelling that he needed to look out for his woman.

Making a quick decision and hoping it wouldn't come back to bite him on the ass, he took a deep breath. "Actually, could you look into a man named Robert Hunt? He's Laurel's youngest brother. He showed up at her house the other night. Scared the living daylights out of her by hiding in the yard. He said the reason he didn't come to the door and try to talk to her was because he wasn't sure she would give him the time of day. After hearing why, I understand, but I still want to make sure he's on the up and up. And, while you're at it, could you make sure her father and other three brothers are still in Womack, West Virginia, and oblivious to Laurel's whereabouts?"

Will just stared. "Boy, you don't ask for much, do you?"

Tristan screwed up his face. "I know. But I just need to make sure she's safe. There's already a killer after her. I don't need to be blindsided by her relatives too."

Will made a note on the legal pad on his desk. "I'll see what I can find out."

"Thanks, Dad."

"Anytime, son."

Tristan headed for the door to rescue Laurel from his mother. They needed to go get their marriage license before he went to work.

A thought hit him and he paused in the doorway. "Dad?"

Will looked up from where he flipped through the rolodex on his desk.

"When you look into Laurel's family—" He broke off. It was difficult keeping things from his father, but he wanted to protect Laurel's privacy. She could forgive him for looking into her family, but he knew he would have a much harder time gaining her forgiveness if he broke her trust. "Look into *just* her family. Please don't go digging into Laurel's past."

Will nodded. "I won't. Names and locations of family members only."

Relief made Tristan's shoulders sag. "Thank you."

Will waved a hand. "Go. Do wedding things."

With a nod, Tristan went to find his bride.

Eighteen

Walking fast, Tristan headed for his desk in the bullpen, well over an hour late. After prying Laurel from his mom, they'd driven into town to apply for their marriage license. Paperwork for that completed, and the fee paid, he took Laurel back to his mom and dad's, so she and his mother could go shopping. His dad had promised to go along to keep an eye on things, easing Tristan's mind about Laurel being out in public. Will may have sat behind a bench to enforce the law, but he was every bit as big as his son and fitter than most men his age. Laurel was in safe hands with his father.

"Hey, Jake." Tristan shrugged out of his coat and tossed it over the back of his chair, sitting down to boot up his computer. "Sorry about that. We get anything new?"

Typing in his password, Tristan realized his partner was suspiciously silent. He peered around his computer monitor to see Jake sitting there, a stony look in his pale blue eyes.

"What?"

"You care to tell me what's going on? You have been distracted and unfocused since we caught this case."

Tristan sighed and rubbed his neck. Jake was right, and he

was owed an explanation. Glancing around, he motioned to the conference room. "In there."

"Huh?" Confusion was written all over Jake's face.

Tristan stood and started walking. He could hear Jake's chair roll back as he hurried to catch up.

Inside the conference room, Tristan leaned on the table.

"Start talking," Jake demanded, closing the door.

"I'm getting married."

Dark eyebrows shot up, and Jake's eyes widened. "What? When did this happen? I'm assuming Laurel's the bride?"

Tristan nodded. "I asked her yesterday. The wedding is Saturday."

Shock widened Jake's eyes further. "Saturday?"

"She's pregnant."

Jake sank into one of the chairs. He stared at the wall for several seconds before turning wide eyes on his partner. "Did you know that when you went after her?"

Tristan shook his head. "She'd just found out herself. She told me while we were holed up in the cabin."

"Well, shit. That sure explains a lot. She doing okay?"

"Yeah. Just tired."

Jake nodded, still processing. "Good. My sister had a baby last year. She was sick as a dog from day one until she was like six months along. I'm glad Laurel's not feeling like that."

So was Tristan.

Sinking into another chair, he rolled to face Jake. "I'm sorry I've been thrusting a lot of the work for this case onto you. If it's any consolation, you've done a great job."

Jake grinned. "Well, duh. Seriously, though, I'm here. She and your baby should be your priority. I can continue to take the lead on this."

Tristan patted Jake on the shoulder. "Thanks, Jake. I appreciate it. I'm going to try to do better now that things have settled down a bit. We enlisted my mom to help with wedding plans, so hopefully there won't be too many disruptions to my day. I'm sure my evening will be full of flowers and a million other little things, though."

"So, am I invited to this shindig?"

"Of course. It's at my Mom and Dad's. I'm not sure what time yet, though. Probably mid-afternoon after it's had a chance to warm up."

The conference room door swung open, startling both men. Ben stood in the doorway. Dread knotted Tristan's stomach at the intense look on his face.

On shaky legs, he stood. "Laurel?"

"She's fine, as far as I know," Ben hastened to assure him. "We've got another body. Young woman, late teens or early twenties. She matches Miranda Benning's description."

Tristan and Jake both cursed. Rising, they headed for the door. Ben passed Jake a paper with the address, then snagged Tristan's arm, bringing him to a halt.

"Congratulations on the wedding."

"How did you know?" Tristan asked in surprise.

Ben shrugged. "Caroline called Gemma, and Gemma called me. The women in your family move fast."

Wasn't that the truth?

"Let me know if there's anything Gemma and I can do."

Tristan nodded. "Will do," he called over his shoulder, rushing to catch up with his partner.

The scene that greeted them was not one Tristan would soon forget. The young woman had been dumped into the river near the Tennessee border. After floating downstream, her body had hung up on a bridge trestle about halfway between Hot Springs and Foggy Mountain. A passing motorist saw her and called it in.

Completely naked, she had a bullet hole through her temple, just like Veronica Chapman. Bloated and mottled from lividity, scavengers had picked several areas of the body clean of their flesh, leaving behind gaping holes and exposed bone.

Dr. Tate and the forensics crew had already arrived and were busy processing the scene.

"Cullen, what have we got?" Tristan asked, coming to stand next to the coroner, where he crouched over the victim.

The doctor looked up, a grimace marring his face. "A mess brewing. She looks like she was killed the same as that other girl. I don't know if they're connected, though. The bullet went straight through her skull, so we can't compare it to any from the first crime scene. I can tell you, though, that this is not Miranda Benning. According to her arrest record, she had a tattoo of a bird on her shoulder blade. This woman doesn't." He huffed out a breath. "If I can even call her that. Just from a cursory look, I would be amazed if she's over eighteen. The medical examiner's office will be able to tell us more once they conduct their autopsy."

Tristan rubbed the area between his eyes. This just kept getting worse. Now he had an unidentified dead woman—a teenager, most likely—to go along with his missing one.

"Okay. Anything else you can tell us?"

Cullen shook his head. "Just that she's been dead about a week, I think. The water's throwing things off a bit, but I'm fairly certain she's been dead at least that long. Again, we'll know more after the autopsy."

Tristan nodded, scanning the bank. Other than the area right around the body, they weren't going to get much from this scene. There was no way of knowing where she went into the water or how far the current carried her.

He felt a headache brewing. Cases like this made him wish

he had picked a different line of work. It was like banging his head against a brick wall.

"Am I the only one who feels like this case is bigger than we think it is?" Jake asked as they walked around to canvass what little the area might yield in clues.

"Nope." Something huge was coming, and he had a feeling it was going to blindside them all.

Nineteen

When the front door to Will and Caroline's house opened that evening, heralding Tristan's arrival, Laurel nearly groaned in relief. She liked Tristan's mother, but the woman was a bigger whirlwind than Gemma. She had dragged Laurel all over Asheville today in search of wedding supplies, including a dress. While they made a huge dent in what they needed to do before Saturday, Laurel was exhausted and just wanted to go home.

Tristan looked similar. The lines on his face were more prominent and his shoulders weren't quite so straight. Some of the weariness disappeared, though, when he saw her and smiled.

She smiled up at him from her seat on the couch. He came around to stand in front of her, taking her hands and pulling her into his arms.

The kiss he laid on her was enough to make her forget she was tired.

After a moment, he pulled back to rest his forehead against hers. "I needed that," he said softly.

"Bad day?"

He nodded, standing straighter. "Yeah. But I don't want to talk about it. How about we get out of here before my mom drags me into a retelling of your day, and we go get something to eat? I have a surprise for you."

Intrigued, Laurel nodded. "Sounds good to me. I can fill you in on what we did over dinner."

"I like it. Let's go."

Yelling down the hallway at his mother that they were leaving, Laurel couldn't hold back the giggle as Caroline called out, asking him to wait.

Tristan was helping her into her coat as Caroline came around the corner. "Tristan Andrew. Really? Laurel and I worked hard today. Don't you want to see what we accomplished?"

"Mom, I'm tired and I'm hungry. I just want to take Laurel out for dinner and then go home and crash. She can fill me in on it all while we eat."

A thrill went up Laurel's spine at his reference to home. It was both weird and wonderful to have him think of her house as home.

Caroline frowned. She shook a finger at him. "You are not going to get out of planning this wedding completely, young man."

Tristan held his hands up in surrender. "Wouldn't dream of it. I already told Laurel to tell me what I needed to do, and I'd do it."

"Good. You have a tux fitting tomorrow at noon. Laurel has the name of the shop and the address in her purse. They said they could have it ready by Friday if you came in tomorrow."

Laurel pressed her lips together to hold in the giggle at the look of torture on Tristan's face.

"This is when I miss my service dress uniform," he

mumbled. "All I had to do was get it dry cleaned, and it was ready to go."

Unbidden, images of Tristan in uniform crept into Laurel's mind. She bet he had been a sight to behold.

"Just make sure you go to the appointment," Caroline told him, hands perched on her hips.

"I will, Mom." He took Laurel's hand. "Come on, honey. Let's go before she makes me smell flowers or something." His mouth tilted in amusement at Caroline's glare.

"I'm so sorry, Laurel. I tried, but he still turned out snarky. I blame the Army."

Laurel didn't try to suppress her laugh this time. "It's okay. It gives him a bit of charm."

Caroline laughed. "It gives him something, that's for sure."

Tristan rolled his eyes, a smile hovering on his mouth. "Tell Dad we said bye."

"I will. You bring her back in the morning. We have more to do," Caroline called as Tristan pulled Laurel through the front door.

Laurel continued to laugh as he just waved, hauling her toward his truck. She half expected him to pick her up and start running. When they reached the vehicle, he opened the passenger door and grasped her waist, lifting her up to deposit her on the seat. Laurel's laughter rang out through the chilly evening.

"We're getting out before she reels us back in," Tristan stated emphatically, his expression comical, a teasing smile lifting one corner of his mouth.

He ran around the front of the truck to climb in beside her.

"She doesn't bite," Laurel said, her giggles calming. She wiped the tears of laughter from her cheeks.

"Oh, yes, she does. You just haven't been around long enough."

"I get the feeling that had more to do with you than with her."

He flashed her a devilish grin in the dim light of the truck cab. "Maybe."

She grimaced playfully. "I'm getting a glimpse of what this child is going to be like. I think your mother is probably laughing in glee that you're going to get a taste of your own medicine."

He groaned. "I hope it's a boy. I don't know how to deal with a girl with my attitude."

Laurel leaned her head against the headrest and smiled. "We'll figure it out."

He took her hand, linking their fingers as he drove.

As tired as she was, it took her several minutes to realize they were heading south and not north toward her house.

"Where are we going?"

He flashed a smile at her. "I told you I had a surprise. It's in Asheville."

"Do I get a hint?"

"Nope."

Disgruntled and now extremely curious, Laurel frowned and tried to figure out what it could be.

"So, tell me about your day. My mom wasn't too terrible, was she?"

"No, but she was definitely a hive of activity. She pulled out this binder from Gemma's wedding right after you dropped me off and took everything out of it, except the checklist. From that point, it was game on. It helped, though. We got a lot done. I went with soft colors. Cream, a dusky pink and a pale yellow.

"After we hammered out the details of everything we would need, she dragged me to Asheville, and we went flower shopping. I think I sniffed every flower in the shop and viewed every possible floral combination of the colors I wanted. There's drapey flowers for the trellis, and roses and lilies for the bouquets and boutonnieres." She waved her hands in exasperation. "It's all coming Friday. Your mom agreed to handle the deliveries since I have to work."

"You're going to put your notice in tomorrow, right?"

Laurel nodded. As much as she hated to admit it, he was right. She couldn't work the hours demanded of her job anymore. The last few days she worked before she found out she was pregnant as well as since had left her absolutely exhausted. She couldn't keep up that pace and stay healthy.

"What else did you do besides sniff flowers?"

Laurel giggled. "We went dress shopping." She smiled fondly at the memory. Caroline had been wonderful. The older woman had been nothing but supportive in Laurel's efforts to find a dress that was both pretty and warm and could be ready by Friday. She had corralled the shop manager, told her exactly what they needed, and how much time and money they had to spend. The staff did the rest. Laurel had felt like a princess as they brought her dress after dress until she found the one that made her feel the way she'd always wanted to feel on her wedding day.

"We also stopped at some restaurant your parents frequent. Caroline talked the owner into catering. We ate lunch there and picked out a menu. Mr. D'Amica said we just need to get him a final tally of how many people we're expecting by Thursday."

She sighed. "Tomorrow, she wants to go pick out tableware and centerpieces." She leaned her head back again. "I need shoes too."

"Mom didn't insist on paying for everything, did she? I told her to get invoices and I'd pay them."

"She tried. I put a deposit down on the flowers and

bought my dress outright. She put her foot down, though, on the dinner. Said it was their contribution to the wedding since we weren't having a rehearsal."

He nodded. "Remind me to give you my credit card in the morning so you can get the rest of the decorations. I meant to today, and I forgot."

Laurel bristled. "I'm not poor, Tristan. I can buy a few table covers and flowers."

He expelled a breath. "I didn't mean to imply you were, but Laurel, you need to know I'm very well-off. I haven't paid rent in years because Mom and Dad's house is paid off. I invested nearly all of my salary while in the military, and I've continued to invest since then. I could buy their house in cash and not bat an eye."

Laurel's eyes widened, and she stared at him. He had said they wouldn't be hurting if she stayed home to raise their baby, but she had no idea he was rich.

"Why are you just now telling me this?"

He shrugged sheepishly. "It's not exactly something I broadcast. And we haven't had the most conventional relationship, so it hasn't come up before now."

Laurel sat back and stared out at the dark night, her mind spinning. She didn't know what to make of this.

"Anyway, it doesn't matter," Tristan continued. "It doesn't change who I am or the values I hold. I mostly did it so that when I retired, I would have the resources to do the things I'd always wanted to do, like travel. The investment choices I made turned out to be better than I thought they would be, and they've allowed me to live off of their profits alone if I so choose. I don't, because that's just ridiculous. I'd go crazy if I didn't work."

She could just imagine Tristan sitting idle. No, he would not do well without something to occupy him.

"Okay. So you're rich. I hope you don't think that means I

won't want to contribute to our household. I've been a kept woman, and I won't be again."

"God, no, Laurel. You're free to do as you please. As soon as we're married, we can move everything into one account. You can add to it and withdraw from it however you want. The only thing I ask of you is that you put your health and that of our child over everything else. You and this baby are the most important things to me. I just want you both safe and happy."

Something cracked inside Laurel at his words. Any doubts she had remaining about this marriage evaporated. No one had ever cared about her wellbeing except her mother and Rob. Laurel barely remembered her mother, and the care Rob had shown to her in the past had been cursory at best.

Blinking back the moisture pooling in her eyes, Laurel just nodded, not trusting herself to speak without breaking down. He didn't know it, but he'd given her a gift greater than financial stability.

The remaining miles into Asheville flew by in a content silence as Tristan drove. When he pulled the truck into a parking spot on a busy street in the downtown shopping district, Laurel was a little reluctant to leave the cozy confines of the vehicle.

She peered out the window at the shops lining the street. "What are we doing here?"

"You'll see." She glanced over in time to see a wicked grin on his handsome face.

Narrowing her eyes suspiciously, she climbed out of the truck. Tristan came around to take her hand and lead her down the sidewalk. When he stopped, they were in front of a jewelry store.

He shrugged as she arched an eyebrow. "We need rings." Suddenly, his face broke out into a grin. "Come on."

Laughing softly, she let him tug her inside.

"Out of curiosity, why didn't you buy me a ring on your own? Why bring me along?"

His cheeks reddened, which Laurel found utterly endearing.

"Honestly? I've never bought a piece of jewelry for a woman in my life. Not even my mom. I have an idea of what you might like, but I have absolutely no idea what size to get. I figured since it's something you're going to wear for a long time, I wanted you to love it."

Laurel's heart tried to swell out of her chest at his implication that they would be married for many years to come. She sincerely hoped that was the case.

She was prevented from replying by the arrival of the saleswoman. She eyed Tristan up and down, but barely spared Laurel a glance. Immediately, Laurel's hackles rose. She was used to being looked over because she was tiny, but never so blatantly dismissed.

"Hi. My name is Deana. Can I help you find something?"

"We're here looking for wedding sets," Tristan told the woman, wrapping an arm around Laurel's waist, his eyes telegraphing he was only interested in the jewelry the woman sold.

The woman's expression fell slightly, giving Laurel a perverse sense of satisfaction. She wrapped her arm around Tristan's back and smiled brilliantly at the woman, making it clear that this hunk of man was hers.

Deana motioned them toward the counter. "We have many to choose from. Is there something in particular you were thinking?"

Laurel looked up at Tristan, but he just gestured at the jewelry case. "I told you, I want you to love it, so you pick. Whatever you want." He looked up at the saleswoman. "Whatever it is, though, we need it by the end of the week."

Her eyes widened slightly, but she quickly covered it up

with a bright smile. "Of course. We offer rush orders. By Friday would be no problem."

Laurel perused the bevy of rings on display. There were so many to choose from, it felt a little daunting. She sucked her lip in, worrying it as she looked.

"Is there a particular style you like?" Deana asked.

"Um, nothing too flashy. Or heavy. I'm tiny, so anything large would just look out of place on me."

A frown creased the woman's brow as she looked down. "Okay. Let's see. Delicate, understated, but elegant. Hmm..." Opening the case, she pulled out several styles and set them on the counter.

One near the end caught Laurel's attention. It was platinum, with an intricate filigree. A central oval cut diamond was set low in a bevel setting with smaller diamonds set into the filigree. It was breathtaking.

Tristan, who had crowded next to her to look as well, noticed her hesitation over that one. He picked it up. "You like this one?"

She nodded, blushing. "It's pretty."

He took her left hand and slid it onto her ring finger. It sparkled under the overhead lights, showing off its beauty. But Laurel was more entranced by the sparkle in Tristan's sapphire eyes than the diamond on her hand. He looked utterly transfixed as he stared down at her. She felt like the only woman in the world.

"I like this one too," he finally said, quietly. Lifting her hand, he placed a soft kiss on the back of her fingers before turning to the saleswoman. "We'll take this one. We need wedding bands too."

The woman nodded, smiling at them. She replaced the engagement rings and began setting out trays of wedding bands.

Tristan's phone rang before they could try any on.

His sudden frown had her wondering what was going on. "Everything okay?"

He nodded, sliding his thumb to answer. "Yeah. It's the lab. I'll be right back. You go ahead and find something you like."

She nodded, and he stepped over to the window to take the call.

"You're very lucky, you know," the saleswoman said, breaking into Laurel's thoughts. "I'd give my eyeteeth to have a man like that look at me the way he looks at you."

Laurel glanced back at Tristan and smiled. She was very lucky indeed.

Twenty

"Detective Mabley," Tristan answered as he wandered away from Laurel.

"Tristan, it's Cullen. I found something in my initial exam, and I wanted to give you a heads-up."

Intrigued and a little worried now, Tristan frowned. "What'd you find, doc?"

"I think our victim recently gave birth, just like Veronica Chapman."

"What?" Dread pooled to sit low in Tristan's gut.

"Her body shows signs of recent childbirth. I'm talking less than a week post-partum."

Tristan cursed.

"Exactly."

"Okay. I'll put out an alert to law enforcement and contact the hospitals. See if anyone has gotten a baby in without a mother. Can you give me a tighter time frame yet?"

"At this point, I'd say the baby is two weeks old, max. Based on river temps and her state of decomp, I think our victim was dumped about five days ago."

"All right. Damn. I'm glad you're handling the autopsy this time, and we don't have to wait for Asheville's M.E. to do it." That wasn't always the case. Cullen was a trauma surgeon, in addition to being the county coroner. More often than not, he was too busy to perform autopsies, so the cases were sent to neighboring jurisdictions. But he'd made time for this case, for which Tristan was grateful. It meant quicker answers.

"Same here. Time is of the essence in this case, I think."

"I agree. Thanks for the heads-up. I'll see you in the morning for the autopsy." Tristan hung up and resisted the urge to punch the window. Now, he had an unidentified killer after his fiancée, a missing woman, and *two* missing infants. He had a bad feeling this case hinged on those babies.

A theory began to take shape in his mind. Opening the note app on his phone, he quickly jotted down a few things to check out the next day. If he was right, this case was going to get a whole lot bigger real quick.

He called Jake and let him know what was going on. His curses matched Tristan's.

"Are you thinking what I'm thinking?" Jake asked.

"That someone is abducting pregnant women and taking their babies?"

"Yep."

Tristan's gaze drifted to Laurel, who was bent over the jewelry counter looking at rings. Her role in this case had just become much more dangerous.

"Can you call the hospitals and see if any of them have had any abandoned newborns come in? I have a feeling you won't, so I'll stop back at the station in a bit and put out a BOLO to law enforcement for the second infant. Laurel and I are out doing wedding things."

"Sounds good. Tell Laurel I said hi, and I'll see you in the morning."

Putting the phone away, Tristan did his best to push the case to the back of his mind for the moment. Worrying about it now wouldn't accomplish anything, and Laurel deserved to have his undivided attention.

Walking back up to the counter, he saw she had several rings lying on a black mat in front of her.

She arched an eyebrow questioningly.

"Jake says hi." His words were casual, but he knew his face told her there was much more to the call than a few pleasantries.

She nodded, understanding.

"Did you find one you liked?"

"Maybe. I can't decide, though. I like the idea of a plain band for when I want to work in the yard or paint, but then it's a choice of width. Then there's the one that goes with the engagement ring and it's just beautiful." She bit her lip again and pointed at the intricate filigree band dotted with small diamonds. "I'm just worried it won't hold up to an active lifestyle."

He picked up the dainty ring. It very much suited Laurel. Delicate and feminine, but he could feel a sturdiness to it as well. "I think it would be fine. If it's the one you like the most, then get it. They make those plastic bands now that you could wear for really active stuff like hiking or camping if you're worried about damaging or losing it."

She worried her lip some more. Tristan cupped her chin and popped her lip free with his thumb. "Do you like it?"

Hesitantly, she nodded.

"Then get it." He wanted her to have what made her happy. If that ring was it, he would buy it a hundred times over.

"Do *you* like it?" she asked.

In answer, he put it and the engagement ring on her

finger. The sight of those rings on her tiny hand sent his masculine pride into overdrive. In four short days, she would be his, and those rings would hopefully grace her hand for the rest of their lives.

Swallowing around the sudden lump of emotion in his throat, he nodded. "They suit you perfectly."

Her smile was nothing short of blinding. Reaching up, she kissed him quick before releasing him to turn back to the saleswoman.

"He needs a ring now."

Deana smiled and put several styles of men's wedding bands on the counter. "You look like a rugged individual. Any of these will compliment hers, but stand up to just about anything you can do to it."

Tristan quickly picked out a thick platinum band with edge grooves, giving the ring a little definition and personality.

After taking a measurement of their fingers, she wrote up the order and Tristan paid for their purchases.

"We're getting food now, right?" Laurel asked as they headed for the truck. "I'm starving."

He nodded, helping her in. "I'm afraid it's going to have to be something quick. I need to stop at the station briefly. I got new information about my case. You and I need to talk about that, but it can wait."

"You're sure?" she asked, frowning up at him.

"Yeah. I'd rather we be home and comfortable for the conversation we need to have." He fastened her seatbelt for her before dropping a quick kiss on her lips. "It's nothing pressing, just some information you need to know."

Still frowning, she nodded. "Okay."

Rounding the truck, Tristan climbed in and quickly took them through a drive-thru for tacos before heading to the station. They didn't linger long. He filled out the BOLO and sent it to area law enforcement while they both scarfed down their dinner.

Task complete, they piled back into the truck and headed home.

Home. It really had begun to feel that way, Tristan thought as he pulled into the driveway. He knew it was because of the tiny woman beside him. Home would be wherever she was.

As he put the truck in park, something about the property registered as different. Growing still, he surveyed the house and yard. Laurel started to climb out of the truck, but his hand on her arm stopped her.

"Tristan?"

"Hang on a minute. Something doesn't feel right." It was a gut feeling that had served him well as a Ranger. He never ignored it.

"I'm going to go check things out. As soon as I get out of the truck, you lock it behind me and climb into the driver's seat. If things go bad, I want you to call 911 and get somewhere safe. Whatever happens, you *stay in the truck*."

"Tristan—"

"Promise me, Laurel. Even if I'm hurt, you will stay in the vehicle until help arrives. If I'm not able to protect you, it makes you easy pickings. Please. Stay here."

Worrying that lip again, she nodded. "Okay. But please be careful."

"I will. Give me your house keys."

She dug in her purse, pulling out the key ring and handed it over.

Taking the keys, he kissed her hard and quick before opening the truck door. "Lock it behind me."

She nodded and was moving into the driver's seat before he had even closed the door. He heard the soft snick of the locks engaging as he drew his gun and moved silently toward the house. Now that he had time to study the building, he realized the porch light that was on an automatic timer hadn't come on and there was no glow coming through the front window from the small lamp Laurel had there.

Hoping it was just a power outage and he was being paranoid, he crept closer. Ducking low, he crab-walked under the windows to the front door. Testing the knob, he noted it was still locked and skirted around the side of the house, checking windows as he went. When he got around back, he immediately noticed that the kitchen door had a shattered windowpane.

Sending up a silent curse, he took out his phone and called for backup, then called Laurel and told her it looked like someone had broken in and to honk if anyone came out the front. He hated leaving her alone, but he didn't want to leave the back of the house unattended. If there was someone inside, he wanted to catch the bastard.

Staying low, he kept an eye on the door and listened for the sound of someone moving within. After several minutes, a rustling to his right made him rise, gun trained on the side of the house.

A Northridge officer walked around the corner, his own weapon at the ready.

Forcing his heart rate back to normal, Tristan identified himself.

"Do you have anyone with you?" he asked the officer.

The man shook his head. "There's only two of us and the other officer is on a call. If you want more backup, we'll have to wait for the county."

"How close is the nearest deputy?"

Using his radio, the officer asked for an estimated time of arrival for a sheriff's deputy. The dispatcher told them at least ten minutes.

Tristan wasn't willing to wait that long. "Tell her to start them en route, but we're going in. You go around front and come in through the front door." He handed the officer Laurel's keys. The man took off around the side of the house.

Taking a few deep breaths, Tristan forced a calm on himself that he didn't feel. He was quickly discovering that how he felt about the situation was vastly different from how he would feel if the house belonged to a perfect stranger.

Reaching over, he turned the knob and pushed. The door swung inward and Tristan followed it. His boots crunched on the broken glass as he stepped inside. Quickly clearing the small room, he moved into the living room. The officer stood near the door, eyes trained on the hallway.

"Hold here," he told the officer. "There's a garage off the kitchen I haven't checked yet, so keep an eye out. We'll do it last."

The man nodded, planting his feet.

Moving silently, Tristan moved down the hallway, quickly clearing the small office and bathroom. Opening the basement door, he made his way down the stairs. He walked down the line of Laurel's paintings to check the well created between them and the back wall. Like the other rooms upstairs, it was empty.

Heading back up, he stopped outside the bedroom door. The *closed* bedroom door. It had been open when they left that morning.

Weapon ready, he thrust the door open and stepped inside. Like the rest of the house, this room was empty as well. No one hid under the bed or in the closet. But someone *had* been in here. It was subtle, but things had been moved. A pillow on the bed. The hangers in the closet.

Teeth clenched, Tristan went back to the living room. He still needed to clear the garage, but he didn't think he would find anyone. Whoever had been here had been gathering information, not lying in wait.

Collecting the officer, he walked back into the kitchen to the interior garage door.

"You go right," Tristan said. At the officer's nod, he opened the door.

Laurel's car sat cold and silent in the dark space. Moving as a team, Tristan and the officer moved around the car to the far side. Seeing no one, he quickly checked Laurel's car, but it was also untouched.

Frustrated, he blew out a breath and hit the button to raise the garage door. He jogged over to his truck. Laurel had the door unlocked and was out of the car as he rounded the hood.

She launched herself at him, and he caught her easily.

"I don't think I like your job," she muttered against his neck.

He pulled back to look at her. "It's not normally like this. Not anymore."

"Did you find anything?" She motioned toward the house.

"Someone was inside. Things have been moved. I need you to take a walk through it and tell me if anything is missing. I don't think there is, but you'll be able to tell better than me."

She nodded and released him except for his hand.

"Why were the lights out? Did he cut the electricity?"

"No. He just turned the switches off. He was probably afraid of being seen, and it was less noticeable to turn off the lights than to draw the curtains closed."

The first sheriff's cruiser pulled up, quickly followed by a crime scene unit.

The next couple of hours were a hive of activity as CSU techs combed the house for evidence, finding little. Whoever had come in had been wearing gloves. When the last official car left, Tristan was beat. Laurel was asleep on the couch, fatigue and her pregnancy combining to let her tune out the noise around her.

Locking the front door and making sure that the board

over the broken kitchen door was secure, he scooped Laurel up and headed for the bedroom.

She woke as he put her on the bed. A huge yawn cracked her jaw. "Is everyone gone?"

He nodded, sitting down next to her. Resting one foot over his knee, he untied the laces on his boot. "You can have the bathroom first."

Nodding sleepily, she climbed off the bed and grabbed her pajamas from the drawer, padding softly out of the room.

While she changed, Tristan removed his boots and placed his gun and badge on the nightstand before stripping down. When she emerged, they traded places and Tristan quickly brushed his teeth before returning to the bedroom to climb into bed beside her.

She snuggled into him, her cool hands resting on his chest. "Are you cold?"

"A little."

Wrapping her up tighter, he used his body heat to warm her.

She toyed with the edges of his collarbone, her tiny hands like butterflies on his skin.

"So, what was it you wanted to talk to me about?"

He sat up, pulling her with him. In the excitement, he'd forgotten about the conversation they needed to have.

"We found what we think is a second victim today. She may have actually been dead longer than the first girl, though."

Laurel looked up sharply. "Another girl? Why do you think it's the same killer?"

He twisted a lock of her silky blonde hair in his fingers several times before replying. "Because Dr. Tate—our local coroner—thinks she had recently given birth as well."

Her eyes widened. "They both had just had babies?"

Tristan nodded. "That's what I wanted to talk to you

about. Other than our immediate family and friends, I don't want it to get out that you're pregnant until we can't hide it anymore or I catch this guy. I think we've stumbled onto an underground baby ring."

Her mouth dropped open in shock and her hands flew to her stomach. "Oh my God. That's terrible. Those women were killed for their babies?"

Tristan nodded, covering her hands with one of his. "I think so, yes. I can't prove it yet. I don't even know if the second woman is connected to the first, but it's just too much of a coincidence that we've had two recently post-partum women turn up shot to death, their infants missing for me not to wonder."

His free hand cupped the side of her head, and he held her gaze. "You're already on the killer's radar. I don't want to give him a bigger incentive to come after you by it getting out that you're pregnant."

She sucked that lip between her teeth and looked over his shoulder in thought.

"Laurel, I promise you I am going to do everything I can to keep you safe. I just want you to be aware of the increased danger if this is indeed about an underground baby ring."

"Okay," she whispered.

Tristan hated that she was frightened, but he would rather she be frightened and aware than oblivious and caught off-guard.

Tucking her close, he slid them down so they were lying flat again. His hand drifted over her belly and hip in a soft caress. She had a slight swell starting between her hip bones, her small frame already expanding to accommodate their growing child. That little detail was enough for the reality that his baby was indeed growing within her to hit home hard. A rush of love for that tiny life blindsided him and wrapped itself around his heart, squeezing it tight. He would do anything to keep their child safe. To make sure it had a chance to be born and to grow into a kind, honest, and loving adult.

Placing a tender kiss on the top of her head, he settled deeper into the mattress, his mind a jumble of thoughts both about the case and the months to come. They had a lot to do to get ready for this child.

"You know, we're going to need a bigger house," he murmured, thinking out loud.

Her head rose off his chest, and she quirked an eyebrow. "How did you go from warning me about bad guys stealing babies to we need a bigger house?"

He shrugged. "It got me thinking about our baby and all that we need to do to get ready for it. The furniture, the clothes, the car seats—all of it. That led me to the fact that this house doesn't have a second bedroom. Just that tiny office. And we're certainly not living with my parents, even if they do decide to start traveling again."

She propped her head on her fists on top of his chest and frowned thoughtfully. "You're right. I hadn't given it all that much thought yet."

"I'll call a realtor and set up some appointments for us next week. We need to make a list of what features we want and then we can go from there. Do you own this house or do you rent it?"

"Rent."

"Good, that'll make things simpler. How would you feel about living closer to Foggy Mountain? Or would you rather stay here in Northridge?"

"I don't think there's anything for sale here. But it wouldn't matter. I don't mind moving towns. Even if I did decide to go back to being a paramedic after the baby's born, there's no guarantee it would be for Northridge. They might not have any openings at that point."

They stayed awake a while longer, discussing what they wanted in a house and where they wanted to live, until Laurel was unable to keep her eyes open any longer.

Tristan stroked her silky hair as she slept on his chest, his own eyes drifting shut finally as a sense of peace stole over him.

Twenty-One

The next morning, Tristan dropped Laurel off with his parents again and headed straight to the county morgue for the autopsy on the Jane Doe pulled from the river. Jake met him in the anteroom to the exam suite.

"Heard you had some excitement last night."

"Yeah."

"Everything okay?"

Tristan nodded. "Nothing was taken. I think they were just looking for information."

Jake frowned. "What kind of information?"

He shrugged. "Maybe what she knows. Her routine. Info on me. I complicate things, and I think they're trying to find a way around me."

Jake snorted. "Good luck with that."

That's what Tristan was hoping. It wasn't being cocky to say he was a formidable opponent. His background meant he was more than just your average cop. Getting through him to get to Laurel would not be an easy task.

"You get anything from the hospitals?" Tristan asked,

changing the subject. He grabbed the vapor rub and rubbed some under his nose to mask the smell of the autopsy.

Jake shook his head, frowning. "No. They all said they'd keep a lookout and report any abandoned infants to me, as well as through their standard channels."

"I didn't think you'd get any hits. I think they're selling them." He ran a hand through his hair. The thick waves fell over his forehead, reminding him he needed to get it trimmed.

"You haven't said anything to anyone about Laurel's pregnancy, have you?"

"No."

"Good. Don't. I don't want it getting out. She's already a target."

Jake's eyes closed briefly as the implications hit him. "Jesus, I hadn't even thought of that. Did Ben put a guard on her?"

"When she's not with someone I trust, yes. She's with my parents again today. Tomorrow, she has to work again, though." He made a face behind his mask.

"Do you not trust her partner?"

Tristan shrugged. "It's not that. I just don't know him. And they can get sent to some shady places. No one would notice someone creeping around, waiting to ambush them. I'm just glad she's putting in her notice tomorrow. The sooner she quits, the happier I'll be."

The exterior door swung open and Cullen Tate strode in. "Hi. Sorry I'm late. I had a patient I had to see this morning. It took a little longer than I expected. Let me go change and we'll get started."

The doctor was quick, and within a few minutes the three men were standing beside the stainless-steel autopsy table, their Jane Doe's body lying on top, washed and ready for the procedure.

Tristan hated this part of his job. He'd gotten his fill of the dead as a Ranger. It wasn't any easier to watch an autopsy than it was to see Afghan civilians—or even his brothers-in-arms—lying dead in the sand. All of it was senseless. This girl shouldn't be lying here on Cullen's morgue slab. She should be caring for her newborn, warm and safe in her home.

For the next two hours, he and Jake watched as Cullen carefully dissected the woman, looking for any abnormalities or clues that would lead them to her identity or that of her killer. They did learn that the woman had been gravely ill at the time of her death. Infection from childbirth had set in, and she likely would have died within a day or two if she hadn't been executed.

Cullen tied the last stitch on the Y-incision he'd made and stripped off his gloves, stepping back from the table. He motioned Tristan and Jake back to the anteroom.

Glad to get away from the smell that no amount of vapor rub could cover up, Tristan hurriedly stepped out of the exam suite.

"I'll try to get her fingerprints, but her hands aren't in the best condition, so no guarantees. I wish I could have told you more."

"You told us plenty. In the absence of a concrete connection, I think you've given us a solid basis for the theory we've been tossing around."

"Which is?"

"Babies for sale."

Cullen cursed. "That makes sense. It would also explain why they killed this one instead of keeping her alive. Her illness made her a liability."

"And why Veronica Chapman was on the run," Jake replied. "I'm betting she escaped with her baby and they tracked her down."

"But why wouldn't she go to the police?" Tristan argued. "Why would she just run?"

"Maybe someone on the force is involved. Not necessarily ours, since we think she was just passing through, but Asheville's," Jake argued.

Tristan's jaw clenched, doubly glad that they were keeping Laurel's pregnancy a secret.

"God, I hate the idea of a crooked cop. I took the extra training to be a coroner to do my part to catch guys who do that." Cullen hooked a thumb toward the exam suite and the body on his slab. "And to give victims and their families some closure. To think that someone who is supposed to do the same is the one you're after is disgusting."

Tristan agreed. He hoped they were wrong. Stripping off their exam garb, he and Jake bid the doctor farewell and left.

"Where to?" Jake asked.

"I'd like to check out that homeless encampment again. See if Debbie can identify our dead woman." He unlocked his truck and opened the door.

"Sounds good." Jake climbed into the passenger seat.

Tristan started the truck and pointed it toward Asheville. Once in town, they made a quick stop to get some groceries to butter the woman up with, then made their way to the homeless camp. They parked outside the alley where they found her the last time and climbed out of the car.

Walking straight to Debbie's little area of the alley, they didn't stop to talk to anyone else this time.

"Miss Debbie?" Tristan called as they got close. "Miss Debbie, it's Detectives Mabley and Maxwell."

The older woman's gray head popped out from her shelter. "M&M, you're back?"

Tristan grinned at the nickname she gave them the other day. "Yes ma'am. We brought you some things." He held up the grocery sacks he carried. "And we were hoping you'd look at a picture for us."

She came out of her shelter and took the bags, poking

through them, exclaiming over several items. "You boys brought some good stuff." She pulled out a pack of Oreos and opened them, removing one from the package. "Especially these. A girl loves her chocolate." She cackled and took a bite.

After finishing her cookie, she sat in one of the lawn chairs and motioned them to join her. "So, where's this picture you want to show me?"

Tristan took out his phone and pulled up the photo he took of their Jane Doe. "I have to warn you, it's of a dead woman and she's been in the water. I know it will be hard to tell if she looks like anyone you know, but if it sparks any kind of recognition, we need to know."

Eyes serious now, Debbie nodded and held out her hand. Tristan handed her the phone.

Debbie sucked in a harsh breath at her first glimpse of the image. "You weren't kidding. She hardly looks like a person."

"Does she remind you of anyone?" Jake asked.

Debbie pursed her lips as she studied the image. Slowly, she shook her head. "I can't say that she does. But it's hard to tell with the way she looks. Can you tell me anything about her? Maybe it'll jog my memory. What was she wearing? People around here tend to wear the same things all the time."

Tristan frowned. "She wasn't wearing anything. She did recently give birth, though. Were there any pregnant women around here that you haven't seen in a while?"

Debbie ate another Oreo as she thought. After a moment, she shook a half-eaten cookie at them. "You know, there was one. Real young girl. Her name was Kaylee. She had blonde hair just like that girl. She showed up one day, scared out of her wits. Said her parents turned her out because she was pregnant. I gave her what little food I had. She's one of those ones that went off with that man."

Tristan shared a look with Jake. Their search of the name on the card had turned up nothing. Even the reverse look-up on the phone number had come back as a burner cell, not registered to anyone. They were planning a sting operation to lure the guy out, but it would take some time. They had to get someone established undercover in the area, so it wouldn't raise his suspicions.

"He took a pregnant woman to prostitute?" Jake asked.

Debbie shook her head. "She said she did cleaning. Ran a few errands. She saved every penny she made, except what she spent on food, trying to get enough to get a place to stay. I tried to tell her to go to social services, but she didn't want them to take away her baby because she was homeless. I told her they had halfway houses for people like her, but she was adamant they were going to take her baby away."

"Debbie, how old was Kaylee?" Tristan asked. If she was a minor, it could explain why she was so afraid to go to the authorities.

"She said she was eighteen, but I think she was lying. She just seemed so young," she said, confirming his suspicions.

"When did you see her last?" Jake asked.

"Oh, it's been a month or so now, I guess. I thought maybe she finally got some sense and went to see social services since she was ready to pop."

"Kaylee ever tell you her last name?" Tristan asked.

Debbie shook her head. "No. And I didn't ask. We don't get too personal out here."

"Okay. I don't suppose you've heard from Miranda Benning, have you?"

She shook her head again.

"Has that man been back around?" Jake asked.

"No."

Tristan pulled a business card from his wallet along with enough change to cover the payphone at the convenience store around the corner. He wrote his cell number and Jake's on the back.

"I want you to do me a favor. If that man or someone he sends to collect people comes back around, I want you to take this change and call me or Jake immediately. If you can get it without being seen, get the license plate on the vehicle." He handed her the card and the change.

She tipped her head and stared up at him. "What's in it for me?"

"All the Oreos you can eat. Plus, a hot meal from that diner we took you to the last time."

Eyes narrowed, she considered their proposal. "You add a pair of nice tennis shoes to that and you've got a deal." She held out a foot ensconced in a threadbare black shoe. Tristan had no idea how she didn't have severe frostbite on her feet.

"Done."

"We'll even bring new socks," Jake added.

"Deal," Debbie said.

They bid her a good day and headed back to their car.

"You think she'll see anything?" Jake asked.

Tristan shrugged, unlocking the car and climbing behind the wheel. "I hope so. She strikes me as the nosy neighbor who knows everything about everyone in the neighborhood. If that man comes back, she'll know."

He hoped it was soon. They needed a break before those babies were out of their reach. They might be already.

Twenty-Two

Laurel stared out the windshield of the ambulance as she drove back to Northridge from Asheville. They had just dropped off a patient at the hospital and were headed back to the station. The winding road was shrouded in darkness, the truck's headlights bouncing off the wet roads. It had warmed up considerably since the snowfall over the weekend, and now everything was just wet. She was glad it was warmer, but she missed the purity of the snow.

"So, you're really getting married tomorrow?"

She glanced over at her partner in the cab's dim interior, and nodded. Because she had put in her two-week notice, she'd had to tell her boss why she was quitting. It had only seemed fair to tell her partner too.

"I still have a hard time seeing you with Detective Mabley. He just doesn't seem like your type."

Laurel frowned. She wasn't aware she had a type. After her disastrous marriage, she'd rarely dated. She'd had one serious relationship between Johnny and Tristan, and that had been a couple of years ago. Paul had been nice, but boring. She'd thought she wanted boring, but he was too boring, even for her. Even their intimate relationship had been blah. No sparks whatsoever. They never made it past heavy petting, and after six months, she finally called it quits.

"What is my type, exactly?"

Wade shrugged. "Smaller? Less intimidating? You're rather quiet and shy, and the detective is, well, not."

Her mouth tilted. "Can't argue there. He is very bold. But he's also kind. And charming."

Wade shook his head. "Ted Bundy was charming."

Laurel laughed. "Tristan is not Ted Bundy. Trust me when I say I would not be marrying him if I didn't think he was 'The One'." And she wouldn't be. She loved Tristan. Had from almost the very beginning. He was it for her. Baby or not, she would have eventually succumbed to that incredible charm and married him anyway. Her pregnancy had just given the timetable a boost.

"Why so soon, though? Even with a baby on the way, that doesn't mean you have to rush. Not in today's world."

It was her turn to shrug. "We didn't see any reason to wait, and neither of us wanted a big wedding. I don't really have much family, and all the people Tristan cares about live in Foggy Mountain. It just makes sense to have the wedding sooner rather than later. Then we can focus on getting ready for the baby."

Wade glanced in the side mirror, a frown forming. "I suppose. Hey, are we being followed? That car has been back there since we got off the interstate, and it doesn't seem to want to give us much space."

She looked into her side mirror. She had noticed that as well. Unease skated through her belly.

"There's a pull-off coming up," Wade said. "Turn into it and let him pass."

Deciding that sounded like a wonderful idea, Laurel sped up slightly. She rounded the bend and glanced in her mirror. A wave of fear shot through her. Increasing her speed hadn't opened up any distance between them and the car. The vehicle had sped up as well, and was now even closer to their back bumper.

"Geez, is this guy nuts? If you have to brake hard, he's going to bury himself in the back of the truck."

Laurel agreed. Her heart flip-flopped in relief when she saw the sign for the scenic overlook. Pressing harder on the accelerator, she headed straight for it.

Just as she was turning, she heard a pop, and the ambulance swerved wildly. They had blown a tire. Laurel hit the brakes hard as the guardrail loomed in front of them. When another tire popped, she realized she hadn't run over something, but that the car following them had shot out the tires.

Horror filled her veins as she fought to control the top-heavy ambulance. Using all the strength she had, she tugged on the steering wheel, turning the tires away from the looming drop-off rushing up to meet them. With a shuddering skid, they came to a stop just inches from the guardrail.

Relief rushed through her, only to be quickly followed by stark terror. She turned in her seat, looking for the car.

No headlights shone in the darkness, but that didn't mean anything if the other car had turned them off.

Reaching for her phone, she quickly dialed Tristan. He picked up on the second ring.

"You get off early?" he asked in lieu of greeting.

If only. "No. Someone just ran us off the road and shot out two of our tires. We're at the overlook on Highway 25."

"Shit. I'm on my way." She heard the ding of his truck as he climbed inside. "You stay in the ambulance. Do not get out unless it catches on fire, do you understand?"

Laurel bobbed her head. "Yes."

"Is the other vehicle still there?"

She looked around outside again. "I don't know. I don't think so, but I'm not a hundred percent certain they're not just sitting out there with their lights off." She unbuckled her seatbelt. "Let me go look out the back windows."

Climbing through the pass-through, she turned to Wade briefly. "Wade, turn off the lights in the back."

Her partner, who had been on the radio with dispatch while she talked to Tristan, reached out and flipped a switch on the dash.

She crawled through into the back and slid alongside the stretcher to peer out the rear windows.

"I don't see anything back here. I think they left."

"Good. I'll be there soon. Stay in the truck." The line clicked as he hung up.

She picked her way back up front.

"Tristan is on his way."

"So is a cruiser from the sheriff's department. Dispatch sent one. There's a wrecker on the way, too, to replace our tires. Did someone really just shoot them out?"

Laurel sucked her lip in, worrying it, and nodded. "This is all my fault."

"No. It's the sicko who murdered that woman who is at fault."

She shook her head. "If I had stayed home like Tristan wanted—"

"They would have tried to burn down your house. Or shoot you through a window. It's not your fault, Laurel." He covered her hand with his.

"But you wouldn't have been involved. I don't want anyone else to get hurt because of me." And she didn't. It would haunt her forever if someone else was hurt or killed because of her.

"Again, not your fault. We need you, and I am thankful you didn't just quit outright. So are the rest of the crew. None of us wants to work double shifts. I'm just glad I managed to talk an old buddy of mine into moving up here to take one of the open spots. At least it won't be any worse on us after you're gone."

She smiled sardonically. "Well, after tonight you might have to work doubles. I'm not a hundred percent certain that Tristan won't chain me to my house."

Wade chuckled. "You just turn those pretty eyes on him and he'll do anything you want."

She hoped that was the case. She was about to test Tristan's promise to work on his overprotectiveness, because Wade was right. She couldn't quit yet. Too many people were relying on her to finish out her two weeks. Unless she was incapacitated, she wasn't quitting early.

Headlights rounded the bend ahead of the overlook, and Laurel tensed, sure that the car that had shot out their tires was coming back to finish them off.

Instead, she recognized Tristan's truck. He drove past and did a U-turn, pulling up behind them. Laurel reached for the door handle, but his shout telling them to stay in the vehicle stopped her.

She watched as he drew his gun and walked down the road the way they'd come. He briefly disappeared around the curve before he jogged back to them, gun holstered.

Laurel took that as a sign that all was well and jumped out of the ambulance.

He scooped her up before she cleared the back of the vehicle.

He buried his face in her hair, his hands clutching her tightly. "No more, Laurel. You stay home now."

She pulled back to look him in the eye. "I'm fine, Tristan. We'll just have to be more cautious."

His eyebrows shot up. "How? You were driving a route you take all the time and still managed to get ambushed. Short of having a deputy follow you on every run—which the department doesn't have the resources for—this could very well happen again. I'm sorry. You're done."

She stiffened in his embrace and pushed away. "I know you're only trying to keep me safe, but it's my decision."

"Laurel—"

"No." She held up a hand. "I'm not quitting early. This is not up for debate."

He opened his mouth to protest again, but her glare stopped him. Instead, he growled and spun away, swiping a hand down his face and over his jaw. He paced away before spinning back around and leveling a fierce look on her.

"Okay. But you will check in with me every fifteen minutes unless you're occupied with a patient. *That* is not up for debate. I will hunt your fanny down if you miss more than one check-in in a row."

Her eyes narrowed at his ultimatum. She *really* didn't like the fact that he was hovering, even though she understood why. It chafed that she was back to having a keeper. The only reason she wasn't telling him to get lost and canceling their wedding was the fact she knew his intentions were good.

She huffed. "Fine."

"Good."

"Okay."

"Stop being stubborn." Wade said, stepping around the side of the ambulance. "Laurel, he means well. And detective, we need her. Deal with it. Both of you."

"I didn't ask for your opinion, Carpenter."

"Tristan!" Laurel admonished. She couldn't believe the way he was acting. This was not the man she had fallen for.

He held up a hand in apology. "I'm sorry, Wade. This is just—frustrating, to say the least."

Wade nodded. "I know. It's not like she's enjoying this either."

Tristan sighed and pinched the bridge of his nose. "You're right. I apologize."

"It's not me you should apologize to."

He walked back over to Laurel and took her hands. Fatigue and worry deepened the lines on his face, making him look older than his thirty-five years. Laurel felt a pang of guilt for making him worry about her so. But sparing his feelings didn't outweigh the cost to her co-workers if she quit now.

"Wade's right. I'm sorry, honey. I just don't want anything to happen to you. This independent streak of yours is as frustrating as Gemma's was last year."

Some of the fight leached out of her. She was still ticked, but she knew she would get over it. She didn't blame Tristan for being overprotective. It was her own hang-ups that were causing her to react the way she was. She just needed some time to come to terms with everything.

"I'm sorry too. I know you're only trying to keep me safe. I will do everything I can while I'm at work to keep something like this from happening again. I won't stay home, though."

Wordlessly, he nodded.

Lights flashed around them as a sheriff's cruiser pulled up. Parking behind Tristan's truck, a lanky deputy emerged from the car and called out to them.

"Everyone all right?"

With one last long look at her, Tristan turned to the deputy.

"They're fine. Once the wrecker gets here, we'll need to get the tires. See if we can pull any slugs from them." The deputy nodded, then radioed dispatch to get an ETA on the wrecker.

Laurel sighed and leaned against the side of the ambulance. This was not how she had envisioned spending the night before her wedding.

She glanced around her at the flashing lights, and at Tristan and the deputy wandering up and down the road, looking for clues.

Nope. Not at all.

Twenty-Three

Saturday morning dawned cool, but clear. Laurel stared out the window of Ben and Gemma's guest room at the still morning. Sunlight glinted off the frosty grass, the first rays bathing the world in a warm golden glow. Pressing her left hand against the glass, her ring reflected the early morning light. It sparked like fire, reminding her of the fire that had lit Tristan's eyes last night when he slipped it on her finger. It had been a moment she would never forget.

When they had finally returned to the fire station after the tires on the ambulance were replaced, Tristan had pulled her aside and took her engagement ring out of his pocket. All the arguing they did earlier had faded away in that moment as he slid it on her finger with shaking hands.

Her heart had been so full in that moment she had almost blurted out that she loved him. It had been the fear he wouldn't say it back that stopped her. No one had ever loved her except her mama, and Laurel didn't want to open herself up to the vulnerability of loving someone who didn't love her back. She thought he did, but until he said the words, she was going to keep her own feelings to herself. Her heart couldn't take it if she said it and he didn't say it back.

The sun rose higher, chasing away the shadows remaining in the yard. She had been awake for a good hour now, waiting on it to be late enough that it was acceptable to wander downstairs. Sleep had been elusive last night. She'd been forced to sleep alone. When she and Tristan finally arrived home, Gemma had been sitting in the driveway, waiting. She told Laurel to pack a bag, claiming it was bad luck for the bride and groom to spend the night together before their wedding. Tristan tried to argue with her, but Gemma just ignored him and railroaded Laurel into packing.

Laurel shook her head, a smile playing on her lips. Her husband-to-be couldn't hold a candle to his sister in the pushy department. She just steamrolled, and you either went along with her voluntarily and maintained a little control, or got caught up anyway and spent the rest of the time trying to figure out which way was up. Laurel had elected for control. It meant she got to pick her own clothes.

While she liked the traditional aspect of spending the night apart, she hadn't realized how hard it would be to sleep without Tristan's bulk alongside her. It hadn't taken her long to get used to it, and she had missed him more than she thought she would.

Pushing away from the window, she grabbed a pair of jeans and a t-shirt from her bag and quickly dressed. They weren't having many guests, but there were still things to do before the ceremony this afternoon.

As she walked downstairs, she realized she smelled coffee. Entering the kitchen, she saw Ben lounging on a barstool at the island, drinking a cup and frowning down at his phone.

"Are you working this early on a Saturday?" Laurel asked, heading for the coffee pot. She probably didn't need it—

nerves had her wide awake—but she needed a bit of normalcy right now.

One side of Ben's mouth quirked, and he laid down the phone. "Just reviewing some stuff."

Laurel rested against the counter and blew over the hot brew. "Anything new on the baby case?"

Grimacing, he shook his head. "No."

She'd been afraid he'd say that. Tristan hadn't mentioned anything and had been coming home every evening with a frustrated and weary look on his face.

Not knowing what to say, Laurel grabbed a muffin out of the basket.

"Laurel, can I ask you something?"

Surprised, she sat down at the island and nodded.

"Are you sure you're okay with getting married today?"

She frowned. "Why wouldn't I be?"

"Because I know what Tristan is like and how unrelenting he can be. He gets an idea in that brain of his and it's full steam ahead." Ben sighed. "I'm not saying you shouldn't marry him—I've known him a long time. I've seen him with other women, and I can honestly say I've never seen him look at a woman the way he looks at you. I just don't want you to rush into something because it's the 'right' thing to do. And I want you to be sure that it's what you want too. That you aren't just going along with it to make him happy."

Laurel appreciated that Ben was looking out for her. "I'm not. He offered to help support me and the baby if I didn't want to get married. The truth is, I've never met a man like Tristan. Even before the baby happened, I thought he was special." She smiled as she thought back to her first impressions of him. "He scared me at first, honestly. Not because he's frightening or mean, but because he provoked such an intense and immediate response in me. I didn't know what to make of it. I resisted because I'd never really had a positive romantic relationship with a man. What happened after your wedding was an anomaly for me. I think it was the romance of the evening that got to me. Once I got some distance and perspective, I fell back to my old ways of holding people at arm's length.

"This baby has changed all that. I can't keep Tristan at arm's length and still be fair to my child. I guess it's forced me to take a good look at what held me back before I found out I was pregnant and to realize that Tristan is a good man whom I can trust."

Ben studied her for several long moments. "He told me he thought you'd been abused."

Laurel's eyes widened. She started to speak, but he waved his hand, cutting her off.

"He didn't give me any specifics, just that he thought you had been. That you acted scared of him and it was the only reason he could think of why you would be. My point is that I'm glad you realized he isn't like whoever abused you. Tristan would sooner hurt himself than hurt you."

She smiled. "I know. Once I figured that out, it helped me to lower my guard. I know this marriage is fast, but it *is* the right thing, and it is what I want. Could we have taken a little longer to plan it? Sure. But I don't want to be figuring out the ins and outs of married life at the same time I'm trying to take care of a newborn."

Ben nodded. "So long as you're going into this with your eyes wide open and not buckling to the steamroller that is a Mabley, then I'm all for it."

Laurel laughed. "They are all a bit like a freight train, aren't they?"

His grin was wide. "Yes. Will's not too bad, but he's more understated than the others."

Her laughter fading, she smiled at Ben and laid her hand

on his arm. "Thank you for looking out for me. My big brothers certainly never did. It's nice to have one now."

He patted her hand. "You're welcome, Laurel. And welcome to the family."

∼

Eyes huge, Laurel stared at herself in the mirror. She was set to walk down the "aisle" to marry Tristan in just a few minutes and she hardly recognized the woman staring back at her now that Gemma had gotten ahold of her. Her eyes had never been so bold, her lips so plump. The woman was magic with a makeup brush.

"What do you think?" Gemma asked, her face appearing next to Laurel's in the mirror.

"Wow."

Gemma's face broke out into a huge smile. "You're going to knock my brother right out of his size thirteen shoes."

She felt ready to float out her size sixes.

A knock on the bedroom door drew their attention. Gemma walked over and opened it a crack.

"You can't be here, Tristan," Laurel heard her say.

She heard his low voice on the other side of the door, but couldn't make out what he said.

Finally, Gemma sighed and looked at her. "He wants to talk to you."

Nervous he had changed his mind, she hurried over to the door, trying not to let dread get the best of her.

Gemma stood in the crack. "You still can't see him."

Not willing to waste the time arguing with her, Laurel rolled her eyes. "Tristan?"

"Honey, so I did a thing."

Laurel frowned. That was not what she had expected to

hear. After last night, she figured he would be coming to tell her he needed more time—that *they* needed more time.

"What thing?"

"I know we didn't talk about it, and I'm not sure how you'll feel about this, but I invited Rob to the wedding."

Shock rendered Laurel momentarily speechless. "You did what?" she finally breathed.

She heard him sigh. "Invited Rob. I didn't want you not to have anyone here for you. I know your relationship with him is complicated, but he seems genuine in wanting to make up for the past. I thought it would be a good way for you two to start over. New beginnings and all that."

Laurel just stared at the bedroom door, her thoughts spinning. Part of her—the part that shunned anything to do with her past—was screaming for her to tell him to make Rob leave. The other part that wanted to get to know the man her younger brother had become, rejoiced. It was an internal conflict that momentarily rendered her dumbstruck.

"Laurel?" The concern in his voice registered in a distant part of her mind, but she continued to stare and think. Could she really let Rob in on what was sure to be one of the happiest days of her life? Would it ruin that happiness to see his face standing there watching her get married? The last thing she wanted was a reminder of her first wedding.

But she did want a relationship with Rob. He was family —the only family who had ever treated her decently after her mother died. As nice as it was to have Tristan and his family, it would be nice to have other family. A connection that went beyond marriage. And just maybe, her baby wouldn't have to grow up without knowing part of her family after all.

"Laurel?" Gemma wrapped her hands around Laurel's biceps and bent down to bring them eye to eye. "Hey. Are you okay?"

Coming back to herself, she took a deep breath and nodded.

"You sure?"

She nodded again. "I'm fine. He just took me by surprise."

"Okay. Who's Rob?"

"My brother."

Gemma's eyes widened. "I didn't know you had any family. You never mentioned anyone."

"For good reason. Most of them aren't worth a thought, let alone a mention."

"But Rob is?"

Laurel sucked in a breath and held it for several moments before blowing it out slowly. "I think so."

"Laurel?" Tristan's voice came through the door again. "Baby, I'm sorry. He's downstairs, but I'll tell him you're not ready."

"No!" She took a quick step forward, then stopped, reigning in her emotions. "No. It's okay. He can stay."

There was a long pause. "You're sure?"

"Yes, I'm sure. New beginnings, right?"

"Yeah, honey. New beginnings. I'll see you outside."

"Okay."

Gemma shut the door. "Okay. Now that we've got the drama for the day out of the way, what do you say we go get you hitched?"

Laurel's smile was bright and genuine. Her tension fading in the face of Gemma's enthusiasm. She looped her arm through her soon-to-be sister-in-law's. "Let's."

Tristan ran a finger under his collar as he waited for Laurel to make her appearance on his father's arm. He hated wearing a suit and tie, but Laurel asked him to, so here he stood, dressed to the nines in his parents' backyard.

Ben nudged him from behind. "Stop fidgeting. It's your wedding, not a firing squad."

Tristan dropped his hand and shoved it in his pocket. "I'm not nervous. I just hate wearing a tie." He lifted his hand briefly to flick the offending accoutrement.

"You can take it off as soon as the ceremony is over. She comes out and sees you messing with your collar like that, she's going to think you've got cold feet."

Tristan swiped a hand along his jaw, knowing Ben was right. Laurel had agreed to marry him, but she was still skittish. He didn't want to spook her at the last minute.

He stared at the back door, willing her to come out. "What the hell is taking so long?" he whispered fiercely.

Ben shrugged. "Women things. And besides, she's not late yet. It just feels like she is because you're standing up here. Waiting. Trust me, I remember the feeling. I thought Gemma would never make an appearance and then suddenly, there she was." He smiled fondly at the memory. "Just try to relax. She'll come out soon."

Tristan stuffed his hands back in his pockets and tried not to stare at the door. Instead, he looked around at the area of the yard that Laurel, Gemma, and his mother decorated. They had taken the arched trellis his mom had in her garden and completely covered it in flowers. Some creamy flower with a hint of pink—he thought Laurel had called it wisteria—draped down softly. Light pink roses and several different kinds of lilies were woven throughout. It was delicate and beautiful, just like Laurel.

Because there were only a handful of people present, they hadn't bothered with chairs. Instead, the women found some off-white columns to set up and attached a floral arrangement to each one and then grouped the columns in a semi-circle in front of the altar. His mom, Jake, and Rob stood there quietly waiting.

He was still on the fence if he'd done the right thing inviting Laurel's brother. But he'd gotten the sense it bothered her there was no one on her side on their guest list. When his dad got back to him with the results of his inquiry into the whereabouts of Laurel's family—who were all still going about their lives in the tiny town of Womack, West Virginia—he had surprised Tristan with a full private investigator's report on Rob Hunt. Will told him he just wanted to make sure his new daughter-in-law was safe. And that no, he hadn't violated her privacy by having the PI compile a report on Rob.

After leafing through the report, Tristan was glad his dad did it. It allowed him to offer Rob a modicum of trust and give Laurel the family she was missing.

His eyes went back to the door, willing it to open. This ceremony could not happen fast enough for him. He didn't care about the whole wedding thing. He just wanted to know that she was his and he was hers. That they were a family.

When the back door finally swung open, Tristan's shoulders dropped in relief. He had been moments away from pacing back and forth.

Gemma came through first. Dressed in a gauzy, soft pink dress with long, lace sleeves, she had a bright smile on her face as she stepped out the door, a small bouquet of pink roses and white lilies clutched in her hands.

His dad came through the door next, dressed much like Tristan and Ben. He paused, waiting for Laurel to step outside.

Suddenly, Tristan couldn't breathe as Laurel stepped out into the bright sunshine. Her blonde hair rained down over her shoulders in soft ringlets, shimmering in the sunlight. Her tiny frame was ensconced in a gown much like Gemma's, only it was white and had intricate beading covering portions of the bodice. It nipped in at her waist, showing off her small but curvy figure. Wreathed around her head was a ring of small white and pink flowers, a gauzy veil attached at the back. She looked like a woodland fairy come to life.

Ben poked him in the side. "Breathe, man."

Breath whooshing out in a rush, Tristan sucked fresh oxygen into his lungs. She looked so beautiful.

In what felt like slow motion, Will led her through the grass. When she finally reached his side, he held out a hand to her. With a tremulous smile, she took it.

Twenty-Four

Laurel looked up at the man at her side in shock and disbelief that this was truly happening. After her first disastrous wedding, she hadn't ever let herself consider a second one. She hadn't even imagined what it would be like. Not until Tristan.

Now that it was actually happening, she could hardly believe it. The entire past week had been surreal. Logically, she'd known she was planning her wedding, but it hadn't hit her until just now that she was really getting married.

Nerves had her hands shaking, and she clenched her free hand into a fist and clutched Tristan's hand with her other. He looked down at her, concern in his bright blue eyes. She smiled up at him as best she could. Laurel didn't know why she was nervous. Tristan was nothing like Johnny and never would be.

But this *was* a major life change for her. In the span of a week, she had gone from a single woman who had been scared out of her wits about dating a man to married with a baby on the way. Nothing would ever be the same again.

As Tristan squeezed her hand, though, she decided she was

okay with that. She was going to embrace her new beginning. It was time for her to leave the past completely in the past.

"You know," Judge Huston began, pulling Laurel out of her thoughts. "I was quite shocked when Will called me to ask if I would officiate at your wedding. Tristan, I've known you nearly your entire life. I know you're impulsive, but this seemed a bit much, even for you. Seeing the two of you together right now, though, I understand. When it's right, you just know."

Laurel looked up as Tristan looked down. As their eyes met, she understood what the judge meant. There wasn't ever going to be anyone else for her. Tristan had captured her heart truly and completely.

Her nerves melted away. Shoulders straight, she faced the judge, listening calmly as he read the marriage vows. She repeated the words without reservation. A smile bloomed over her face as she listened to Tristan's rich voice ring out over their little group. Her joy couldn't stay contained.

With a hand that didn't shake, she slid Tristan's ring onto his finger, marveling at the sight of it on his strong hand, knowing she had put it there. That he wore it for *her*.

When the judge finally pronounced them man and wife, Laurel felt like she was floating. Her heart was light and a pure joy permeated every pore of her body as she melted into Tristan for their first kiss as husband and wife.

After a delicious dinner, Laurel stood with her new sister-in-law and mother-in-law in the living room, listening to stories of Tristan's youth. She prayed fervently that their child inherited her calmer demeanor. She wasn't sure she could handle a miniature Tristan. He had been a hellion.

A tap on her shoulder had her turning to look into her

brother's eyes. She smiled at him, glad Tristan thought to include Rob in their day. It had been nice to have someone who was there for just her.

He returned her smile and nodded a greeting at Gemma and Caroline. "Can we talk for a minute?"

"Sure." Laurel excused herself and followed Rob out of the living room into the kitchen.

"I wanted to thank you for inviting me," Rob said once they were alone. "You didn't have to, and I appreciate it. I wasn't lying when I said I wanted us to start over."

"I know. That's why I didn't turn you away when Tristan told me he asked you to come. You were the only one in our family besides Mom who ever cared about me. I'm tired of being alone. The last couple months with Tristan have shown me that."

"He's a good guy. I was shocked when he showed up at my door and asked me to come today. I thought he was there to tell me to stay away from you, not to help us cultivate a relationship."

Laurel grinned. She would have thought the same thing in Rob's shoes.

"He also told me about the baby. Congratulations. You're going to be an awesome mom. You were to me. I never thanked you for that."

Tears welled in her eyes. She had done her best. It was nice to know it had been enough and that he hadn't turned out like their older brothers.

Rob reached out and pulled her into a hug. Laurel clung to him, her emotions in a blender once again. She was happy to have someone who was connected to her in her life once again. It was nice not to be alone anymore.

"There you are."

Laurel looked up as Tristan walked into the kitchen. He

paused just inside the doorway, frowning at the tears coursing down Laurel's face.

"Honey, are you okay?" His face hardened, and he glared at Rob. "What did you say?"

"He didn't say anything," Laurel hastened to assure him. She pulled away from Rob and walked over to Tristan. "At least nothing bad. Everything is fine."

His face softened as he looked down at her. "You're sure?"

"Yes."

He cupped her face and stroked a thumb lightly over her cheek. "Okay. I came to see if you were ready to go. Do you two need a few minutes?"

"No," Rob said, coming up alongside them. "I just wanted to congratulate Laurel on her marriage and the baby. I'll let you two get on your way." He held out a hand to Tristan. "Take care of my sister. If anyone deserves a happy ending, it's her."

Laurel's eyes filled again. *Damn hormones.*

Tristan took Rob's hand and gave it a firm shake. "I know, and I will."

"Good." He looked down at Laurel. "Call me next week? Maybe we can have dinner or something?"

Laurel nodded. "I'd like that."

With a nod and a smile, Rob left, leaving them alone. Tristan immediately gathered her into his arms.

"You sure you're okay?" His blue eyes were dark with concern.

She wrapped her hands around his neck and nodded. "Yeah. I'm good." She raked her nails over the back of his head, his earlier words about leaving finally registering.

Desire lit his eyes. He bent at the knee and wrapped his arms around her waist, lifting her so her mouth was level with his, and kissed her.

Laurel kissed him back, eager for their honeymoon to

start. She had been dreaming of their wedding night since they called a halt to things earlier in the week. She was done being patient.

Spearing her hands into his thick hair, she tilted her head and bit down lightly on his lip.

He growled, pulling back. "Let's go. My parents' kitchen is not the place for this."

Laurel nodded, biting her own lip this time as he set her down, her body sliding along his. She hoped they weren't going far.

Tristan took her hand and towed her out of the kitchen and back to the party to say their goodbyes. Laurel fought the blush threatening to stain her cheeks at the knowing look in Gemma's eyes as they bid everyone farewell.

"Where are you taking me?" Laurel asked as Tristan ushered her into his truck.

He clicked the seatbelt around her, leveling that devilish grin of his on her and making her weak in the knees. His eyes twinkled merrily in the waning light.

"Our honeymoon."

Laurel rolled her eyes. "I know that. Where are we going on said honeymoon?"

He huffed out a laugh. "We're not going far. And not home. I thought it would be nice to get away for a night. Reality will show back up soon enough."

Well, he wasn't wrong there, Laurel conceded. Because of his investigation, he couldn't take much time off. In fact, he was still on call. But Jake had promised not to bother them unless something major happened. Laurel prayed that it didn't.

Tristan rounded the truck and climbed inside, quickly buckling up and starting the engine.

Laurel let her head rest against the seat, her adrenaline finally ebbing and reality sinking in. She was *married*.

Her fingers fiddled with her new rings, the weight feeling odd. It had been a long time since she had worn a wedding ring, and it felt weird. It wasn't as scary as she thought it would be, though.

That had a lot to do with the man beside her. Laurel had no worries that Tristan would mistreat her. Her only fear was that he would smother her with overprotectiveness. She had become her own person over the last ten years. Their biggest challenge as a couple was going to be compromise. She would have to get used to letting him know when she had plans and he would have to learn to let her have some space. Right now, she understood. She had seen a killer's face. But once this case was over, she was not going to be followed around and tracked twenty-four-seven. By him, or anyone else.

Sighing, she shoved those thoughts away. Now wasn't the time to worry about any of that. There were other thoughts more pressing. Like where they were going. And what was going to happen when they got there.

A tingle raced up Laurel's spine. Tristan had promised to erase the memory of her first wedding night. If their night together in January was any indicator, tonight would be enough to render her permanently boneless.

As he drove south, Laurel's anticipation ratcheted up with every mile. Surely he would stop soon.

They cruised into Asheville, the city lights twinkling in the darkness. As they neared downtown, she thought he would turn off for one of the hotels that populated the city center, but he kept going.

Left wondering just how far he deemed "not far" was, she settled in to wait. Buildings flew by as they cruised the interstate system through downtown and into the residential areas. Just as the lights began to fade, Tristan hopped off the highway heading west.

Interest peaked at the change in direction, Laurel peered

out the window for any clue to where they were going. When he drove through the entrance to Biltmore Village, her mouth dropped open.

"We're going to Biltmore?"

Tristan glanced over at her, a smile on his handsome face. "They have a cottage that's completely private." He shrugged. "I wanted something special, and this is the best place I could think of without having to travel far since we can't get away right now."

Laurel knew her eyes were as big as saucers. "You booked an entire cottage? On the Biltmore estate. For one night?"

He nodded, his mouth turning down. "Is that okay with you? I can turn around and we can go somewhere else."

"No!" she practically shouted. "I'm not complaining. I'm just a bit flabbergasted. It seems a bit much for one night."

He took her hand in his as he steered the truck down the lane leading to the magnificent inn. "I told you I wanted tonight to be a one-eighty from your first wedding night. I meant that."

"Tristan, you could have taken me to the Hampton downtown and it would have been a thousand times better than that. We could have even stayed home. It will be better because of you, not because of where you take me. I still would have had an awful night with Johnny in a place like this. *You* make the difference, not the surroundings."

His mouth flattened, and he gave her a half-shrug. "Regardless, you deserve to have a beautiful memory of your wedding night. Don't argue with me. I *want* to spoil you."

She blushed, a little uncomfortable with the idea of being spoiled. No one had ever done that before.

"Thank you," she whispered. Ducking her head so that he wouldn't see the tears shimmering in her eyes, she tried to focus on the stunning building that had just come into view. Rising five stories in front of them, the hotel was lit up brightly. Through the front doors, she could see people milling in the lobby.

Tristan parked under the portico and unbuckled. "I'm going to go check us in. You can wait here if you want. We have to drive down to the cottage from here."

Laurel nodded and settled back into her seat to wait. He was only gone a few minutes before he returned with a set of key cards and a map.

Handing both to her, he turned them back the way they came, and soon they were pulling into the drive at the cottage.

"Stay there. I'll come help you out."

Laurel unbuckled, but nodded. She wasn't about to try to get out of this behemoth of a vehicle in this dress without assistance. She would end up flat on her face on the driveway if she did.

Running around the front of the truck, Tristan opened her door and helped her down. He grabbed the duffel with their clothes from the backseat and slung it over his shoulder. Laurel took a step toward the sidewalk leading up to the house, but that was all the further she got. The ground and sky whirled as Tristan lifted her off her feet.

"Tristan! What are you doing?"

He grinned down at her devilishly. "Carrying you over the threshold."

She relaxed into his arms, her merry laugh twinkling through the night. Of course he was.

At the door, she inserted the keycard and gave the heavy wood a push. It swung open silently to reveal a lavish interior. Beautiful, dark hardwoods and rich colors greeted her, but she paid the décor little attention. Her eyes were on her husband, who looked down at her, fire lighting his too blue eyes.

He stepped over the threshold, never taking his gaze off of her, and kicked the door shut with his foot. Laurel reached up to thread her fingers in his thick, wavy hair, pulling his mouth down to hers, her control vanishing.

That familiar burn licked through her at the first touch of his lips to hers. Gripping his shoulders, she held on as he headed for the stairs, his urgency matching her own.

"I hope you're not picky about which bedroom we end up in," he said, pulling away, so he didn't trip as he climbed the staircase.

"There's more than one?" she murmured against his neck. She kissed his scars, the raised skin smoother than the stubble-roughened skin around it.

A groan rumbled through his chest, and he quickened his pace, reaching the second floor landing in just a few long strides. He turned into the first room he reached. Again, Laurel took little note of the dark hardwood furniture and rich colors.

Making a beeline for the bed, Tristan laid her down before dropping the duffel on the floor and climbing up beside her.

"I promised myself I was going to take my time this time, but I don't think I can."

Laurel looped her arms around his neck and pulled him down. "I don't want you to," she said before sealing her mouth to his in a searing kiss.

It was like her words lit a fire under him. He shucked his jacket and kicked off his shoes. Laurel didn't wait for him. Her heels dropped over the side of the bed and she reached back to begin unfastening the buttons on her dress. She was regretting now that she'd chosen a dress with so many buttons. It hadn't really occurred to her at the time that she might want to get out of it quickly. She picked it because she thought it was pretty.

By the time Tristan had removed his shirt and pants, she had only managed to unbutton three of the tiny pearl buttons. Her hands dropped into her lap, and she stared at the mostly naked man standing in front of her. He was as magnificent as she remembered, all hard planes and golden skin.

"Why are you still dressed?" he asked, frowning down at her in confusion.

She pointed behind her. "Buttons."

He pulled her to her feet and spun her around. She couldn't stifle her giggle at the groan he let out at the sight of what greeted him.

"Can I just cut it off? I brought my knife."

Laurel's giggle turned into a full-fledged laugh. "No, you may not. I like this dress."

"It's not like you're ever going to wear it again," he mumbled as he forced the tiny buttons through their holes.

"But if we have a daughter, she might want to one day."

His hands paused momentarily. She looked back to see a thoughtful frown on his face, as well as another emotion she couldn't quite figure out.

He smiled down at her. "Baby, I hate to break it to you, but not a single one of our children is going to be as tiny as you. Not with me as their dad."

Laurel dipped her head in acknowledgement. He wasn't wrong there. Unless he carried some recessive short gene, she was doomed to be the smallest of them all.

"There. Done." Tristan pushed the material off her shoulders and cool air hit her sides. She pulled her arms free of the sleeves, and he pushed it down over her hips. His quick intake of breath as he revealed the lace panties and garter set she wore underneath told her he liked what he saw.

His hands ghosted over her hips to flip open the tiny tabs holding up her stockings. She shivered at the touch of his fingers on her bare skin.

Tabs undone, he moved back up to the strapless bra she wore and quickly unfastened it, letting it drop heedlessly to the floor at her feet. His hands quickly took its place.

Laurel leaned back into his bare chest as he cupped her breasts, kneading her flesh in his large palms. Arrows of want shot straight to her core.

"Tristan." Her voice came out as a breathy moan. She was barely staying upright, her knees rapidly turning to water as he continued to run his big hands over her body.

Taking pity on her, he spun her around and lifted her, depositing her on the bed. Laurel scooted backward until she was leaning against the mountain of pillows. Tristan followed, settling over her. She relished the feel of his warm weight pressing her into the mattress.

Hands on his shoulders, she tried to pull him down, but he resisted. She frowned up at him. "Tristan?"

Holding his weight on his elbows, he pushed the hair off her cheek and stroked her skin. His expression was tender as he stared down at her.

"You're beautiful. I thought so when I was dying in that helicopter last year, and I still think so. I could drown in your eyes. They kept me alive all those months ago. I just wanted to see them again. Now, I get to stare into them for the rest of my life. Thank you for marrying me."

Tears leaked out of Laurel's eyes at his words. She grasped his face, swallowing around the huge lump in her throat. "Thank you for being patient with me these last months. I know it wasn't easy."

Instead of answering, he kissed her, pouring all the tenderness and emotion that had been in his eyes into his kiss. Laurel felt her tears trickle down her face as she kissed him back. She had never dreamed—had never let herself dream—she would have a man like him in her life. He was every fantasy she had ever had for a husband and so much more.

The emotions tumbling through her only served to heighten the sensations his touch evoked as he ran his hands along her small frame. Laurel felt like she could float right off the bed. Only his heavy weight kept her in place.

He took his time exploring her, much to her frustration. Every cell in her body was crying out for him, wanting them to become one, but he refused to give in to her urging. It was like the short, tender pause he took had reset everything and allowed him to slow the pace down.

It was maddening.

When he finally shucked his boxer briefs and peeled her stockings off her legs and tugged her panties down over her hips, she felt like a quivering, electrified mass of gelatin. As he entered her, she could swear sparks jumped between them. The jolt was enough to send her blood pulsing through her body. It rushed through her ears as her climax built. When it finally hit, she felt like she was soaring over the highest mountain peaks, the thrill and the rush like nothing she had ever experienced before.

Vaguely, she was aware of Tristan's form stiffening and his muffled shout as he buried his face in her neck as his own climax hit. Breathless, completely sated and utterly boneless, her limbs went lax and she melted into the bed. Tristan's body relaxed, his weight pressing her down briefly before he rolled to her side with a satisfied groan.

"I told you the anticipation would make it better."

Her mouth quirked. She didn't think the anticipation was totally to blame for the conflagration that just erupted between them. It certainly didn't have anything to do with the feelings currently filling her heart and soul.

Twenty-Five

The ringing phone jolted Tristan awake the next morning. He slapped at the nightstand, trying to stop the noise before it woke Laurel. She needed the rest, especially after he had kept her up until all hours.

He saw Jake's name on the screen as he silenced the phone. With a stifled groan, he slid from bed and padded silently into the hall to answer.

"My honeymoon is getting cut short, isn't it?" Tristan asked, in lieu of a greeting.

Jake's sigh said it all, and Tristan cursed. "What happened?"

"Debbie called," Jake said, putting Tristan instantly on alert. "Said that man was back. I called Asheville PD and asked them to send a unit over, but he was gone by the time they got there. You're closer and time is of the essence on this. Can you go find Debbie and talk to her? Find out who went with him? See if she got a license plate this time or even a direction of travel?"

"The uniforms can ask her all that," Tristan argued, unable to see why his presence was necessary.

Jake sighed again. "They can't find her. I traced the number she called on to the payphone at that convenience store down the street from the homeless camp. I called the store and the kid working said she used the phone and left. Asheville is keeping an eye out for her, but so far, no luck. It's been two hours since she called, Tristan."

Tristan pinched the bridge of his nose, frowning. That changed things. Debbie didn't stay away from her campsite for long. People in the camp knew she watched out for them and their belongings, so they tended to bring her a lot of the things she needed. If she was still gone that long after using the phone, there was a damn good reason.

"All right. Give me a few minutes to get dressed and I'll head over there."

"I'm sorry to disturb your weekend, Tris. I just have a really bad feeling about this."

Tristan did too, which was why he was agreeing to put on pants and to disturb his naked wife, sleeping on the other side of the door. He bid Jake goodbye with a promise to call him as soon as he knew anything.

When he walked back into the bedroom, he was surprised to see Laurel awake and half-dressed.

She looked up at him as she stepped into a pair of leggings. "I heard the phone. No one but Ben or Jake would dare disturb us this weekend and only in an emergency. What happened? They didn't find another dead woman, did they?"

He walked over to his duffel and pulled some clothes out, stepping into his underwear and pants as he talked. "A man who we've been trying to find to question about the dead women showed up at a homeless camp here in the city. I need to go find the woman who called it in. She disappeared after she called Jake. We're worried something happened to her."

"I'm going with you," she said as he buttoned his flannel shirt.

He paused mid-button. "Honey, no. It's a terrible part of town and the guy we're looking for might actually be the one who shot Veronica Chapman. I can't take the chance he's still in the area and sees you. I shouldn't be gone more than a couple of hours." He hoped it didn't take that long, though.

She was shaking her head before he even finished talking. "You said you're worried something happened to the woman. You might need me if she's hurt. The killer has already seen my face, so it's not like seeing me again can put me in any more jeopardy." She crossed her arms and arched an eyebrow at him, daring him to contradict her.

His frown was fierce. "Laurel, no. It's just too dangerous."

"So is leaving me alone." She walked up to him and took the shirt plackets out of his hands, and started buttoning. "Look, either way, I'm in some semblance of danger. I'd rather be with you—and possibly be of some help—than sitting in this house twiddling my thumbs and hoping no one followed us down here yesterday. I'll stay in the truck unless I'm needed."

He continued to frown down at her as he thought about what she said. While he didn't like the idea of taking her into a potentially dangerous situation, he didn't relish the thought of leaving her alone and vulnerable, either.

Wrapping his hands around hers where they rested against his chest, he stared down into her warm brown eyes. "You swear you'll stay back and do exactly as I say?"

She nodded. "Yes."

Knowing he would be less distracted if she were with him, he finally nodded. "Okay. But you stay in the truck."

Smile bright, she pecked him on the chin, then spun away to stuff her feet into her boots. Tristan made quick work of putting on his own shoes, all while praying he wasn't making a colossal mistake.

The homeless camp was a dismal place, Laurel decided as she stared out of the truck window, waiting for Tristan to return. This wasn't the first one she'd seen. She had been on numerous ambulance runs to places just like this more times than she cared to think about. It was terrible what drugs, alcohol, and mental illnesses did to people; that it reduced them to living in such conditions.

Her eyes darted around the area, looking for anything out of the ordinary.

She scoffed. It was all out of the ordinary. Trash littered the sidewalk and graffiti covered the sides of the decrepit buildings. If the truck windows were down, she knew she would be able to smell the stench of the camp. This area was extremely depressed. The city had tried to clean it up, but there just wasn't enough economic opportunity in this part of town to dig the area out of the gutter. The drug epidemic wasn't helping, either.

Tristan walked out of the alley, a deep frown on his face. He strolled straight to the truck and climbed inside.

"Did you find her?"

He shook his head. "Let's go over to the convenience store. Maybe she showed back up or someone saw her leave."

Unease settled low in Laurel's belly. Tristan seemed rather concerned the woman was still missing. It had her concerned as well that something bad had happened.

Within moments, they were pulling into the small convenience store, the truck bumping over the deep potholes littering the parking lot. He pulled into a space and put the truck in park, turning off the engine.

"I'm going to run in and talk to the clerk."

She nodded, watching as he ran inside. Glancing around,

she noted that things were no nicer here than they were two blocks away.

Tristan had parked on the corner of the building, and she could see the dumpster at the back of the parking lot behind the store. It looked like the store's employees were rather lazy. Trash bags sat outside the dumpster, their sides torn from animals trying to scavenge what they could from the bags. Napkins, food wrappers, and assorted papers spilled from the torn plastic. There was even some clothing mixed into the pile.

Just as she was about to glance away, the pile moved. Laurel squinted, looking for the animal scrounging for food. At this time of day, it was probably a stray dog. All the wildlife would stay hidden until dark.

The pile moved again and something flopped onto one of the trash bags. Laurel sat forward, trying to get a better look. That didn't look like an animal.

It moved again and Laurel's brain finally registered what she was seeing. It was a bloody hand.

Eyes wide, she hit the horn and jumped out. Tristan flew out of the store just as she rounded the front of the vehicle.

She pointed frantically toward the dumpster even as she ran that direction. "There's someone hurt back there."

With a curse, he ran ahead of her, his long legs eating up the ground. Reaching the dumpster, he began pulling bags away from the person lying amongst them.

Laurel reached him just in time to hear him curse again and see that he had revealed a fiftyish woman in heavy clothing. Her face and hands were covered in blood, some of it dried. Her eyes were swollen to slits and heavy bruising marred her face.

"It's Debbie," Tristan said, softly.

Figuring as much, Laurel knelt next to the woman. "Debbie? My name is Laurel. Can you hear me?"

The older woman moaned, one bloody hand reaching out blindly.

Gently, Laurel pushed it back down to the woman's side. "Everything is going to be okay, Debbie. We've got an ambulance coming. Try not to move." She glanced up at Tristan, who already had 911 on the line and was giving their location to the dispatcher.

Hanging up, he leaned over the woman. "Debbie, it's Detective Mabley. Help is coming. Was it the man you told me about who did this to you?"

She nodded imperceptibly and moaned.

"Don't try to talk," Laurel cautioned. She wished she had her kit now. She desperately wanted to assess her and give her some medicine for the pain.

"Do you have a first aid kit or some gloves in the truck?" she asked Tristan.

He nodded and quickly ran to get what she requested. Returning moments later, Laurel took the latex gloves he offered her and the small first aid kit.

Quickly pulling on the gloves, Laurel took Debbie's wrist with a gentle but firm touch to check her pulse. It was fast, but strong.

"Debbie, I'm a paramedic. I'm going to check you for injuries. I know you can't talk well, so if something hurts, just make a noise."

Noting the obvious injuries to Debbie's face, Laurel turned to the woman's chest and abdomen. She made swift work of the buttons and zippers on the heavy overcoat the woman wore. Sliding her hands under the heavy sweater so she could better feel her anatomy, Laurel probed the older woman's abdomen. When she pressed on her ribs, Debbie moaned.

"I think she's got a few broken ribs, and I can't rule out internal injuries. They feel pretty crunchy, so it's possible one of the broken ends punctured a lung," Laurel said quietly to Tristan, who squatted silently next to her. His expression was still pinched as he continued to stare down at the semi-conscious woman.

Sirens sounded in the distance and Laurel offered up a silent prayer of thanks. She ran her hands over Debbie's extremities but didn't feel any abnormalities, and Debbie stayed quiet. The ambulance screamed into the parking lot just as Laurel finished her assessment.

She quickly identified herself and gave the responding medics a report on what she had discovered. Making quick work of packaging the woman for transport, they lifted her onto a stretcher and transferred her into the ambulance. Laurel jumped in to help attach monitoring equipment and start an IV. She wanted to see the poor woman get some relief.

Quickly, they worked, checking Debbie's vitals and starting some pain medicine. Within just a few minutes, the ambulance crew was ready to take her to the hospital.

Laurel stepped down out of the ambulance into Tristan's arms. He hugged her hard before taking her hand and leading her back to his truck. "Come on. We'll follow them to the hospital."

Tristan forced his jaw to relax before he broke a molar as he and Laurel sat in the waiting room while the medical staff worked on Debbie. It had been nearly an hour since they found her. He wanted to get in there and ask her some questions about who had assaulted her so he could go after the bastard. He knew she couldn't talk thanks to the swelling, but he hoped she would be able to write. A cursory description of the vehicle the guy was in would at least give them something to go on. A license plate would be even better.

The door to the waiting room opened and Jake walked in. "Any word?"

Tristan shook his head. "They're still working on her. Laurel thinks she broke some ribs and might have some internal bleeding. Her face is a total mess. Whoever did it wanted her dead. She probably would be if she hadn't managed to get a hand out between the bags and Laurel hadn't spotted her moving. They buried her in a mountain of trash."

Jake's pale eyes turned flinty. "We need to find these assholes. I stopped at the convenience store before coming here and looked at their surveillance footage. They have surprisingly good cameras. It caught a glimpse of a silver sedan driving around the side of the building shortly after Debbie walked out of the store. No license plate, though."

That peaked Tristan's internal radar. Rob Hunt had said he'd seen a silver sedan outside of Laurel's house.

"Do any of the other businesses nearby have cameras pointed that way?" Laurel asked, jumping into the conversation. "There was a laundromat across the street and a smoke shop on the other corner."

"I have the uniforms on scene looking into that very thing," Jake replied. "Did she tell you anything?"

"She couldn't talk," Laurel said. "There was so much swelling. She probably has several broken facial bones in addition to her ribs."

"I asked her if it was the same man who was coming around looking for people to work and she nodded." Tristan stood and started pacing. Someone was getting nervous. They would never have attacked Debbie in broad daylight if he and Jake weren't on the right path. Whoever was coming around the homeless camp was definitely involved in their murder case.

The door opened again and the same doctor who had treated Laurel after their journey through the woods stepped inside. "Well, we meet again," Dr. Kessler said with a smile. "I trust you're doing better?"

Laurel nodded and moved to stand next to Tristan.

She smiled at the doctor. "Yes, thank you." She had suffered no ill effects from her hypothermia.

"Good, I'm glad. Are you here for the homeless woman who was beaten and brought in by ambulance?" She eyed Laurel with a questioning look on her face.

"We are," Tristan replied. "My wife was with me when my partner here, Detective Maxwell, called." He motioned to Jake. "Debbie is an informant on a case we're working. We think her attack is related to it. How is she?"

"She's got several fractures to her face and ribs and some significant bruising. She seems to have escaped internal bleeding, however, which is surprising considering how badly she was beaten. She's going to be taken to surgery in the next few hours to set the bones in her face. In the meantime, we're keeping her comfortable."

"Can we see her? I know she can't really talk, but I'm hoping she'll be able to write a description of the man who attacked her or of the vehicle he was driving."

The doctor frowned. "You can see her briefly. I want her to rest. She's been through enough. Give me a couple minutes to make sure she's feeling well enough to talk to you, and I'll send a nurse to get you." With a short nod, the doctor left.

Tristan tried not to pace again as they waited.

Thankfully, the wait wasn't long. A nurse poked her head in several minutes later and led them down the hall to Debbie's cubicle.

He tried not to wince as he looked at the older woman's face. It had swelled even more since the ambulance took her away. He was glad she was on some pain killers now.

Quietly, they made their way to her bedside. Tristan nudged her gently and called her name. Debbie groaned but didn't open her eyes. He nudged her again a little harder and called her name again. When she still didn't respond, he glanced at Laurel, who looked down at the woman in concern.

He could see the wheels spinning in her mind as she assessed the unconscious woman. Moving closer to him, she opened one of Debbie's eyes as best she could.

"What?" Tristan asked. He could tell something about the homeless woman's state had her worried.

"She shouldn't be this unresponsive. Something's not right."

The words barely left her mouth when the monitor blared.

Tristan's eyes shot to the screen in time to see Debbie's heart rate go berserk.

He whipped his head back around. "Laurel?"

"She's crashing." With swift movements, she hit the code blue button on the wall before lowering the side rail on the bed and climbing up to straddle the woman and begin CPR.

Medical personnel poured into the room. Laurel called out information fast and furiously as she continued to perform chest compressions. Tristan and Jake melted into the wall to let the staff work.

In shock and disbelief, he watched for the next twenty minutes as the staff and his wife tried to save Debbie, to no avail. Finally, Dr. Kessler called a halt to the code and pronounced time of death.

Moving out of the throng and back to his side, a pink flush lit Laurel's cheeks and sweat dampened the tendrils of hair around her face from the effort she had exuded during the code. "I'm sorry, honey. We tried."

He pulled her into his side and placed a soft kiss on the top of her head. "I know you did."

Leaving the staff to finish up with Debbie, Tristan led Laurel out of the cubicle behind Jake. Anger simmered as the injustice of it all hit him. Debbie had only been trying to help. She did not deserve the fate that had befallen her. And, to top it off, he didn't have anything to go on other than the fake name of the man Debbie had described and the silver sedan that may or may not have been involved. Anything Debbie could have told them had followed her to her grave.

Back in the lobby, his mind still whirling, Laurel jerked him from his thoughts as she tugged on his hand and pulled him off to the side. She motioned for Jake to follow.

Tristan frowned down at her. Worry pulled at her eyes as she looked up at him. She had that lip between her teeth again.

"What? What's wrong?"

"I think you need to have an autopsy done on Debbie. I don't think her injuries killed her."

Jake stepped forward. "What do you mean?"

Laurel paused, gathering her thoughts. She glanced back and forth between the two men before continuing. "She was seriously injured, but in the absence of internal trauma, she should have been fine with time. Unless she threw a blood clot, her injuries didn't kill her."

Tristan's frown turned fierce. "You think someone slipped her something? Someone at the hospital?"

Laurel nodded hesitantly. "I know it sounds crazy, but I really don't think she died from her injuries. And if she did, then the doctor missed something."

Spinning away, he paced several feet before turning back. He ran a hand over his jaw and into his hair as the implications hit. If Laurel was right, then someone at the hospital was involved.

He looked at Jake, who had a similar expression on his face.

"Call the judge," Tristan said. "Get a warrant to have Debbie's body sent to Dr. Tate, and only Dr. Tate. If someone here is involved, I don't want the local M.E. handling her body. Too big of a chance she'll go missing. I'll go down to security and have a look at their tapes and see who went in and out of Debbie's room."

Jake immediately pulled out his phone.

Tristan grabbed Laurel's hand. "Come on. Let's go look at some video footage."

~

File folder in hand, Tristan pushed open the door to the interrogation room with Jake hot on his heels. They had gotten a hit from the security camera footage from the smoke shop across the street from the convenience store. It led them to the young woman now seated at the table in the room, a healthy measure of fright written all over her face. Her blonde hair was mussed, like she hadn't been able to keep her hands out of it, and the skin puffed around her wary blue eyes.

She should be scared, Tristan thought. Her car had been seen leaving the scene of a murder. While probably not their killer, this woman still had a lot of explaining to do.

Crossing to the table, Tristan and Jake sat down across from her. "Do you know why you're here, Ms. Evans?" Jake asked.

She worried her hands as she looked back and forth between them. "The officer who brought me here said it had something to do with my car being used to commit a crime. I don't know how that's possible. The only time it ever leaves my possession is when my boyfriend borrows it."

Tristan shared a look with Jake.

"What's your boyfriend's name, Ms. Evans?" Tristan asked.

"Logan Taylor."

"Did he borrow your car today?"

"No. I was at work until noon. I worked a short shift."

"Where do you work?"

"Mission Hospital. I'm a nurse."

Tristan shared another look with Jake. She might not be the one who murdered Veronica and Kaylee, but she could very well be involved in this whole mess.

"What department do you work in?"

There had been several nurses in the hospital's surveillance footage outside of Debbie's room, but none who looked like this woman had actually gone inside that Tristan saw.

"The E.R."

Warning bells went off in Tristan's brain. Too many coincidences. This woman was involved somehow, purposefully or not. He made a mental note to go back and look at the surveillance footage again. He was going to track Ms. Evans' movements through the emergency department from the time Debbie arrived until she died. If she was involved, he would find out.

"Can you tell us what your boyfriend looks like?" he asked, circling back to the only other person she indicated had access to her vehicle.

"Why are you asking about Logan? It's my car. I had it with me today. You have to be mistaken."

Sensing that Kara Evans was about to get obstinate, Tristan opened the folder and pulled out the still image from the smoke shop's surveillance camera. "This is your car leaving our crime scene at nine a.m. The license plate confirms it. Are you still sure you had your car today?"

Eyes wide, she stared down at the photograph. With a shaky hand, she touched the edge before pulling her fingers back to clutch the table. "It was still in the same parking space when I got off work. I don't understand."

Tristan pulled out another paper from his folder and slid it in front of her. It was a forensic sketch of the man Laurel had seen.

Kara's eyes widened to the point Tristan thought they might pop out of her head. She picked up the drawing and stared down at it, disbelief all over her face.

"Is that Logan?"

Horrified, she nodded. "It looks like him, yes."

Tristan resisted the urge to pump his fist as they got their first real break in this case.

"Ms. Evans, what kind of car does your boyfriend drive?"

Eyes wide, she looked up at him. She swallowed hard. "A small pickup. It's red."

He turned to Jake. "Get surveillance from the hospital parking garage. See if we can get an image of him entering in that truck."

Jake nodded, standing. "I'll put out a BOLO on it, too. Do you know the license plate, Ms. Evans?"

She shook her head numbly.

With a frown, Jake left. Tristan settled into his chair and leaned back, crossing his arms. "Now, Ms. Evans. Tell me about your boyfriend."

"I don't know what you want to know. Why are you asking about him and my car, anyway? What did he do?"

Tristan eyed the woman speculatively. While scared, she seemed genuinely surprised her boyfriend—and her car—were involved in a crime. Or she could be involved and just surprised they had messed up and gotten caught. He was betting she wasn't that good of an actress, though.

"The crime your car was seen leaving was a murder. A homeless woman who's been an informant on a series of missing persons cases. We think someone has been using your car in conjunction with not just the murder, but with the missing persons as well. And, according to you—and the DMV photo I'm going to pull up on Logan Taylor—he matches the description of the suspect in another murder a week ago."

Her eyes widened to the max again, and she stared at him, mouth agape. "You can't be serious," she finally managed to say. "Logan wouldn't hurt anyone."

Eyes narrowing, he leaned forward. "Then how do you explain your car showing up at my crime scene and our suspect matching his description to a T?"

Tears welled in her eyes and she clutched her hands together. "I don't know," she whispered. "I just don't know."

Twenty-Six

Yawning, Laurel pushed the button on the coffeepot to start it. One more week. She just had to get through this week and then there wouldn't be any more early mornings or long days.

At least until the baby came.

She skimmed a hand over the slight swell of her belly under her uniform pants, a soft smile spreading over her lips. She couldn't wait.

The creak of the floor alerted her to Tristan's presence as he ambled down the hall from the bathroom. Still sleepy-eyed, he walked into the kitchen. Fine lines stood out at the corners of his eyes as he squinted against the bright light.

Wordlessly, he walked over to her and dropped a kiss on the top of her head before he grabbed a coffee mug from the cabinet, filling his cup from the half-brewed carafe. He leaned one hip against the counter and took a healthy swig of the hot brew.

The toast she put in the toaster minutes before popped up, and she busied herself with buttering it while Tristan continued to lean there, sipping his coffee, his eyes unfocused as he tried to wake up.

She had eaten an entire slice of toast and was halfway through the second when the sleep finally cleared off his face. Laurel couldn't blame him for being tired. After they left the hospital yesterday, he dropped her off with Gemma and Ben, then spent the day chasing leads with Jake. From what he told her on the drive home, they had made some real progress and finally had a name to go with the face she had seen. Between the long day yesterday, their sleepless—but very pleasant—wedding night, and all the extended hours he'd already logged in the last week, she was amazed he was even able to crawl out of bed.

When they returned home last night, it had been late, and they went straight to bed. She had used the bathroom first and by the time she finished her nightly routine and walked back into the bedroom, he had been sprawled across the quilt, shirt off, jeans unbuttoned and his stocking feet hanging over the edge, sound asleep. She had silently climbed into bed beside him and fallen asleep almost as quickly, the long hours and her pregnancy taking its toll. She hadn't wanted to get out of bed this morning any more than he did.

Laurel popped the last bite of toast in her mouth and reached for the coffeepot. She filled Tristan's travel mug, then her own, savoring the scent of the warm brew as she added a splash of cream to hers to cool it down. Taking a sip, she relished the thought of the caffeine that was about to course through her system, even as she knew the single cup wouldn't sustain her long. The inability to drink as much coffee as she wanted was one of the few drawbacks of being pregnant. She looked up to hand Tristan his mug, only to see that he was frowning down at her.

"What?"

"That all you're going to eat?"

Laurel's eyebrows slammed down into a frown. They had covered this ground already.

He seemed to read her mind and threw his hands up in surrender and his face smoothed out. "I know. You can take care of yourself. It just doesn't seem like much when you're going to be working all day." His frown returned. "You sure you have to go to work today?"

Resisting the urge to roll her eyes, she picked up her mug and headed for the living room. "I have some snack bars in my bag. If I eat more than just that toast right now, we're going to be cleaning your truck later. And we've talked about the work thing, Tristan. The department is still down one medic and his replacement doesn't start until Wednesday. Unless I'm deathly ill, I can't take any time off." She didn't want to go to work any more than he did. The incident Friday still had her shaken up, but she couldn't stay home and let her colleagues down. If she didn't go in, someone else would have to work a double shift. Having done that in the past, she wasn't going to willingly subject any of her co-workers to that.

He caught her hand as she reached for her coat, spinning her back to hold her against his long, hard frame.

Heat licked up her spine as one muscled arm banded around her waist while his other hand swept up her arm to cradle the side of her face. His brilliant eyes gleamed as he stared down at her. An intensity that should have unnerved her, but instead made her feel safe and cherished, glowed brightly from their depths.

"Still doesn't mean I like it." He kissed her soundly, making her knees go weak. She was glad she had put her coffee down on the entryway table to put on her coat or it would be all over the floor.

After a moment, and with a herculean effort, she pulled back, her eyes connecting with his. Softly, she ran one finger along the ridge of his jaw, feeling it flex beneath her touch. It was smooth now, having just been shaved, but she knew by tonight it would be rough with his dark beard. "I'll be careful," she promised.

He rested his forehead against hers. "I know. But you can't predict everything, and we still don't know where Logan Taylor is. He hasn't returned to the address his girlfriend gave us, nor has he shown up at her place. Until we catch him, you aren't safe." He straightened. "Hell, even after, you're not until we round up everyone involved in this."

And if that wasn't a bucket of ice water on the blaze he had ignited in her veins, she didn't know what was.

The face of the man she saw murder Veronica Chapman flashed in her mind, and she suppressed a shudder.

Logan Taylor.

It was such a normal name. She had even tossed the name Logan around as a name for the baby, if it was a boy. Not anymore.

Tristan let her go and just stood there, eyeing her. His mouth was a tight line and his hands rested on his hips.

"I know you want to go in, but I still don't think you should. I can tell you're scared. How about I take you to Mom and Dad's? You can talk baby stuff with my mom. She was fairly bursting at the seams at our wedding. She's very excited about becoming a grandma."

Laurel sighed. "I would love to stay home, but you know I can't. I've told already told you—"

"You're short-handed. Yeah, I know. But I don't care about that. Your safety is more important." He pulled out his phone.

She frowned. "What are you doing?"

"Calling you in."

Anger shot through her. Taking a step forward, she snatched the phone from his hand.

"No. I am going to work. You're just going to have to deal with it. I promise I'll be careful, but I'm going."

For a moment, she thought he would argue further, but finally, he nodded. Taking her coat off the rack by the door, he held it open. Laurel spun around so he could help her into it before he changed his mind. She knew she was pushing his boundaries and didn't want to find out what would happen if she pushed further. And she would, if he made her. He might be her husband now, but it was still her life.

"I know you don't want me to hover, but I'm going to be texting you all day just to check in on you. A simple smiley face in return will appease me."

Turning back around, she zipped her coat, a grin on her face. "Mollify you is more like it. I'll do my best, but if I'm on a call, you'll have to wait."

He nodded. "Fair enough. I'll call dispatch if it takes you too long."

Laurel's grin quickly turned down. "Tristan."

"No arguments on that one, babe. Taylor's murdered at least one woman, probably two others, and he knows you know his face. If I get even the least bit concerned about you, I'm going to track you down."

He kissed her nose. "I won't always be like this, but right now, consider me big brother. I just wish I had the cameras and audio to go with it."

This time Laurel didn't hold back the eye roll. "I'm honestly amazed you haven't put a GPS bracelet on me."

His grin was quick and wicked. He pulled his coat off the rack and shrugged into it. "Don't think I didn't consider it. The only thing the department has, though, are the house arrest monitors. Even if I wanted to put one on you, I can't because of the laws regarding them."

She glared up at him. She would have liked to have seen him try something like that. It would not have ended well for him. He would have been finding out how comfortable the front seat of his truck was to sleep in. He could be her bodyguard from *outside* if he tried that.

He dropped another quick kiss on her lips before picking up his own mug from the table beside hers. "Come on. As much as I don't want you to go to work, I know you don't want to be late."

With one last stern look, she picked up her coffee and her bag and followed him out the door.

Twenty-Seven

Back aching and limbs heavy with fatigue, Laurel closed and latched the last bin in the back of the ambulance as she finished restocking after their last run. With any luck, it really would be their last run. There was only a half hour left in their shift. She prayed fervently it was uneventful.

Sighing heavily, she climbed out and shut the door, heading into the common room. Her partner, Wade, had gone in to file all their paperwork while she finished the restock.

Spying him at the long bar that separated the kitchen from the sitting area, talking to one of the other paramedics, she headed for the chairs positioned in front of the big screen television hanging on one wall. Gratefully, she sank into one of the plush recliners. She popped out the footstool and sighed as her feet left the ground. She was so glad this day was almost over.

A change in the air around her warned her she was no longer alone. Opening her eyes, she saw Wade standing over her, a bottle of water clutched in each of his hands. He held one out to her.

Smiling in thanks, she took it. Cracking open the cap, she took a swig as he sat down in the chair next to hers.

"You sure you want to leave all this behind?" he asked jokingly, gesturing to their utilitarian surroundings.

Laurel smiled. "It'll be rough leaving you bozos to your own devices, but I'll manage." Truthfully, while she was going to miss everyone, she was looking forward to starting a new chapter in her life. Her art—and her growing family—were dreams she had given up on years ago. The chance to resurrect them and let them thrive was a dream come true in and of itself.

"So what are you going to do with yourself while you wait on that baby to finish cooking?" Wade motioned to her still flat stomach.

"Paint. Decorate whatever new house Tristan and I move into. Get the nursery ready." A sudden yawn cracked her jaw. "Sleep," she said with a laugh.

Before Wade could respond, the alert tones sounded.

Laurel tipped her head as she listened. *Please don't say Unit 4!*

"Unit 4. Report of an unconscious person. Please respond."

She couldn't stifle the groan as the dispatcher called their unit.

Wade chuckled and stood. "Looks like you're going to have to wait a little longer for that nap." He held out a hand to help her out of the chair.

Groaning again, Laurel took his hand and got to her feet. "No rest for the wicked, Carpenter. Let's go."

Pushing past the fatigue, she hurried behind Wade to their rig and climbed into the passenger seat. Donning her headset, she radioed dispatch that they were en route and received an address in return. It was in a fairly remote part of their jurisdiction.

"Must be one of those mountain recluse people," Wade commented as he drove.

Laurel nodded, thinking of the elderly Mrs. Preston. She needed to get out there again next week for a visit. Hopefully, all this craziness with the killer would be over by then.

In the meantime, though, it wouldn't hurt to be careful. She pulled out her cell and texted Tristan that she and Wade had drawn a late call and that she would keep him updated. Knowing him, he would keep an ear on the dispatch traffic and meet them at the hospital in Asheville if they had to transport a patient, then follow them back north.

The miles flew by as Wade steered the ambulance up the winding mountain road that would lead them to their call. Laurel went over a mental checklist for what she might need for a call like this. A myriad of things could be wrong. Anything from a fall to a heart attack or stroke, or even an overdose.

The disembodied voice of their GPS unit advised them of the upcoming turn. Laurel sat forward and squinted, looking for a driveway. Wade slowed.

Metal glinted through the overgrowth lining the road.

"There!" Laurel pointed. "Is that a mailbox?"

Creeping now, Wade pulled closer.

"Looks like it. There's a two-track here." Cautiously, he turned onto the drive that was little more than two dirt ruts through a cut in the forest.

Unease skated up Laurel's spine. She didn't like this. They were miles from anything, and this place had the look and feel of being abandoned.

Tree limbs slapped the sides of the ambulance as they slowly bounced up the rutted drive. Laurel grabbed the chicken bar and held on tight.

Thirty seconds later, the drive opened up into a small clearing, and a dilapidated cabin came into view, a light glowing in the window. An ancient pickup truck sat next to the cabin under a lean-to that looked ready to fall over.

Wade parked near the door, and Laurel radioed dispatch of their arrival before climbing into the back to grab their gear. He came around to the rig's side door and took the duffel from her while she carried their portable monitor and defibrillator.

"Does this strike you as a little weird?" Wade asked as he rapped on the cabin door. "I mean, we weren't exactly quiet coming up that drive. Shouldn't someone be out here to greet us if the person they called about is unconscious?"

Laurel nodded, thinking the same thing. "Unless it's a drug overdose, and the caller doesn't want to get in trouble for drugs." She had her doubts about that, though. They rarely got calls this remote for drug overdoses. The people who lived this far out of town were more prone to overdoing the moonshine, not heroin.

Wade knocked again, louder this time. "Northridge EMS. Open the door, please."

No footsteps or voices came through the cabin door. Only the light shining through the window showed them any sign of life.

"Try the door," she suggested. "Maybe the caller left it unlocked."

Wade twisted the handle, and the door swung inward, revealing a sparse, dusty cabin. He stepped over the threshold. "Hello? EMS."

Laurel saw movement to his left as a man stepped forward, swinging an axe. Before she could shout a warning, he hit Wade square in the head, imbedding the tool in his skull. With a sickening wet squelch, the killer pulled the axe free. She watched in horror as her partner dropped like a ton of bricks to the rough cabin floor, his head nearly cleaved in half. Blood flowed out of the wound to soak his clothes and the wood beneath him.

A scream lodged in her throat. She dropped the monitor and backpedaled toward the rig. Strong arms wrapped around her, trapping her hands to her sides. The scream ripped free, and she kicked and twisted for all she was worth, trying to get away.

The axe wielder dropped the tool with a thud and stepped over Wade's body, a gun now in his hands. Fear tangled her insides as she realized the man in front of her was the same man she'd watched murder Veronica Chapman—Logan Taylor.

"Stop struggling," Taylor snarled. "That cop husband of yours isn't here to save you this time."

Shock rendered Laurel immobile. How did he know she and Tristan were married? It had only been two days. She turned her head to look at the man holding her. Was he someone she knew? His bland features, muddy eyes, and short blonde hair didn't ring any bells. Was he someone Tristan knew?

Taylor's eyes flicked past her to the man holding her. "Put her in the van and let's get out of here. Make sure she loses her radio."

That galvanized Laurel's brain back into action. Refusing to heed Taylor's warning, she renewed her struggles, cursing at them up one side and down the other. Tears streamed down her face, but she refused to be a meek victim. She had spent the first nineteen years of her life timid. Meek. Not anymore. She fought for all she was worth as Taylor's partner dragged her around the side of the cabin.

The man holding her was big—as big as Tristan—and just as strong. At the van, he swung her under one arm, holding her like a football while he opened the van's back doors.

The yawning, steel interior, bare of everything except a

plastic sheet over the floor, stared back at her. She renewed her struggles. The notion of what that plastic was for sent terror streaking through her veins.

But it was no use. The man was just too strong for her. He ripped the radio off her belt and threw it down on the ground, then lifted her off her feet and thrust her inside. Laurel hit the floor of the van hard. Pain ricocheted through her at the hard contact, momentarily stunning her. The doors slammed shut, leaving her in darkness.

She pushed up on her hands and knees and scrambled for the door. "No. No, no, no, no!" With a yank, she pulled the handle, but the asshole had locked it behind him.

She pounded on the door. "Let me out of here!"

The front doors opened as Taylor and his partner climbed into the van. A half panel with a cage at the top separated her from the front seats. Changing directions, she thrust herself against the screen.

"Let me go, you assholes!" She curled her fingers through the thick wire, wishing the gaps were big enough she could get her hand through.

"Shut up," Taylor growled.

"I will not. You need to let me go. My husband is going to come down on you so hard when he finds you. He might not rip off all your limbs and let you bleed to death if you let me go now."

The man's laugh was nothing short of evil. "He has to find me first, and he has no idea where to look for me. Now, sit back and shut your damn mouth, or I swear I will make your life a living hell when we get to the farm."

Laurel frowned. "Farm?" Why were they taking her to a farm? And what was there?

He didn't answer her, just maneuvered the van down the two-track back to the main road and headed down the mountain.

With a frustrated screech, Laurel sat back, saving her strength and taking stock of what she had on her person. They hadn't searched her or bound her hands and feet before they tossed her in here. Why, she had no idea—maybe because of her size they didn't see her as a threat—but she planned to take full advantage of their mistake.

Butt against the half wall so they couldn't see her, Laurel felt her pockets. She had her trauma shears and her multi-tool in the left cargo pocket of her pants. She also had her pen light, a couple of hypodermic syringes, and two rolls of tape in the other. She could do some damage with several of those items. Timing would be key, though. She knew she was too tiny to overpower either of them or to outrun them. If she wanted to get away and not get caught again immediately, she would have to pick the right moment.

Shifting again, she turned until she could see out the windshield. She wanted to know where the jerks were taking her, so when she escaped—and she was determined she would—she would know where to go to get help quickly. It bothered her they hadn't blindfolded or bound her, but if they had wanted her dead, she would be. Cleaved into pieces just like Wade.

Tears welled in her eyes at the thought of her partner. They had only worked together for a few months. Wade had been new to the squad. He'd been a paramedic in Asheville for years before he had decided he needed a change of pace. Something where shootings and stabbings weren't so commonplace. He had moved to get away from the violence. It seemed ironic he had met such a violent end.

Pushing thoughts of Wade's mutilated body from her mind, Laurel concentrated on where they were going. Taylor had headed southeast toward Asheville into a valley. The van wound down the mountain and into the valley for nearly half an hour before he veered right onto a single-lane dirt road.

Laurel struggled to see through the darkness, but could only make out the looming shapes of the trees lining the roadway.

About half a mile down, Taylor slowed and turned left onto a gated driveway. His partner hopped out and opened the gate. The van bumped through and stopped long enough for the man to climb back in, then continued down the drive through the trees.

Knowing they were near their destination, Laurel absorbed all the information she could about her surroundings. It was wooded, but as they bumped up the drive, the area opened up into what looked like a large meadow. Laurel couldn't see the edges of the field because of the darkness, only what was illuminated by the pole lights mounted near each of the three outbuildings and the barn. A two-story farmhouse that would have looked bucolic under other circumstances sat in the midst of it all, its white paint gleaming in the bright lights.

Disappointment shot through Laurel as she surveyed what she could see of the yard. There wasn't a lot of cover past the buildings that she could see in the dark. If she tried to escape now, they would catch her easily.

She prayed they continued to be lax with her and didn't search her once they hauled her out of the van.

Taylor drove past the house and the first outbuilding—a large garage—to the larger of the two remaining buildings. Bigger than a shed, but smaller than a barn, it was long with only a few windows and a single door set into the middle of the long side facing them. Lights glowed in the windows, which were covered with bars. Curtains blocked anyone from seeing inside.

The van lurched to a halt and Taylor cut the engine.

"Get her out and inside, then come up to the house. I need to call in that the op was a success."

The big blonde man nodded and climbed out. Laurel

turned and faced the back of the van, body tensing, ready for a fight.

The doors flew open, and the man loomed in the opening. "Get out."

Laurel hesitated and her eyes darted around behind him, looking for anything that could help her.

"Lady, if I have to come in there after you, you won't like the consequences. Get. Out."

Deciding to heed his warning this time, she inched forward. When she was within an arm's length, he grabbed her wrist and pulled her out, immediately wrapping one large hand around her biceps so she couldn't run away.

With a rough jerk, he pulled her toward the building. A set of keys appeared in his hand, and he selected one, putting it in the lock. Pushing the door open, he thrust her ahead of him through the doorway.

What Laurel saw inside stopped her in her tracks. Six women, all in various stages of pregnancy, stared back at her.

Twenty-Eight

Tristan looked at his watch for the hundredth time in about five minutes as he sat in his truck outside the Northridge Fire Rescue station. Laurel should have texted him already. It was now a full half hour past the end of her shift. Even if they had taken their patient into Asheville for treatment, she should have let him know where she was by now.

Pulling out his phone, he dialed the direct line to Northridge dispatch.

When the dispatcher answered, he quickly identified himself and inquired about the status of Laurel's last run.

"We've been unable to contact their unit since they reported that they were on scene. It's not unusual for us to lose contact with a unit temporarily when the call is in the mountains."

Maybe not, but when it was his wife they couldn't contact and there was a killer after her, it made the hair on his neck rise.

"Dispatch a deputy to check on them. She should have checked in by now. Give me the address. I'll meet the deputy up there."

The dispatcher rattled it off. Tristan thanked her and hung up, immediately starting the truck and putting it in gear. Nerves had him pressing the accelerator a little harder than he should as he wound his way up the mountain, but he didn't care. He had a bad feeling about what he was going to find at that address.

Tristan slammed his hand against the steering wheel. He knew he should have insisted on someone following her on her runs. Hell, he should have been more insistent that she quit without giving notice. She would be safe at home right now instead of missing in action.

He could be overreacting. He knew firsthand how spotty reception was in the mountains. Just over a week ago, he had experienced that very thing when he'd been searching for Laurel.

But he didn't think lack of reception was the case. Not this time.

Pushing his driving abilities to the max, he made it to the address in a fraction of the time it should have taken, nearly missing the drive, the overgrown two-track barely visible. Turning sharply, he bounced up the lane to come to an abrupt halt behind a sheriff's cruiser and Laurel's ambulance.

His gut sank to his toes at the sight of it. There was no way they should have still been on scene.

Throwing the truck in park, he flew out of the vehicle.

"Laurel!"

The same deputy from Friday night ran around from the side of the cabin at his shout.

"Drake! Where's Laurel?"

Face paler than Tristan had ever seen it, Tim Drake stopped just feet away and shook his head. "I don't know, Tristan. But you need to see what I found inside." He pointed at the open cabin door.

Dread pooled in Tristan's gut as his gaze swung toward the

cabin. Shadows hung heavily, but the light from inside and the vehicles' headlights glinted off something wet. A dark shape lay motionless on the floor.

In several long strides, Tristan crossed to the door and got his first look at what had Deputy Drake so pale. Laurel's partner lay on the weathered cabin floor, his head split wide open, a wood cutting axe next to his body.

Tristan swallowed hard several times as worry, fear, and horror threatened to send his stomach contents back up. Hand shaking, he swiped it down his face and rubbed his jaw, trying desperately to regain his composure.

He cleared his throat and looked at the deputy. "Did you find any sign of Laurel?"

Drake shook his head. "No. I've been canvassing the area around the cabin looking for clues. There are some footprints leading around the side of the building that stop where there's a set of tire tracks. I found a radio back there too. She either ran into the woods or whoever did that to her partner took her with them. I already called it into dispatch. Dr. Tate and his team are on their way, and so is Deputy Townsend with his K-9, Maverick."

Tristan took several steps back until he came to rest against the bumper of Drake's cruiser. His legs threatened to give out as the implications hit him. From the pattern of footprints, he didn't think Laurel ran. There were drag marks in the dirt where it looked like someone had struggled. For the first time in his life, Tristan felt an overwhelming sense of fear. The killer had Laurel hostage, and he didn't have the first clue where to start looking.

∼

The echo of the door closing behind the blonde behemoth was the only sound in the room as six sets of eyes stared at

Laurel. She didn't need them to talk, though, to understand how they felt about her presence. Pity, despair, apathy, and resignation blared from the women's eyes as they took stock of the newcomer. These women had lost all hope they were ever going to see the outside world again.

Squaring her shoulders, Laurel moved further into the room.

"Hi. I'm Laurel."

The women stared back at her for several moments before one, a willowy woman with short dark hair, stood, cradling her belly.

"I'm Tessa. This is Emma and Livvy. Nora, Miranda, and Jackie." She pointed to the women on either side of her, then to the others seated around the room.

Laurel waved.

"So, what'd you do to land in here? You don't look pregnant," Nora, the lone black female in the room, asked.

Deciding to keep that tidbit to herself for now—it wouldn't do for her captors to learn she was pregnant—she moved further into the room and sat in an empty seat next to the young blonde woman named Miranda.

Laurel hiked a thumb toward the door. "I witnessed our dear Mr. Taylor murder Veronica Chapman."

Shocked murmurs moved through the room, and several of the girls started to cry.

The young woman next to her gripped her arm tightly, tears shimmering in her hazel eyes. "Veronica's really dead?"

Laurel nodded, compassion in her eyes. "I'm sorry."

Miranda sniffed. "What about her baby? We all hoped when she got out of here that she made it away safely. If she's dead, then where's Haley?"

"I don't know what happened to her baby. My guess is Taylor got a hold of her when he killed Veronica. I ran after I saw him shoot her, so I don't know what happened after that."

"You know what I don't understand?" Tessa said. "Why they didn't just kill you? Why bring you here?"

Laurel bit her lip and clenched her hands in her lap to keep from pressing a hand to her belly. "My husband is the lead detective on Veronica's murder case. They might be holding me as leverage."

More murmurs went through the room.

"So, he's going to be looking for you then, isn't he?" Jackie asked.

Laurel nodded. "Tristan won't stop until he finds me. They should have killed me. I'm grateful they didn't, but they're going to regret it." She was sure of that. Whether she lived or died, Tristan would keep digging until he found the people responsible.

Hope lit the women's eyes.

Brow furrowed as her mind raced, Laurel's eyes scoured the room. "Is this place being bugged or videoed?"

Tessa pointed at the vents high on the walls. "We think there are cameras in there. They seem to know what we're doing all the time. They can't hear us, though. We said some things to get a reaction from them—plans to escape—and they didn't change their security routines."

A plan forming, Laurel nodded. "Good. They didn't search me before they shoved me in here. My pockets are full of things we can use against them."

Tessa's eyes lit up, and she moved closer. "What did you have in mind?"

Leaning on the counter in the men's room at the precinct, Tristan tried desperately to hold it together. When Ben had briefed the other deputies on the situation, it had been all he could do to stand there and listen to him describe his wife's disappearance like any other missing persons case. As soon as the briefing was over, he fled to the restroom.

He turned on the faucet and splashed some water on his face, hoping it would help dispel some of the fear that had taken root. His normally calm, level-headed mindset had completely disappeared. It felt like his world was crashing down around him and he was powerless to do anything about it.

The door swung open, and he fought not to groan. It was probably Ben or Jake, coming to talk him out of his funk. He didn't want any company right now.

He turned, intending to tell him to get lost, but stopped when he saw his sister standing just inside the door.

"Gemma? What the hell are you doing in here? This is the men's room."

She crossed her arms. "I know. Ben told me you disappeared in here after the briefing."

This time, he didn't bother to hide the groan. "Go away. I don't want to talk about my 'feelings'," he air-quoted and turned away. Hands braced on the counter, he looked down and closed his eyes, willing her to leave.

But, of course, being Gemma, she didn't.

The rustle of fabric nearby had him opening his eyes. She'd invaded his personal space and was leaning against the sink right next to him.

He groaned again. "You're relentless."

She smiled without mirth. "Duh. But only because I know you need to get what you're feeling out in the open or you're going to blow at the least opportune moment. Nobody wants that. Ben wants to bench you, but I talked him out of it by reminding him that he was in your shoes less than a year ago.

But you have to get it together, Tristan, or he will sideline you."

Tristan expelled a harsh breath. He knew she was right, but he was having a hard time pulling himself out of the deep, dark hole he was in. It felt like he had lost a piece of himself and he was just spinning, trying to find it.

Gemma laid a hand on his arm. To his horror, he felt tears welling in his eyes. He didn't cry. Ever.

Swallowing hard, he pushed them back.

"I don't know where to start," he finally said quietly.

"At the beginning."

He shook his head. "I meant where to start looking for her. I have no clue where to start. Taylor left very little evidence behind at the cabin to point to where they were headed. I've got a set of tire tracks—that disappear before they reach the road—and little else."

"You'll figure that out. You just need to dig a little deeper. Give it some time. You'll find something."

His head shot up. "Time?" Anger shot from his eyes. "She may not have time. The longer she's missing, the more likely they've—" He broke off, unable to say the words. The tears welled once more, and this time, he couldn't stop them. They flowed freely down his face.

"God, this is all my fault. I should have made her stay home. I have to find her, Gemma," he whispered, voice raw.

She gathered him into a tight hug. He wrapped his arms around her and hugged her back. The fear and the guilt threatened to swallow him whole, and he didn't fully understand why. He hadn't been this crazed with worry when Gemma had been kidnapped.

But with Laurel, he just couldn't focus. Couldn't figure out which way was up. Her disappearance had knocked him off his center, and he was having a hard time finding it again.

"You *will* find her, Tristan. If there's one thing I know, it's that you will do anything for the people you love. You pulled out all the stops for me and you will for her too."

Love? Was that why he was so off-kilter? So scared? Did he love Laurel?

Like a lightning strike, things were suddenly crystal-clear. Love for the pint-sized woman who had saved his life and made it a life worth living hit him so hard it made his knees wobble.

Dear God, he did love her.

He had struggled to make heads or tails of how he felt for her for so long. Now, it was glaringly obvious.

Pulling back, he straightened, some of his equilibrium returning now that he knew why he was so fearful.

"You're right, Gems. I do love her. More than anything. I will do whatever it takes to get her back." Determination steeled his muscles and tightened his jaw. A plan took shape in his mind for what they would need to look into to get an idea of where Taylor might have taken her.

Gemma smiled up at him brightly. "There's the brother I know. The wheels are turning again."

He kissed her on the cheek. "Thank you for pulling my head out of my ass."

She laughed. "That's what little sisters are for."

With a quick uptick of his mouth, he ushered her out of the restroom. He had work to do.

Twenty-Nine

Keeping it casual, Laurel sat with the other women to discuss her plan. In the end, it was simple. Escape.

"So, the cameras are in the vents?"

Emma nodded. "We're pretty sure. We know they can see us from things they've said, but we can't see any cameras."

"How did Veronica get away?"

"She wasn't in here with us, so we don't know," Jackie said. "They came to get her to take her up to the main house for a check-up with the doctor after she had her baby. She never came back. We heard shouting and looked out the window and could tell something was going on. The next time Jeremy came back, he was livid."

"Is Jeremy the big blonde who brought me in here?"

All the women nodded.

"Are there any others besides Logan and Jeremy?"

"Just the doctor who lives up at the farmhouse," Tessa said.

"Why did Veronica still have her baby after she'd given birth? My husband said that the infant was a couple of weeks old. Aren't they taking them and adopting them out illegally?"

Tessa's hands wrapped her belly protectively. Of all the women in the room, she looked the farthest along. "Yes. But Haley was a little early, and the doctor thought it best for Veronica to nurse her for a couple of weeks to help her get stronger. The day she went up to the house for her exam was the day they were probably going to take Haley away."

Laurel's gut clenched at the thought of anyone taking away her baby, especially if she had bonded with the infant. She could only imagine the fear these women had been living with.

"So, what's your plan?" Nora asked. "We all want out of here. The quicker the better."

Laurel once again surveyed her surroundings. The room they were in was a communal living space. She could see the edges of a fridge through a doorway that she assumed led to a kitchen and dining area, and there was a stairway on the far wall that likely led to their sleeping quarters.

"I want to get the lay of the outside tomorrow once it's light. If there's a way to get into the trees without being seen, we might be able to get out of here."

"What about the cameras?" Livvy asked. The girl—and she was a girl—sat meekly in her chair, curled into a ball.

Laurel grinned. "That's where a little subterfuge and the things in my pockets are going to come in. Are there any cameras in the bathroom?"

"We don't know," Jackie said. "There's only two vents in there. The fan and the heating duct. But they're both up too high for us to look in without having to climb up on the counter. None of us are exactly nimble right now, so we haven't looked."

Determination settling in her belly, Laurel stood. "Well, I am. I think I'll go use the restroom. Tessa, could you show me where it is?"

Frowning slightly at the request, Tessa's eyes lit with an

understanding as Laurel leveled a direct gaze on the willowy woman. Heaving herself from her seat, she nodded. "It's this way." She pointed toward the hall and ambled that direction. Laurel followed.

Eyes moving, she looked all around as they moved into the hallway. No vents lined the walls, nor was there any art where a camera could be concealed. They passed a doorway for the laundry room, and she peaked in. Like the hall, it didn't have any air vents. Just two sets of washers and dryers with a set of shelves in between, holding various laundry products.

In front of the bathroom, Laurel stopped and turned to Tessa. "How far along are you?"

"Thirty-seven weeks."

"Perfect. You're going to fake labor to get someone over here. If you can create enough of a commotion, the rest of us can get a jump on whoever it is."

Tessa cradled her belly, worry creasing her brow. "Even if we can capture whoever comes, how will we get away? There's almost always at least one other person on the farm. Like Jackie said, we're not exactly nimble. Or quick."

"I've been thinking about that. It might be best if it's just me who runs off. I can move faster than any of you and can bring back help. I think you all will be fine even with you helping me. I doubt they'll harm any of you. You and your babies are too valuable."

Tears welled in the young woman's eyes. "I know we have to try this, but I'm still scared to hope. I've been here for months. I've watched five other young women give birth and then just disappear. I keep telling myself they're just going to live somewhere else. Somewhere where they can move on, but I know I'm probably lying to myself. I don't want to end up like them." She ran her hands over her swollen stomach. "I don't want my baby to end up with strangers. I may not have planned this child, but it doesn't mean that I don't want her."

Laurel wrapped the young woman in a hug. "We get out of here and I promise you that my husband and I will help you start over. *With* your baby."

Tessa sniffed and nodded. She pulled back and swiped the tears from her cheeks. "I'd better get back to the living room. They don't like us to be out of camera sight in groups for too long."

Laurel nodded and watched Tessa waddle away for a moment before going into the bathroom and closing the door. The room was small, but clean and neat.

Bending down, she opened the cabinet beneath the sink and started rummaging. Cleaning products and toilet paper greeted her. She took her penlight from her pocket and shined it inside, looking at each screw hole and imperfection for any sign of a listening device. She even stuck half her body inside so she could see the front and run her hands along the edge.

Finding nothing out of the ordinary, she backed out and climbed up onto the counter so that she could reach the vents in the ceiling. She aimed the light at them, but didn't see anything poking out or anything glinting from inside.

She hopped down and checked the rest of the bathroom, including the linen cupboard, but didn't find anything to indicate her captors were watching or listening to what went on in the small room. Doing a mental victory dance, she emptied her pockets of everything except her pen and notebook in case someone finally decided to search her and buried it all in the linen cabinet behind and beneath the towels.

With a final glance at the stack of towels to make sure they were straight and showed no sign of the treasure beneath, she closed the cabinet door and flushed the toilet just in case someone somewhere was listening. She ran the faucet for several seconds before exiting the bathroom and heading back to the living room.

Now, she just had to wait.

Noise echoed all around him in the bullpen, but Tristan didn't hear any of it. His sole focus was on the evidence that the crime scene unit had gathered and on locating Logan Taylor. Their new K-9 officer, Maverick, had tracked Laurel to the back of the cabin and then the scent had disappeared, confirming his fear that whoever murdered Wade Carpenter had kidnapped Laurel. Tire tracks indicated they had likely driven away in a utility van. Her radio had been smashed by one of the tires, but Cullen's team had managed to lift two sets of prints from it. They were being run through the database now. They had also lifted prints from the axe that had been used on Wade. Those were also being tested.

While they waited, Tristan and Jake did a deep dive on Taylor, looking for anything that might lead them to his whereabouts. The man still hadn't returned to his apartment or contacted his girlfriend. His truck was missing too. Jake was calling the list of friends Kara Evans gave them, while Tristan poured over the bank and credit card records that came in an hour ago.

Frustration clawed at him. The financial statements only told him Taylor was in the area. He had made few credit card transactions in the last month, and all of them were at the stores near his apartment. More than likely, the man carried cash so he couldn't be tracked.

He checked his email again, hoping the prints on the radio or axe had been identified. The same messages that were there five minutes ago stared back at him.

He suppressed a groan. This hurry up and wait crap was for the birds. The longer it took for them to get a worthwhile lead, the longer Laurel was at Taylor's mercy. He couldn't even bring himself to think about what she might be going through right now. If he did, he would be right back to where he'd been in the restroom, and less than useless to the team Ben had formed to track Taylor down and end this.

Shoving away from his desk, he stood abruptly, grabbing his empty coffee mug. "I'm going to get some coffee," he told Jake and headed for the break room. He could honestly use something stiffer than the bitter brew, but that wasn't going to happen anytime soon. But it was better than nothing. He picked up the half-empty carafe and filled his mug.

Just as he was about to take his first sip, the break room door opened and Ben walked in. Seeing the mug in Tristan's hand, he walked over to the pot and grabbed a paper cup, pouring himself some of the hot coffee.

"Clayton is at Judge Warner's house now to get the warrant signed," Ben mentioned one of the other detectives. "You should have it in hand soon."

"Good. Jake and I have come up with nothing so far. Maybe Taylor's apartment will yield some clues."

Tristan swiped a hand through his hair. "God, Ben. This is a nightmare. We have to find her." It had been twelve hours now since they discovered Wade Carpenter dead and Laurel missing. He was excruciatingly aware of every second that had passed. He had managed to get past most of the fear, but guilt still gnawed at his belly.

Ben laid a hand on Tristan's shoulder and squeezed. "We will. It's a good sign they didn't kill her outright."

"Yeah, but what's their plan? No one knows about the baby, so they can't be keeping her for their baby ring. Why do they want her alive?" He groaned in frustration. "I should have been more adamant about her staying home. Done something that would have convinced her."

"This is not your fault. Laurel's a lot like Gemma. No amount of sweet talk would have convinced her not to go to work. I may not have known her long, but I've learned that she knows her own mind and has a very strong set of personal convictions, just like you and your sister. I also don't think she regrets her decision to go to work, even knowing where it landed her and what happened to Wade. Might she have done things a little differently, like asking another unit to go on the call? Maybe. But she still wouldn't have stayed home."

Ben shook his head. "I don't know what they want with her, but we know she holds some value to them. It could be something as simple as they want to know what she knows. What *we* know. But we have to operate on the assumption that she's still alive." He squeezed Tristan's shoulder again. "Please don't blame yourself for this. We will find her."

Ben's words made sense, but knowing he was right and feeling no guilt were two very different things.

Tristan ran a hand through his hair, his feelings still in turmoil. He would deal with the guilt later. He just hoped to God Ben was right and they hadn't killed her yet.

He didn't know how he would live without her.

Together with Jake, Ben, and K-9 officer, Carter Townsend, Tristan breached the door on Logan Taylor's apartment. With the dog in the lead, the four of them quickly cleared the small one-bedroom flat and found it as empty as Tristan expected.

"You can tell he left in a hurry and didn't come back," Jake commented as they began their search. Dirty breakfast dishes cluttered the sink and a half-empty coffee mug sat on the small table squeezed into the tiny kitchen.

The rest of the room and the living room were clean and tidy.

"At least he's not a slob," Carter remarked, heading into the kitchen with Ben.

Tristan listened with half an ear as he yanked open the top drawer on the small desk in the corner of the living room. Pens and a checkbook greeted him. Yanking open the second drawer only yielded more office supplies. He pushed it closed and began rifling through the papers on the desk, but it was all just bills.

Rising, he quickly searched the remainder of the living room before moving down the hall. Jake was already in the bedroom and rifling through the dresser.

"You do the closet yet?"

Jake shook his head.

Tristan pulled open the bi-fold doors. He went through the clothes, checking pockets as he went before moving up to the shelf. There were few belongings other than the clothes in the closet.

"You know, I'm wondering if this guy doesn't have a second apartment or house somewhere," Jake said, closing the last drawer on the dresser. "There's nothing personal here. No pictures, souvenirs from trips, nothing."

Tristan knelt and tugged at the carpet in the corners of the closet, but it was stuck fast. Grimacing, he stood and faced his partner. "It wouldn't surprise me. His girlfriend didn't seem to know much about him when we pressed her about his past."

"I'm thinking she was just a cover. It allowed him access to the hospital and grounds without being suspicious. If anyone asked why he was there, he could just say he was visiting her."

Tristan agreed. It was just too convenient.

He motioned to the bed. "Help me lift this mattress."

Stepping over, Jake grabbed a corner while Tristan lifted on the other side, tilting it up so the top of the box springs was exposed.

"Hello." Jake grabbed a photograph that was sandwiched between the two.

"This woman looks familiar." Jake turned the picture toward Tristan as they let the mattress fall back onto the bed.

Tristan walked closer to get a better look. In the photograph, a much younger Taylor stood with his arm around the shoulders of an older woman. Another man, taller and blonde, was on her other side.

Eyes narrowing as he got a good look at her, a flare of recognition sparked in his mind. He snatched the picture from Jake's fingers to look even closer. There was something about the smile that reminded him of someone.

Like a light, an image popped into his mind. "Holy shit. No way."

"You recognize her?"

Tristan could only nod as fury began to seep through every pore of his being. Oh, he knew her all right.

Thirty

Light streamed through the windows of the bunkhouse, rousing Laurel from sleep. She stretched lazily, reaching a hand out in search of Tristan's solid form. When her hand flopped over the edge of the bed, she frowned, coming more fully awake. As she did, the reality of where she was and what had happened in the last eighteen hours hit her.

Eyes popping open, she looked around. The other women were still sleeping, much more used to their surroundings than Laurel. Quietly, she rolled out of bed and padded to the window facing the back of the property. Edging the curtains aside, she surveyed the outside and immediately frowned. It was a good hundred yards to the trees, with no cover. Escape would be difficult without being seen unless they were sure their captors were occupied.

Letting the curtain drop, she crossed the large room to the windows facing the front of the building and nudged the curtain open. The farmhouse was visible to her right, a silver Mercedes SUV parked out front.

Probably the doctor's car, she mused.

A red truck sat next to it, and the white van that brought

her here next to that. She hoped all except a babysitter left. Her plan wouldn't work if there were too many of their captors present.

A bed creaked behind her. She turned to see Tessa pushing herself into a sitting position.

"I'm sorry," Laurel whispered. "I didn't mean to wake you."

Tessa yawned and stood. She padded silently over to stand next to Laurel at the window.

"You didn't. I'm an early riser. I usually get up and get breakfast started for everyone."

"How long have you been here?"

Tessa sighed. "Almost my entire pregnancy. Logan's the father. I got pulled in by his good looks and charm. When I found out I was pregnant, all that evaporated. He morphed into this greedy, mean, uncaring man I had never met before. He was excited and kept telling me that, with our combined looks, the child would fetch quite a price."

"He's selling his own child?" Laurel was incredulous. She couldn't imagine anyone doing that. She couldn't even imagine what it would be like to *give* her baby away if she wanted to adopt it out. It was just too devastating to think about.

Tessa nodded. "It's not the first one, either. Nor the last. Miranda's pregnant with his baby too."

Knowing her eyes were as wide as saucers, she glanced over at the still sleeping woman. "That's awful."

Rubbing her hands over her belly, Tessa nodded. "I wasn't happy that I was pregnant. Logan tricked me by using a defective condom. But it doesn't mean I don't love this child. It's a part of me. But he doesn't want anything to do with it. He just sees it as a commodity he can sell. I tried to run away, but he caught up to me and brought me here. I haven't left since."

Horror washed over Laurel. "What about your family and friends?"

"I ran away right after I graduated high school last year. My stepdad was abusive, and I couldn't take it anymore. The streets seemed like a better option. When Logan started coming around offering work, I took it. I was starving and just wanted a way to turn my life around. I should have known it was too good to be true."

Laurel slung an arm around the younger woman and hugged her. "We get out of here—and I swear we will—I will help you get that better life. I ran from home at nineteen after my first husband tried to kill me. I know what it's like to be alone and scared. You're not alone anymore, Tessa."

Tears trickled down the girl's cheeks, and she hugged Laurel back, hard. "Thank you," she whispered. With a sniff, the young woman dried her tears with her sleeve and straightened. "So, what's the plan now? I will do whatever you want to get us out of here."

Laurel edged the curtain open again, peering out. "Do they normally all stay here during the day? If this is going to work, we really need just one of them here."

"The doctor should leave anytime. Jeremy and Logan are a little more unpredictable. I think it's Jeremy's day on guard duty, which means Logan will probably head out at some point. But if he's the focus of your husband's investigation, he might stick close to the farm and out of the public eye."

Just as Tessa finished, the front door of the farmhouse opened and a woman stepped out. Laurel squinted, trying to get a better look at her. Something about her looked familiar.

With a light step, the woman descended the porch stairs and climbed into her SUV, quickly starting the vehicle and heading down the drive.

"Tessa, do you know the doctor's name?"

She nodded. "It's Dr. Kessler."

Shock rendered Laurel immobile momentarily. Now she knew why Logan and Jeremy hadn't killed her. They wanted her baby too.

"Got it!"

Tristan rushed around to Jake's desk at his exclamation. They had come back from Taylor's apartment armed with the photograph that showed him with an unknown blonde man and the doctor from the hospital who treated Laurel as well as Debbie. He never would have suspected Dr. Kessler in any of this if it weren't for that photograph.

"Warner came through. The adoption records were sealed, which is why her name never came up in our search on Taylor. When he was fourteen, she adopted him out of foster care. His mother was a druggie and died when he was eight from an overdose. His dad is listed as 'unknown' on the birth certificate."

Jake scrolled down on the report that had just come through. "She also adopted another boy the year before—Jeremy Anders." There was a picture attached to the report.

Tristan tilted his head as he studied the image. "Looks like he's the blonde in the pic we found at Taylor's."

He ran back around his desk and typed the man's name into the database. An arrest record quickly popped up.

"He's got a rap sheet for several counts of soliciting prostitution and drugs. Methamphetamines. His only address on record is way out in the boonies between here and Northridge."

Jake rattled off an address. "That match the one you have?"

Tristan nodded.

"That's Dr. Amanda Kessler's place of residence."

Tristan switched to Google Maps and pulled up the address. Switching the map view to satellite, he was better able to see the property.

"It looks like a farm. There's a house and several outbuildings." Excitement and anticipation that maybe they were finally getting somewhere hit him hard. Laurel could very well be at that remote farmhouse.

Jake picked up his phone. "I'm calling Warner for a warrant and then SWAT. You go tell Ben."

Pushing away from his desk, Tristan stood and headed for his brother-in-law's office. Conviction that they were indeed on the right track lengthened his stride. It was time to get his wife back.

Thirty-One

Chaos abounded around Laurel as Tessa bent double in the living room of the bunkhouse. Her shouts of pain threatened to bring down the walls.

Laurel fought to keep the grin off her face as Tessa faked labor for all she was worth. The girl was a fantastic actress.

It was just after lunch and Logan had been gone a little over an hour, leaving Jeremy alone at the farmhouse. Once Laurel was Logan wasn't coming back, she'd been quick to implement her plan. She had laid out her idea that morning and left supplies on the counter in the bathroom. The girls took turns using the restroom and grabbing something while they were there.

Now it was time to implement the plan.

With a barely perceptible nod, Laurel sent Jackie the okay to call Jeremy on the phone that was hard-wired directly to the farmhouse.

In a performance as Oscar-worthy as Tessa's, Jackie put just the right inflection in her voice to convey a sense of panic as she told Jeremy that Tessa was in labor.

She hung up the phone, barely containing her smile. "He's on his way."

Laurel did a mental fist pump. "Okay. Places everyone. Remember what we talked about. You can do this. There's seven of us and one of him."

The girls acted as naturally as they could, hovering around Tessa as she continued to howl intermittently.

When the door swung open, they all jumped. Laurel forced her heart rate to calm. They needed this to look real if they were going to get him close enough and relaxed enough to get the jump on him.

He zeroed in on Tessa seated in a chair, cradling her belly. She had even managed to force a few tears out, their tracks still evident on her face.

"You can't be in labor yet. The doc says you have at least two more weeks."

"Tell that to this baby." She howled again and doubled over. "Oh, it hurts!"

Indecision lit Jeremy's face, so Laurel stepped in. "I'm a paramedic, and I can tell you she's definitely in labor."

Jeremy huffed as if inconvenienced. "Fine." Stepping forward, he moved to gather Tessa up to carry her to the farmhouse where the other women said they went to give birth. Dr. Kessler had outfitted one of the bedrooms as an exam-slash-birthing room.

As he bent to pick up the distressed young woman, Laurel nudged the cap off the syringe in her pocket. With a nod at Miranda and Nora to be ready, she moved quickly. In one smooth movement, she withdrew the syringe from her pocket and stabbed it into Jeremy's neck, quickly depressing the plunger. Ten CCs of air were immediately injected into the tissues of his neck. It wouldn't kill him, but it was excruciatingly painful.

Bellowing, he slapped a hand over the wound on his

neck and backed away. Laurel dropped the syringe and pulled her Leatherman multi-tool from her pocket and leapt onto his back, holding the point to his throat. She made sure she drew blood, so he knew she would use the knife if necessary.

"You're going to let Miranda and Nora tie you up or you're going to bleed from more than the tiny prick you just got."

She glanced at Nora, who stood hesitantly off to the side. "Do it now."

Both women moved forward and to wrap Jeremy's wrists while he stood there, holding his neck with one hand. Laurel felt his muscles tense as the tape touched his wrist. She dug the multi-tool a little deeper into his neck, halting his movements.

"How did you get that?" he ground out through his teeth.

"You and your buddy didn't search me, idiot. Paramedics carry all kinds of things in their pockets. You should feel lucky I didn't have any medications stashed in my pants."

Sweat started to drip down the sides of her face as she held her position wrapped around Jeremy's back and waist. He was a big man, and at the angle he was bent, it was taking all her strength to maintain her hold and keep the knife in position.

"Done," Miranda said, stepping back.

Laurel hopped down and thrust her hand into her pocket once again, walking around so she could look Jeremy in the eye.

"Now, you're going to sit down on that chair." She pointed to the kitchen chair Livvy brought into the room. She pulled another syringe from her pocket and waved it at him. "This one isn't full of air. I raided the cleaning products in the bathroom. I don't even have to hit a vein for this to cause some serious damage."

His eyes widened as he stared at the yellowish liquid in the syringe.

"And I've got a third one full of bleach just in case you decide to try your luck."

With a gulp, he lowered himself to the chair.

Emma and Jackie stepped forward with a set of bedsheets that had been tied together to form a rope. They circled it around his torso, tying him to the chair. Nora and Miranda taped his shins to the chair legs.

A bulge in the pocket of his pants had Laurel moving forward. She handed the syringe to Tessa, who had stood up and was watching the proceedings. "If he moves, stab him with that."

Tessa took the syringe, stepping closer. "Gladly."

Laurel thrust her hand into his pocket, coming away with a set of keys. On it was the key to the van.

Her smile was enough to light up the room. "Well, ladies. It looks like we're all getting out of here."

"You bitch! I told Logan we should have killed you when we killed your partner. But no. You were too valuable. The wife of a cop? Carrying a baby that had never been exposed to any illicit drugs?" A gasp went through the room at his declaration. He continued like he didn't hear anything. "It was like a dream come true to Mom. She could demand a much higher price for your baby. I knew she'd never be able to keep you hidden, though. I just expected it to be your husband who took us down. Not you."

"You're pregnant too?" Tessa breathed.

Laurel nodded, smiling softly. "I was trying to keep that under wraps so they didn't have any more leverage on me, but Dr. Kessler was the one who did my first ultrasound in the E.R. after I witnessed Logan murder Veronica. She's known all along about my baby. I just didn't know she was involved in this until today."

She faced Jeremy. "Be glad it was me. Tristan would have

done much, *much* worse to you than just a syringe full of air to the neck."

Turning her back on the man hogtied to the chair, she motioned the women toward the door. "Come on. Let's get out of here while we can."

Mindful that Logan could come back at any time, they piled out the door, hurrying across the yard to the white van. Laurel quickly opened the back, ushering all but Tessa inside. As the most heavily pregnant, she got to sit in the passenger seat.

Just as she slammed the doors, she heard a vehicle coming up the drive. Logan, in his red pickup, came into view.

"Shit!"

Tessa's exclamation matched what Laurel was thinking. Thrusting the keys at Tessa, she pushed the woman toward the driver's door. "Wait for me to distract him and then you take off. Go straight to Foggy Mountain to the police station and ask for my husband, Detective Tristan Mabley. Tell him everything. He'll come find me."

"Are you sure? We could all leave now," Tessa pleaded.

Laurel shook her head and opened the driver's door, pushing Tessa inside. "I'm sure. You get everyone to safety and don't worry about me. Go!"

With one last look, Tessa climbed inside the vehicle and started the engine. Laurel ran out from beside the vehicle into Logan's line of sight. He immediately swerved in her direction.

Not hesitating, she took off for the trees. Evading him in the forest had worked once before. She could do it again.

Running as fast as she could, she nearly made it to the tree line when the pickup came to a shuddering halt just feet behind her and Logan jumped out. He was on her in seconds, tackling her to the ground.

Laurel screeched and clawed at his face as he tried to pin her down.

"Stop fighting, bitch! How'd you get out?"

Still struggling, she yanked a hand free and belted him with her fist across one cheek. It glanced off, but it was enough to keep his focus on her. From the corner of her eye, she could see Tessa floor the van down the driveway. A sense of victory stole over Laurel. At least the others were safe.

He heard the roar of the van's engine and turned his head in time to see it disappear into the trees. "No!" His head whipped back around. He stared down at her, fury etched all over his face. "You are going to pay for that!" Fisting a hand in her hair, he stood, pulling her with him.

Laurel fought not to yell from the pain. She grasped his wrist, trying to lessen his hold on her a bit, and stood on her toes. When he shook her, she couldn't hold back the whimper.

"Where's my brother? What did you do to him?"

"He's tied up. In the bunkhouse."

Immediately, he began dragging her back to the bunkhouse by her hair. Laurel did her best to quicken her steps and keep up.

They burst through the back door of the house into the kitchen. Logan hauled her through the room, calling for Jeremy, who quickly answered. He pulled her into the living room and stopped at the sight that greeted him.

"Christ, Jer. You let a bunch of pregnant women get the better of you?" Moving into the room, he thrust Laurel into a chair by her hair. "Don't you fucking move. I will gut you like a fish, baby be damned." He whipped out a knife from his pants pocket and went to work freeing Jeremy from his bonds.

"What the hell happened?" Logan asked as he worked.

"They lured me over here by having Tessa fake labor pains. Then that one," he pointed at Laurel, who sat on the edge of the seat waiting for a chance to run, "jumped on my back and stabbed me in the neck with a syringe full of air."

"Where the hell did she get the syringe?"

Jeremy rubbed his wrists as Logan pulled the tape away. "We messed up and didn't search her. She had pockets full of sharp crap."

Logan muttered another oath and sliced through the tape binding Jeremy's legs to the chair.

"Mom's going to kill us," Jeremy muttered, standing.

"No shit, Sherlock. At least we still have this one."

"Who we need to move. Now. I've heard about her husband from a buddy he arrested. The guy was an Army Ranger before he was a cop. And so was his brother-in-law, who's now the sheriff. If they find out where we are, we're toast."

He wasn't wrong, Laurel thought, watching the exchange. She just hoped Tessa drove like a bat out of hell and got help here before they could move her somewhere safe.

"We need to call Mom and have her come back. The others took off in your van and are no doubt headed for the nearest police station." Logan pulled a cell phone from his jacket pocket and quickly dialed. Once he was connected to whom Laurel assumed was Dr. Kessler, he quickly explained the situation. She had to give him props for having the courage to make that call. She could hear the woman berating him from here.

When he finally hung up, his face was red. "She's on her way."

"So let me get something straight," Laurel quipped, stalling for time. "You two are brothers and Dr. Kessler is your mother? No offense, but you all don't look anything alike."

"She adopted us when we were young."

"And groomed you to be kidnappers, killers, and baby snatchers?"

Jeremy backhanded her before she even saw it coming. She pressed a hand to her lip and felt the warm trickle of blood. He had broken open the spot where she was hit last week.

"She saved us! Do you know what foster care is like for young boys? It's not pretty, I'll tell you that. No one wants a pre-pubescent or a teenage boy whose mommy was addicted to drugs. Amanda Kessler took us out of orphanages and gave us a real home. We would do anything for her."

"So I've gathered," she murmured.

Wiping her lip on her sleeve, she pressed on. "So why babies? Why kidnap and kill their mothers and sell the infants?"

"To save them from becoming unwanted street urchins like we were," Logan interjected. "All the babies go to nice homes with families who are well-off and can give a child anything he or she wants. Unlike their biological mothers, who only care about their next high. Anyway, it doesn't matter." He grabbed her arm and yanked her from the chair. "Come on. We need to go over to the big house and wait for Mom. She'll decide what to do with you."

As he hauled her to the farmhouse, Laurel sent up a prayer that Tessa would get to Tristan and that he would find her before they either killed her or took off with her to parts unknown.

Thirty-Two

Gathering his gear to head out to raid the address listed in the database for Amanda Kessler, a commotion at the front desk drew Tristan's attention. A pack of pregnant women had descended on the desk sergeant, all talking at once. When he heard Laurel's name mentioned in the cacophony, he stepped into the melee.

"Quiet! One at a time, please. Someone mentioned my wife's name. Do you know something?"

A willowy woman with dark hair who looked ready to give birth any moment stepped forward. "Are you Detective Mabley?"

"Yes."

Her shoulders sagged in relief and tears welled in her eyes. "She made us leave her behind and told us to come here."

"Leave her behind? Where?" he demanded.

"At the farm," a young black woman stated.

"Dr. Kessler's farm?"

Six sets of eyes widened at the name.

"You know who kidnapped us? Who's selling our babies?" the willowy woman asked.

"We just figured it out. I was getting ready to leave to raid the place when you all showed up. Is Laurel all right? What happened? How did you get away?"

"We lured Jeremy in and then ambushed him. He had his car keys on him, so we took his van, but Logan showed up again before we could leave. Laurel caused a distraction so we could get away. She made us leave her there." Her voice broke, and she covered her mouth to hold back a sob. "She saved us."

Tristan's heart leapt into his throat before settling back into his chest to gallop at a hundred miles an hour. He swallowed hard. "What was the last thing you saw her doing before you left?"

"She was running toward the trees behind the bunkhouse. Logan was going after her in his truck."

"What about the doctor? Was she there?"

The woman shook her head. "She left for work about seven."

Adrenaline flowing, he turned back toward the bullpen in search of his partner and his brother-in-law. "Jake! Ben!"

Jake quickly holstered the weapon he had been checking and Ben poked his head out of his office, a fierce frown on his face.

Tristan motioned both of them over. "We need to go. These women are from the farm. Laurel's still there. She lured Logan away so they could escape."

Ben looked at Jake. "You got the warrant?"

Jake nodded.

"I'm going with you. Let me grab my vest." Ben hurried into his office.

Tristan turned to the desk sergeant. "Get these women whatever they want and settle them in the conference room."

Ben reemerged, strapping on his vest. He barked orders at the other deputies who were part of the raid team to move out. Tristan and Jake both grabbed their rifles and followed Ben out of the squad room.

Heart lodged in his throat, Tristan prayed that they made it there in time to save Laurel. Now that she had liberated the others, he had no idea what Logan would do to her.

Laurel watched warily as Logan and Jeremy paced, pausing every once in a while to look out the window as they waited for the good doctor to arrive.

She let her hand flutter over her side cargo pocket, feeling the still full syringes hidden there. After they tied up Jeremy, she had recapped the syringe of cleaning fluid and put it back in her pocket alongside the syringe full of bleach. She couldn't believe they still hadn't searched her. She wasn't going to look a gift horse in the mouth, though. Given the opportunity, she wouldn't hesitate to use the needles.

"She better get here soon or those women will have had time to alert the cops," Jeremy said, passing by the window again.

"She'll be here. She knows what's at stake."

For several more minutes, Laurel watched them continue to pace until the sound of a vehicle coming up the drive had her sitting straighter.

"It's her," Logan said. Jeremy opened the door as the car pulled to a halt.

Laurel stood as the doctor's trim form breezed through the doorway.

"You two had one job and you let this pint-size slip of a woman derail our entire operation." Dr. Kessler turned her glare on Laurel. "And you. You have ruined *everything* I have worked for. Everything I have built to provide for my boys. To give them a better life than what they came from."

Laurel's eyebrows practically reached her hairline as she stared at the doctor, incredulous. "You can't be serious. You set them up for this. An operation like this just isn't sustainable. Not when dead women keep popping up. You had to know you would be caught eventually."

"It has been going very well for years, thank you. It wasn't until you stumbled on that accident scene that it all went to pot. This is your fault, and I intend to make sure you pay." She pointed one long, thin finger at Laurel, her eyes snapping in indignation before turning to Jeremy.

"Put her in the car. We're leaving. Logan, grab the files."

As Logan moved off to do his mother's bidding, Jeremy stalked toward her. Laurel shrank back, her knees hitting the chair and causing her to sit down again. She pulled her legs up, intending to fight for all she was worth. If they left the property before the police arrived, Tristan would have a much harder time finding her—if at all. She couldn't let that happen.

When Jeremy reached out to grab her, she kicked out hard, landing a solid blow to his gut. He backpedaled, but grabbed her leg as he went, toppling her out of the chair. She hit the floor with a thud. Pain ricocheted through her already bruised hip, making her freeze for a brief second.

It was all the time the big man needed. He regained his equilibrium and started dragging her by her leg toward the door.

"No!" Laurel clawed at the hardwood floor, trying desperately to hook her fingers over a raised board. Anything to provide some resistance and keep her out of the back of that SUV. "Let me go! Please!"

But her efforts were useless. When they reached the door, she managed to hook her hands around the jamb, but he just gave a mighty tug and pulled her free. Laurel screeched as he dragged her to the stairs.

Reaching forward, he grabbed a fistful of her uniform top and pulled her upright, half-carrying, half-walking her to the car. Logan and Dr. Kessler were hot on their heels. As Jeremy rounded the back of the car with her, he tucked her under one arm to free up one of his hands, much like he had at the cabin.

Laurel writhed, knowing it was getting her nowhere but unable to just stand there idly. She stomped on his foot, making him grunt, and tried to bite any portion of his body within reach.

"God, you are more trouble than you're worth. But that baby of yours is our ticket to starting over. Oh, how I wish it wasn't. I would enjoy killing you."

Just as he lifted the back gate on the SUV, the sound of engines revving and tires crunching gravel reached her ears.

Tristan!

She fought harder, trying desperately to buy some time.

"Shit!" Jeremy hauled her against him and lifted her off her feet, retreating quickly toward the house.

"It's the cops!" Logan yelled. He had a hand on the doctor's arm, pulling her back toward the house, hurrying inside and leaving Jeremy in the open with her.

Laurel screamed and writhed, determined to keep them right where they were. She did *not* want to be a hostage inside that house.

Cop cars roared into view, coming to a halt a few yards away. Jeremy froze, but Laurel kept wriggling and screaming to be let down.

Car doors flew open and suddenly Tristan stood there, looking tall and strong and *fierce*. His brilliant blue eyes were dark with deadly intent as he speared Jeremy with his gaze. He leveled his weapon on the man.

"Jeremy Anders, let the woman go and put your hands in the air." His voice rang out clear and cold through the crisp March air, crackling with authority.

But Jeremy did the opposite. He wrapped his other arm around her and lifted her higher, shielding his body with hers as much as possible.

Deputies moved forward, training their weapons on the man holding her.

Laurel squirmed again. "Let me go!"

His arms only tightened, and he stepped closer to Dr. Kessler's car.

"You have nowhere to go, Anders. It's over. Put her down."

Anticipation surged as he slowly lowered her to the ground. But it was quickly snuffed out when he raised one arm to wrap around her throat.

"Everyone back off, or I'll snap her neck."

Shock and fear rendered Laurel momentarily stunned before anger kicked in and turned her brain back on. Slowly, so she wouldn't alert Jeremy to what she was doing, she edged her hand down her leg to reach into her pocket.

"Anders, you need to let her go," Ben's voice rang out. "Let's end this without anyone else getting hurt. Don't give my detective an opportunity to do what I'm sure he wants to right about now."

Tristan's smile was nothing short of cold and deadly.

She heard Jeremy gulp and bit back a smile of satisfaction. It was nice to have the tables turned on her captors.

Again, though, Jeremy swallowed his fear and backed up another step, his arm tightening around her neck, restricting her airflow to a degree. She clawed at his arm with her free-hand, knowing it was now or never. With a quick flick of her finger, she removed the cap on the syringe and slowly lifted it out. Once clear of her pocket, she gave the man holding her one last chance to end this peacefully. As much as she wanted to see him pay, she didn't want to hurt him. She wasn't a violent person, but she would do whatever it took to keep her baby safe.

"Please let me go. It doesn't have to end this way."

His arm tightened more before loosening slightly. Laurel blinked to clear the stars from her vision.

"No. You're my ticket to getting out of here. They won't dare shoot with you in the way," he muttered in her ear, almost to himself.

"All of you back up!" he yelled at the cops. "I'm going to get in this car and drive away. If you don't let me go, I swear I'll kill her."

Sensing he was about to lose it completely, Laurel said a quick prayer that this would work. In one quick motion, she thrust the tip of the needle into Jeremy's leg and pressed the plunger.

Immediately, he cried out in pain, his arms dropping from around her as he reached for his thigh, the chemicals she had injected burning their way through his tissues.

She didn't hesitate as his arm loosened. Shoving away from him, she ran straight toward her husband.

Tristan caught her on the fly, scooping her up against his long frame to wrap her tightly in his arms.

Taking a peek behind her to make sure she was truly safe, she saw Jeremy on the ground, screaming and writhing in pain. Deputies rushed forward to take him into custody while others ran around to the back of the house to keep Logan and Dr. Kessler from getting away.

With the danger passed, Laurel's adrenaline left in a rush, and she broke into sobs.

Tristan cradled her head, pressing soft kisses to her hair. "God, I thought I'd lost you. I love you, Laurel. I wish it hadn't taken this for me to realize it, but I do. So very, very much."

Tears welled in her eyes as her emotions overwhelmed her.

Just minutes ago, she had been wondering if she would ever see Tristan again, and now she was standing in his arms, listening to him declare his love for her. Her heart threatened to burst right out of her chest. Everything she had ever wanted was right here in her arms.

She swallowed hard, trying to dislodge the emotions clogging her throat. "I love you too," she finally managed to whisper.

He took her face in his hands and pulled back far enough he could look into her eyes. With a thumb, he brushed away the tear that trickled down her cheek. "Are you all right? They didn't hurt you, did they?"

She hiccupped softly and shook her head. "No, I'm fine. Did you find Wade?" Her voice became a whisper as images of how her partner had died flooded her memory.

Tristan nodded solemnly. "We did. I'm sorry, honey."

Choking back another sob, she sniffed. "Logan did it. He stepped out of the shadows and just—" She broke off, unable to put into words what she had witnessed.

He gathered her close again, chasing away the images. "I'm so sorry, sweetheart."

She was too. So many senseless deaths just so this dysfunctional family could make a few bucks.

Angling her head away from Tristan's chest, she peeked back at Jeremy. The deputies had put him in cuffs and were hauling him to his feet even as he still thrashed and moaned.

"Jesus, what did you inject him with?" Tristan asked, looking over at Jeremy as well.

Laurel reached into her pocket and pulled out the last syringe. The liquid inside was yellow. "Bleach. This one is full of all-purpose cleaner."

"How did you even get those?"

She shrugged. "They never bothered to search me. I had

pockets full of stuff, including these syringes. I guess they figured since I'm so small, I wasn't a threat."

Tristan's mouth tilted in a small smile, and he pressed a kiss to the top of her head. "They thought wrong. You might be little, but you're fierce."

Laurel hugged her husband tight. "I had a lot to live for."

His answer was to kiss her senseless.

Epilogue

The noise assaulted Laurel's ears the moment she stepped through the doorway of her house. Voices and joyful laughter echoed down the hall from the kitchen as she wiped her wet shoes on the mat just inside the door. A quick summer thunderstorm had rolled through not long ago, bringing some much-needed rain to the area. The summer had been dry and hot so far, something that Laurel's hugely pregnant body did not like.

Pulling her top away from her sweaty chest, she fanned herself with it as she waddled through the house to get to the source of the noise.

Seven sets of eyes turned her way as she entered the kitchen. Gemma, along with the six women Laurel had helped rescue over the winter, were busy baking cookies for a fundraiser in town tomorrow. Laurel had meant what she had said about helping Tessa and the other women. Along with Tristan, Ben, and Gemma, she had started a foundation for single, pregnant women who needed some help to get on their feet. All six women—and their babies—were thriving now, thanks to the foundation's help. They had also helped three others recently, and with the fundraiser tomorrow, they were hoping to help even more for a lot longer.

"Hey!" Gemma came around from the center island to give her an awkward hug, Laurel's enormous belly bumping against Gemma's smaller, but ever increasing one. "How did your meeting go?"

Laurel couldn't stop the grin that spread over her face. She still felt like she needed to pinch herself. It just didn't feel real. "Great! The gallery owner couldn't say enough nice things about my work and wants to set up an art show next month. I told him he better strategically place some chairs around the room so I can sit whenever the weight of this belly drags me down." With a groan of relief, she settled onto a bar stool at the island and grabbed one of Gemma's cookies, taking a bite of the decadent treat. "I don't know how I'm going to make it through the next couple of months. This baby is already running out of room."

Gemma giggled and cupped her own protruding belly. "You're the one who picked my giant of a brother."

Laurel grinned. "Speaking of babies, how did your doctor's appointment go? Do I have a niece or nephew coming this Christmas?"

Gemma beamed with happiness. "It's a girl."

Exclamations of joy echoed through the room as the others all rushed to congratulate Gemma.

"At least you won't have two boys or two girls ganging up together to cause trouble now," Tessa said. She had her little girl, who had arrived a couple of weeks after the fiasco at the farmhouse, perched on her hip. The baby chewed happily on a teething ring, occasionally blowing raspberries as she watched the adults.

Laurel laughed, smoothing a hand over her swollen stomach. When she and Tristan found out their baby was a boy, Laurel had started praying that Gemma and Ben's wouldn't be. She could only imagine the trouble the two cousins could get into if they were both boys. She wasn't sure they wouldn't, even knowing one was a boy and one was a girl. According to Caroline, Gemma and Tristan had caused plenty of trouble together and they were six years apart in age.

Laurel turned as the door leading to the garage opened and Tristan stepped through. She smiled at her husband as he quickly made his way to her side.

"What are you doing home so early?" she asked, accepting a quick kiss.

"I wanted to hear how your meeting went, and I have some news that you all should hear." He looked at the young women clustered around the island.

Intrigued, Laurel's brow furrowed as she looked up at him. "It went fine. I have an art show scheduled next month. Now, what news do you have? Something to do with the trials?" Logan Taylor, Jeremy Anders, and Amanda Kessler had all pleaded not guilty to a myriad of different crimes, ranging from child endangerment to murder and were currently awaiting trial.

"Not exactly. Everything is still on track for those to begin soon. You all know that we've been combing through the doctor's records, looking for other victims and their babies?"

The women all nodded.

"Well, we've located the baby broker who arranged all the adoptions and arrested him. Kessler had been running this scheme for about five years, and we now have access to all the adoption records and are looking into the families with whom he placed the stolen children. Apparently, many of the families didn't even know the adoption broker wasn't legit. They thought they were going through a reputable adoption agency to build their families."

"So does that mean those children get to stay in their homes?" Nora asked.

"Possibly. I know the state doesn't want to take the children out—especially the older ones who have established bonds with their adoptive parents—unless they can prove the parents knew the adoption was illegal. It's a complicated mess that's probably going to take years to completely sort out."

He paused and looked at Miranda. "We also found Veronica's baby, Haley, as well as Kaylee's son."

A collective gasp went through the room.

"Veronica's parents have talked to Haley's adoptive parents and have decided not to pursue custody. FBI investigators determined that the couple who adopted Haley had no idea she had been stolen from her mother. Same with Kaylee's son. His adoptive family thought it was a reputable adoption. Both families have been cleared of all charges and are in the process of *legally* adopting the infants."

Miranda smiled. "I'm glad her baby will be happy. I wish Veronica wasn't dead, but it's nice that at least her baby got a happy ending."

Tristan's warm, firm hand slid comfortingly down Laurel's back, sending her heart soaring. Love for the man threatened to overwhelm her.

She reached across the island and clasped the younger woman's hand. "We all did, Miranda. We all got a happy ending."

Thank you for reading Smoky Mountain Baby! I hope you enjoyed it. Please consider leaving a rating or review on Amazon and/or Goodreads. It would be greatly appreciated! If you'd like a FREE romantic suspense novella just for signing up and EXCLUSIVE looks twice a month at my latest work-in-progress, you can join my mailing list at ashleyaquinn.com. You can also stay up-to-date on my newest projects by joining my Facebook readers' group, Ashley's She Shed. See you next time!

Keep reading for a sneak peek at Book 3 in the Foggy Mountain Intrigue series, Smoky Mountain Stalker.

Smoky Mountain Stalker

FOGGY MOUNTAIN INTRIGUE
BOOK 3

ONE

The twang of a steel guitar echoed through the bar over the din of dozens of voices. Laughter rang out in pockets around the room. Jake Maxwell let the heavy wooden door swing shut behind him as he walked deeper into the building on his way to the long mahogany bar at the back. Nodding to several people he knew as he crossed the room, he didn't stop to chat. He needed a beer.

Today had been brutal. Most of the time, he welcomed the variety and challenge of being a detective. But today was a case he wanted to forget. A robbery gone wrong that left an eleven-year-old boy in the hospital with a life-threatening stab wound after he tried to defend his mother from a jacked-up teenager, looking for some quick cash to score his next hit.

That mother's pain wasn't something he'd soon forget. If she'd been able to, she would have traded places with her son in an instant.

Sidling up to the bar, Jake motioned to the bartender. The man tipped his head in acknowledgment, then turned back to the beer he was pouring. After delivering it to a customer at the other end of the bar, he walked down to Jake.

"What can I get you?"

"Guinness. Draft, please."

The man nodded and reached for a pint glass, filling it from the dispenser. Jake passed him some cash, waving off the change. Spying an open table against the wall in the corner, he took his drink and sat down. He hoped no one would venture back here to talk. He just wanted to be alone to process his day.

Normally, the cases he worked didn't get to him. But when they involved kids—well, he'd need a heart made of steel not to be affected. It didn't help that he'd worked this one alone. His partner, Tristan Mabley, was out on paternity leave. Without him, Jake didn't have anyone to talk to as things progressed. He knew he could stop by Tristan's house to talk about the case, but it wouldn't be the same. Tris hadn't been there. He didn't see the blood on the woman's hands and clothes, or the pain and disbelief in her watery brown eyes.

He lifted his glass and took a long swallow. More laughter erupted from across the room, and he grimaced. Buying a case of beer at the store and drinking at home might have been the better option. But he didn't want to be alone yet. Or to drink more than one beer. Especially on an empty stomach. His plan was to walk to a local diner and get some food after this to help absorb the alcohol, then come back and get his car and head home.

Another couple came in, holding hands. Jake watched as they headed his direction. He sank lower into his seat and prayed it wasn't anyone he knew. They sat down at a table ten feet away, engrossed in each other.

His phone dinged, and he fished it out of his pocket. Turning on the screen, he saw a text from Tristan. *Ben said you caught a bad one today. You okay?*

Jake sighed. How was he supposed to put the case out of his head if he kept being reminded it of it? Biting back a growl, he replied. *I'm fine. Having a beer and some dinner, then heading home to bed. How's the baby? And Laurel?*

Three dots appeared on his screen, then the message. *They're fine. Stop redirecting. I'm here if you need to talk.*

He shifted in his seat, feeling a little ashamed that he'd gotten angry at Tristan; the man was just trying to look out for him. *I know, and I appreciate it,* he typed. *But don't worry about me. I'm a big boy.*

A laughing emoji appeared. *Fine. Let me know if there's anything I can do.*

Jake smiled and replied. *Will do. Tell Laurel I said hi.*

The dots appeared again, then one word. *Yep.*

Jake turned off the screen and put his phone away. He glanced up, taking a drink, and noticed a waitress had appeared at the couple's table. This girl was new. He'd remember a figure like that. Lean and willowy, but with just the right size curves so a man could get a nice handful. And her hair. Halfway down her back even in a ponytail, it shone a deep, rich, dark chocolate in the low light. He loved it.

She stepped away and turned, looking his way. Something about her face reminded him of someone.

Her eyes widened slightly when she saw him, but she schooled her features and walked over.

"Hello, can I get you anything?"

It hit him as soon as she spoke how he knew her. That husky, velvety tone wasn't a voice a man forgot. "Shay?" He'd interviewed her during the stolen babies case he and Tristan worked earlier in the year.

She blushed. "Hi, detective."

"When did you start working here?" He wasn't exactly a regular, but he came in several times a month. This was the first he'd seen her. "What happened to the motel?"

"I still work at the motel." She paused, her mouth twisting slightly. "Well, a different one, I guess, than the one you met me at. It's here in Foggy Mountain. But I needed some extra income, so I started waitressing a few nights a week. I've been here just a couple weeks." She tucked a flyaway strand of her dark hair behind her ear.

He wasn't sure he liked that she was working in such a rough place. Barney's wasn't a dive, precisely, but the police department got its share of call-outs to this place. "Everything going okay so far?"

She nodded. "Yeah. I haven't had any problems." Her gaze flitted away.

Jake narrowed his eyes. She was lying. He let it slide, though. They didn't know each other well enough—hell, hardly at all—for him to call her out on it. Instead, he nodded. "Good."

"So, can I get you anything?"

"No, I'm good for now." He lifted his glass a couple inches off the table, then set it down again.

"Okay. Well, if you need anything, just yell."

"I will. Thanks."

She offered him a polite, shy smile, then turned and left.

Jake watched her walk away. The woman had a figure to die for. Though he had a feeling, she didn't see it that way. Her tight jeans showed off the curve of her hips, but the oversize t-shirt hid everything else. And he'd noticed she was makeup-free.

Thoroughly distracted from his earlier depressing thoughts, Jake kept an eye on the pretty waitress as she made the rounds of the room. When she reached the raucous party of mostly men across the bar, Jake tensed. One of the men reached out and ran a hand up the back of her thigh.

Red filled his vision. His ass left the seat, but before he could leave the table, she stepped out of his reach and glared at the drunk. The man gave her a lopsided grin and reached for her again. This time, he snagged her wrist and dragged her down onto his lap, slapping a hand over one of her breasts. His friends laughed and egged him on as Shay squirmed in his lap.

Beer sloshed as Jake pushed away from his table and wove his way through the bar.

"Hey!" His voice boomed, silencing the group. Shay looked up, tears streaming down her face. He grabbed her arm and pulled her to her feet.

The drunk peered up at him, an unperturbed smile on his face. "Dude. You ruined my vibe. She was really doing something for me with all that squirmin'."

Disgust twisted Jake's gut. He pushed Shay back, shielding her, as he faced the man. "She's here to serve you beer, not your baser urges. I think it's time for you guys to leave."

That wiped the smirk from the man's face. He stood up, swaying a bit on his feet. "Yeah? You gonna make me?"

Jake took his badge from his pocket. "Do you want me to?"

The belligerent look on the man's face faded. He held up his hands. "You win." He glanced at his friends. "Come on. Let's go find us a place without the law."

"Make sure you settle your bill. And don't drive," Jake called as the group filed out of the booth. One of the women —a meek blonde in skintight leather pants and a cutoff white t-shirt—gave him a wary look, then walked over to the bar to settle the tab. The rest stumbled toward the door.

Once they were gone, Jake turned to Shay. "Are you all right?"

She sniffed and swiped at her face, nodding. "I'm fine." Stooping, she picked up the order pad she dropped in the fray, then spun toward the bar.

Jake frowned and followed her. "Does this sort of thing happen often?" he asked, leaning against the bar as she retreated behind it to get her next order.

"No."

The bartender who served him his beer snorted. "Liar."

She glared at him.

Jake frowned harder, his gaze bouncing between them. Finally, it settled on the bartender. "Where's your bouncer?"

"We don't have one. He quit a month ago, and our manager hasn't found a replacement."

"In a month?" Jake's eyebrows shot up.

The man nodded.

"It's not a big deal, detective." Shay plunked two pints of Budweiser onto her tray, then grabbed the cocktails the bartender slid toward her. "I can handle myself." She picked up the tray.

"Sure you can." He blocked her path. "That's why you were squirming, trying to get off that guy's lap, but only succeeding in getting his rocks off."

Her face colored. "Can you move, please?"

He ignored her and looked past her at the bartender. "Why didn't you do something?"

"I didn't see it until you came barreling across the bar."

Jake looked at Shay again. She stared at the hollow of his neck, unblinking, her jaw tight.

"Is that the worst that's happened since you've been working here?"

A single tear slid down her cheek. "Please move." Her voice came out as a shaky whisper. "I can't lose this job."

"Answer me first. Has anything worse happened?"

She looked up at him, then. A spark of anger flashed in her rich, dark eyes. "No. I just get groped on a nightly basis and called all sorts of inappropriate names. Happy?"

"Hell, no." He took a breath through his nose, then blew it out, reining in his temper. "Are you sure this is where you want to be?"

She snorted. "If I had a choice, I wouldn't be here. But I don't. Now, can you please move?"

What the hell did she mean by that? He wanted to ask more questions, but the look on her face told him she wouldn't answer any. Instead, he stepped back and let her pass. She darted around him without a backward glance.

Jake turned to the bartender. "I want your manager's number." They were going to have a chat about his staff's security.

About the Author

Ashley started writing in her teens and never stopped. Her first novel, Smoky Mountain Murder, came out in 2016, and she has since published two more series and has plans for more. When not writing, you can find her with her nose stuck in a book or watching some terrible disaster movie on SyFy. An avid baseball fan, she also enjoys crafting and cooking. She lives in Ohio with her husband, two kids, three cats, and one very wild shepherd mix.

Website: https://ashleyaquinn.com

goodreads.com/ashleyaquinn
amazon.com/Ashley-A-Quinn/e/B07HCT4QST

Also by Ashley A Quinn

Foggy Mountain Intrigue

Smoky Mountain Murder

Smoky Mountain Baby

Smoky Mountain Stalker

The Broken Bow

A Beautiful End

Wildfire

In Plain Sight

Close Quarters

Scorched

Light of Dawn

Pine Ridge

Sweetness

Loner

Shark

Katydid

Homespun

Milton Keynes UK
Ingram Content Group UK Ltd.
UKHW030626111124
2729UKWH00033B/89